RETRACE

Sigal Ehrlich

Cover designed by Alisha of www.Damonza.com
Cover Art:
Copyright © Shutterstock 104219099
Copyright © Shutterstock 194064680

Editing by Jenny www.editing4indies.com

Formatting by Polgarus Studio

Published by Author Sigal Ehrlich OU

Visit the author website:
http://www.sigalehrlich.com

ISBN: 978-0-9914007-4-4
Version 2014.10.15

For my mom, I simply adore you.

PROLOGUE

Reeves

~3 years ago, somewhere near Lake Erie, Ohio

My heart drums in my ears, beating fast and hard. I'm poised. My face reveals nothing. No stress, no panic, not so much as a twitch of a muscle or a bead of sweat. I do this thing I've mastered throughout the years. I hold my eyes cold and calculated – they tell nothing. I look at the dark, bearded man before me square in the eyes, waiting. No matter what, I cannot blow my cover. We, that is, Ben—who's sitting on the sofa opposite me—and I can't reveal our cover no matter what the cost. I inwardly repeat: there are thousands of lives on the line.

"Did you think you could pull it off?" the man asks. He has a deep scar across his prickled cheek and he holds a semi-automatic at my best friend Ben's temple. "We are onto you, you son of a bitch." He grits his teeth and kicks Ben full in the ribs.

Ben groans and my gut wrenches viciously. We manage to exchange a concealed glance between us, a flit of a glance that says so much, a look that feels more like a goodbye. I take inner deep breaths and summon every bit of willpower I have to stay still. A strong intuition brews within me. Something terrible is about to happen. My entire body throbs with dread. And there's absolutely nothing I can fucking do. Nothing! At the back of our minds, Ben and I have always known that something like this could happen to either of us, if not both of us.

I've looked death in the eyes so many times that it's become habitual. But this time, I'm petrified because it's not my life that's at risk, it's my best friend who I've known for the last fifteen years who's in real danger. There's more talking in this Middle Eastern language that I'm fluent in. Words pronounced deeper in the throat are barked at Ben. I hear but I don't listen. Inside I'm numb. I know what's coming is inevitable, and with each ticking of the clock, the anxiety within me grows. Both tanned, solemn men give me another assessing scan just to make sure they are right, that I truly am one of them.

With a small confirming nod from the guy in the expensive suit who is sitting on the plush sofa across the misty room, the gun goes off once.

For a beat, before mourning enfolds me, I'm paralyzed. I look at the scene before me, because I know I'm expected to. It could be some sick initiation I'm supposed to pass. I look, but I look through it, I don't see it. I'm playing a part. I'm on a mission that can save many civilian lives. That's what's holding me back from losing control and exacting merciless retribution for Ben's life. I cannot break down. I cannot blow this thing up. Instead, I keep my face placid, slouching back in the chair, looking the killer straight in the eyes. As Ben's body drops, my heart stops.

With *his* last breath, I know *my* life would never be the same.

PROLOGUE

Nia

-3 years ago, Fortaleza, Brazil

My eyes are swollen. The purple-black marks have faded some, but nevertheless they are still evident on my face. I study my image as it reflects in my notebook's screen and wince. I carefully touch my lip with the pads of my fingers. It's still tender and has a sickening iron taste to it. My other hand instinctively reaches for my bandaged ribs. No matter how deep the pain I'm still nursing or the way I look, I still want him next to me. Nothing has changed; I love him just the same. Nothing has changed, at least not for me.

The sound of the front door opening pulls me back from my thoughts. There's a jingle of keys as they land in the glass bowl. I listen for the familiar call, asking if I'm home, but it doesn't come. My brows knit as I wait.

I shrug and call out, "I'm in here."

In place of an answer there's a low exchange of words. I can't make out what's being said but the tone itself seeds alarm within me. Footsteps climb the stairs to the second floor of the house.

My parents appear at my door and my heart faints at their expressions. Color has left their faces. But it's what echoes from their eyes that sucks the air right out of me – a dual vision of fatality.

"Nia, it's… Patrick," my mom's voice breaks as she tries to speak.

"They found him earlier…" my dad finishes.

Their lips keep moving but the sounds coming out of their mouths are stretched and heavy, as if they are speaking underwater. My mother's teary eyes caress me. She moves her hand to mine and I flinch back. I shake my head violently from side to side.

"No. No…. No, no, no, no, no." I bring my hand to cover my mouth, muffling the hysterical sounds coming out. "No, no, no, it can't be," I repeatedly murmur. They both look at me in pain, hopeless. I shake my head and move back on my bed, digging into the corner with my feet, resembling a scared animal. My tears almost choke me, and my body shakes uncontrollably.

"It can't be…" I whisper, my words breaking at the tail end of my sentence.

"He is gone, Nia love. He is gone." My mother's words are so soft but yet so powerful, they paralyze me. Something takes over me in a sudden ferocious flash. Something resilient, spreading to every part of me.

Guilt.

And with *his* last breath, I know *my* life would never be the same.

CHAPTER 1

Reeves

Present Day, Cleveland, Ohio

"I'll tell you what, wait for half an hour 'til my shift ends and I'll take you up to my hotel room," I say, bored. I run a damp cloth over the bar's dark surface, deliberately taking my time before rewarding the redhead ogling me with a look. Her eyes dart fire at me. *Now* she has the nerve to start playing innocent? She's been eye fucking me the entire shift and doing everything short of climbing over the bar and jumping my bones for the last fifteen minutes. Aside from actually asking me to honor her with what she's been nearly begging for, she doesn't skip even one of the bimbo commandments.

She's chemically over-red, too artificially tanned, done tits—a nice rack, I must admit, but still unnaturally enhanced. Any other time I'd be all over this. Probably have her take the edge off, gladly. But not tonight. I'm not in the mood. I can't stop thinking about what happened before my shift. I still can't believe that I allowed that kiss to happen. I could kick myself for it. *I should* kick myself for it.

"Oh. Em. Gee!" Hugh Hefner's employee of the month squeaks at me. Even her voice annoys the crap out of me. It's been gradually getting on my nerves, especially when she tried to make it sound sexy, somewhere between shoving a twenty into my right, front pocket to fucking grazing her claws over my chest. "You are so full of yourself! You must be dreaming if you think I'd set a foot in your hotel room," Red huffs, taking a sip of her "classy" cocktail. Her pink banal drink just complements the "sophisticated" look she's trying so hard to pull off. I send my eyes to the black ceiling. A person's alcohol preference can reveal so much. I personally prefer women who appreciate high-class liquor.

I raise an eyebrow at her, not missing the way she's eyeballing the ink on my bicep. "Okay, so no go." I shrug and turn to the guy next to her. "Yep?"

"Two piña coladas."

Are you for real? Who drinks those anymore? I turn to mix the joke of a drink, covertly rolling my eyes. I slide his drinks toward him and take the bills. Putting the notes in the narrow tray, I slam it back with a flat hand. Why did I agree to this shift? I should've just refused Jake. He sounded desperate when he called for the favor earlier this evening, earlier as in right after Katie had kissed me. Fuck! If there was anything in this world I should not have allowed to happen, it was that kiss. How could I? Well, when it comes to Katie, I just lose all my guard, and the little, sweet devil knows that, too well. I close my eyes and scrub my hands over my bristled cheeks, sliding them further up to rest over my dark buzz cut. Exasperated, I heavily exhale my next breath.

"You seem stressed," my stalker determines, drawing me from my thoughts. I bring my eyes to look at her. Oh, Jesus. Miss You-are-so-full-of-yourself raises a white flag. "I could help you release that stress." She sucks on the moon-shaped orange decorating her lame drink... seductively. And I need to keep myself from snorting. Maybe I should just let her suck me off and that's it. Maybe it will help release some of the shit causing riots in my head.

"You think you can help me take this stress away, huh?" I change tactics, sending her a hint of a smile.

"I do."

And 3...2...1... huge surprise, she flings her hair back and raises her 6K boob job at me in the universal slut code of "you'll have me in the first stall before the night ends." I reward her with an encouraging side smile and push myself back from the counter. Saying nothing, I start toward the back office, aka Jake's place, aka hiding space when I've had enough.

"Listen, man, I'm done here for tonight."

Jake nods, stands up, and pats my back in a *thank you, bro* signal. He gazes at me for a long beat. His brown, straight hair falls to almost hide his piercing brown eyes.

He scratches his five o'clock shadow and says, "Thanks for saving my ass tonight. That's the problem with the women staff. You never know when they'll start using cramp excuses."

"You know you can get your ass sued for saying shit like that." I chuckle, and his black, worn leather jacket rises and falls with his shrug.

"Reeves, you okay?" his brows sink together as he searches my eyes.

I sigh and twist my lips into a hard line. "Katie."

Jake shakes his head in overt disapproval. "She is *not* your responsibility." His voice comes out curt, even irritated.

"She is. She'll always be." I regard him with a look that tells him not to go on any further with *this* subject.

"I think I should put you on a new job, send you away for a while." His way of not exactly letting go of the subject.

"Maybe you should," I say pensively, heading to the door. I tap the doorpost. "And Jake? Next time no bartending, okay?"

"Got it," he says and follows me out. I drop the white waist apron to the counter, nod at him, and fling up the little door that sets me free from behind the bar. Jake takes my place and starts flirting with a couple of cute brunettes while taking their drink orders.

"Welcome back." The stress therapist's red lips shine at me as soon as I reach her side. I just send my hand to the small of her back, unspoken, telling her to stand up and follow me. "My name is Neveah." She giggles. *Of course it is.* I don't even bother telling her my name as I know it'll start a series of questions that I'm not in the mood to answer. Anyhow, it's not like she'll ever have to use it. "Oh, God, yes," works just fine. As I direct us to the toilets, she turns to look at me questioningly.

"I can't wait," I lie, seriously debating calling this thing off. She smiles and inches on her toes to kiss my jaw. I manage to fabricate half a smile.

As soon as I lock the door behind us, she is all over me. She licks my neck while I send myself a harsh look over the mirror. Her straightened hair moves slowly from my neck to my chest, while her hands reach to unbuckle my belt. I observe the scene over the small room's mirror as if I'm just a spectator. My face is constricted, the muscle above my square jawline tightly clutched. My eyes are squinted as I rerun the scene with Katie earlier today in my head. Somehow, it feels unholy to think about Katie while the stress relief crusader fiddles with my zipper. She slides her hand inside my boxer briefs, and not a second later, I grab her wrist, preventing her from taking it any further. I collect all possible tolerance I have left in me and help her straighten.

"Babe, I think we'll have to continue this some other time," I lie again. She smiles but her eyes turn a shade gloomier, making me feel like a total dick. "Let me take you back to the bar." I try to make some sort of amends. She composes, blinks at me, and slips her hand to my jean's back pocket. *What the fuck?*

When she's done punching numbers into my phone, she hands it back to me, saying, "Call me." Not waiting for my reaction, she unlocks the door, and sashays her skirt-clad ass back to the noisy, darkened, vast room.

Even before I push open the exit door to the chilled evening, her number is deleted from my phone. What a day. My mood drops a notch lower as I think about not having a real home to go back to. The complex where I bought a duplex will be ready in two days. For the time being, I'm shacked at some hotel within walking distance from Jake's. I crack my knuckles, having Katie's confused look play before my eyes again. I must sort this mess out first thing tomorrow morning.

CHAPTER 2

Nia

"I can't thank you enough for this opportunity, Mrs. Perry." I smile at the older lady with the plaid, lilac suit. She studies me with kind eyes. "I'm thrilled to start teaching at your studio, and I can't wait to meet the girls," I add, genuinely thrilled. She nods in response.

"Make sure to bring your own music, and we'll provide the rest." She writes something with a thin, gold pen in her floral journal. "Some of them might be less... ahem," she lightly coughs, "behaved." She raises her eyes to me.

"That's fine, I'm sure I'll manage. Nothing like a bit of a challenge to make life interesting," I say and inwardly hate my statement when reflected on my private life. The last thing I want is any sort of complication or drama. I'm done with that. I don't have any strength left in me to deal with anything that's remotely emotional. I've already been subjected to much more than I could ever handle.

"It's best to be here about ten minutes before your class starts. I'll be with you in case you need any assistance." A subtle way of telling me that she'll be assessing my first lesson.

"That's kind of you, thank you," I answer and she gracefully stands up, letting me know our time has come to an end. Everything about the lady before me tells me that she used to be a dancer, from her airy motions to her elegant posture. She sees me to the door and wishes me a pleasant evening. I wait for the glass door to close behind me before letting my lips stretch into a broad smile. It's been a long time since I've been this thrilled about something. I can hardly contain my excitement. I button the three buttons of my camel-colored wool coat, lift up the lapel, and secure the white cashmere scarf around my neck. I know that in local weather standards this doesn't count as a cold evening but it is to me. For a tropical climate native, this is borderline torment.

~~~

"Hello," I greet the clerk at the hotel's reception.

"Good evening, miss." He grins at me too lavishly. "How may I help you?"

"I'd like to check in. The reservation should be under Nia Mitchell." I prefer to go with my mom's maiden name. Somehow, with my fresh start, using my real last name just doesn't seem right. Having a sense of being watched, I look out of the corner of my eye at the older gentleman in an expensive suit who blatantly checks me out. The receptionist's voice brings my attention back to him.

"Here you go, Miss Mitchell. You'll be staying in room 255, which is on the second floor. The elevators are to your right." He gestures with his hand to said direction.

"Thank you." I take the offered bundle that holds a key card. I pull my carry-on's handle up and turn on my heels. A hand on my shoulder stops me from taking another step. I turn back to the picture of vanity in the suit. He hands me a business card, held between two fingers, and winks. A room number is written across one side. The only thing I can really see is the shinning gold band on his finger. I force a sweet smile and inch closer to him.

"Wow…" I feign a girlie giggle. "Can I ask for a small favor though?" I add in a low, *Happy birthday Mr. President voice*. His eyes light as he leans toward me with a smug grin. "Can you please add your wife's number to the back of the card, so I'll be able to call her and tell her what a treasure of a husband she's got?" He flinches, and curses something under his breath, not so polished any more. I need to kill the urge to both kick him in his straying chub and flip him off. Asshole.

I take a step closer toward the mirror in the elevator, checking my chapped, reddened lips. This wind is not something that I see myself getting used to anytime soon. I clear smudged mascara from under my hazel eyes, combing my fingers through my long, straight hair. A thought about how my mom calls my dark hair silk sneaks to my mind and the familiar feeling of good mixed with ill surfaces, making my heart twinge. I contemplate whether to call home but decide it's too soon. They know I've arrived safely and that should do for now.

I throw the room a fleeting glance, leave the carry-on by the bed after getting out my purple toiletries bag, and hurry to the shower. I let the warm water stream while getting undressed. I've been looking forward to this shower the entire day. Two more days. Two more days until my own place, my own shower, my own little balcony. As steam starts to cover the glass door, I get under the water, close my eyes, and let the calming warmth wash the day away.

CHAPTER 3

Reeves

I talk to The Russian on the phone while waiting for the cute receptionist to check me in. "Sir, I'm not sure I'll be available before the end of the week." I'm not going on a job before I have my new apartment ready. Anyhow, the thought of the long flight and the predator wife of the man who I'm talking to is not something that I'm willing to even entertain right now. "How about I ask Jake to give you a call?"

My client, The Russian, is not someone who easily accepts no for an answer, but with my current mood, I'm not someone who'll let anyone make him do anything he is not inclined to do. I take my room key from the receptionist who smiles shyly at me. I give the card a brief look, cataloguing the number and send her a thanking nod. I drape my backpack over my shoulder and use the stairs so the call won't drop. Or maybe I should have chosen the elevator for that exact reason. I lean my back against the wall beside the door to the room, ending the call.

"Sir, thank you for the generous offer, but I'll have to pass this time." To his less-than-pleased assent, I press end. I'm done with everyone fucking my brains for today. I'm done with this day, period.

As soon as I enter the room, I do a quick peep, drop my bag to the floor, and kick my shoes off. I toss my wallet, keys, and phone to the small table and pull my black long sleeve shirt over my head. I throw the shirt to the bed, and start unbuckling my belt a step before the bathroom door. I send my hand to the handle, and before I know it, the door flings open.

Holy. Fucking. Sweet. Jesus.

A startled cry rips the silence in the room, but the only thing I can focus on is the impeccable naked body before me.

Those tits.

Fuck. Me. Dead. She's completely shaven. My eyes literally fly out of their sockets.

"Turn around, *turn around*!"

I finally register that someone's talking to me, screaming at me, and I forcefully unglue my eyes from the masterpiece before me to meet her face.

Shit. What a beauty! Straight, silky, dark brown hair, big hazel eyes, pouty pink mouth. She flings her arms to cover herself, still urging me to turn around, completely shaken.

"Talk about room service. Best. Hotel. Ever," I say with an amused bite, still very much facing her. Truth be told, there's nothing I can really do. That's a vision that I'm not willing nor able to stop gaping at, even if I wanted to. She huffs, and turns her back to me, only to reward me with a direct view of the greatest gift in the form of a most supreme piece of ass. My dick twitches, highly appreciating the generosities showered at him.

The bathroom door is slammed in my face followed by, "I'm calling security."

"Hey, it's *you* parading naked in *my room*, babe. No need to call in the Feds." The door opens, and two livid hazel eyes, beautiful but pissed as hell, squint at me from the narrow space.

"Get out of my room *now*!" Her nostrils flare and I find it mighty charming.

I can't subdue the smile crawling back to my lips. "I'll do whatever you want, but the thing is that you are kind of in *my room*."

Her stare narrows to thin slits. I take a step back and reach for the key I've left on the table and flash it at her. When she sees the number on the plastic evidence, confusion takes over her delicate features. Damn, she is pretty. Getting out of the bathroom, she secures a towel over her breasts. She can go ahead and cover herself with cement for all I care. What's needed is already imprinted safely in my memory.

I hold my hands up in surrender with a side curve of my lips, and say, "I guess there must be some sort of a mix-up."

For the first time since this delightful encounter began, she really looks at me, and her guarded, panicked expression gradually fades. I barely hold in a chuckle as I notice it's *her* checking *me* out now.

"Hey, turn around, stop looking at me!" I say, making a production of covering my bare chest with my hand and snort, bringing the livid expression back to her face. Only now, an adorable flush is added to her cheeks. I could be a total dick and ask her to come with me to sort this thing out at reception. I play with the appealing idea for a few long seconds, making myself grin.

"I'm glad you find this amusing. *Can you just leave,*" she says, and when my eyes fly to hers, her lips crack at the edge.

I can't overlook the fact that my mood that was about to cross Hellville's border has surprisingly turned around. "This room is equally mine." I state the obvious, buying time. I don't give a flying fuck about this room, or any other for that matter, but if it gives me more time to drink her in, I'll be damned if I'll make any effort to move. She wrinkles her nose in what seems a pensive trait. Damn adorable.

"Give me a moment to get dressed," she says, taking a few steps to grab a purple carry-on. I run my eyes over her long legs. The view is quite magnificent. The towel is doing a great job of barely covering more than a few inches below her ass. She has mocha, endless legs that glimmer in a velvety kind of way. My dick assures that he got the message my mind just sent him, and I need to adjust myself. The zipper's friction is not something I need against me right now. She shuts the door behind her and I shrug on my shirt for her sake. That's definitely a case of high-class meets good girl. By no means is she my lately "easy type," the one I'd treat like nothing but a piece of ass I'd like to tap and send on her way. I'd have this one for breakfast, snack, lunch, and dinner. Who am I kidding? I'd have *her* via IV.

Even though her body is now fully clothed, it does shit to relax the situation in my pants. It just instigates it even more. She has one of those shoulder revealing kind of loose shirts on. It's obvious that she's braless. My eyes are magnetized to her teasing, pointed nipples that peak from under the delicate fabric. Her incredible legs are stretched below low, very low, cut-offs. That's a first... I'm not sure which version I find more attractive, the naked one, or the hinting one. One thing I can't argue with, she is as sexy as she is exquisitely beautiful.

"I'll just call the reception," she says as she makes her way to the phone on the round table between two embroidered wing chairs. Her back is to me and I can't break my gaze from her ass. In a matter of minutes, I've turned into a horny stalker. Stellar.

"Hi, I'm calling from room 255. Apparently, there's been some sort of confusion. It's seems you've double booked the room. There's a gentleman here who apparently was also assigned this room." I listen to her as she speaks and detect some remnant of an accent. It's quite faint but still there. "Hold on, please," she says and turns to look at me over her shoulder.

"They need your name." She does that nose wrinkling thing again and the corner of my lips tugs.

"It's Mitchell, Reeves Mitchell." Her eyebrows rise and she gives me a curious little gaze.

"Oh, I see," she says in the phone, after giving them my name. "Ah, don't worry about it, it's fine," she adds. "Thank you so much; he'll be there soon." She puts the phone down. She leans her hip against the table, crossing her arms. "Apparently, we share the same last name."

My eyes squint at her, and it's not because of the explanation she's just provided, it's because of her body language as she said it. Something that she just said makes her uncomfortable, as if she were lying. It's probably not about the mix-up as I'll be able to validate it soon. Maybe it's about her name?

Strange... And I'd know it. This is what I do. A part of my expertise is reading people's body language/behavior. One of the many perks of having your life at risk, constantly.

"I see," I grab my backpack. "So, enjoy *my room*, I'm going to thank reception for this bonus..." I gift her with a wicked side smile. She holds her lips with her teeth, but her try is futile, as they pull up enough to reveal a smile. "So, for the sake of proper conduct, Miss Mitchell," I send out my hand for a shake, "you know my name…"

She observes my offered palm for a short moment before she fills it with her soft one. Bare, groomed fingernails, just the way I like. In unison, our stares drop to where our palms link. Something's happening there, something that produces energy with unworldly speed.

"Miss Mitchell," she says, prompting our stares to re-meet. Her expression a transparent tease. I nod, amusement playing on my face.

"Well, we've crossed nudity off the list, so I guess it's safe to say we should be okay on a first name basis…"

She mirrors my glee. "It's Nia."

Nia. I repeat her name in my head. Everything about her is just what I like, neat and natural, and absolutely gorgeous. All the good reasons for me to get the hell out of here.

"It was a pleasure," I say and send her a wicked grin.

She sighs with a smile, in a "what's done is done, I can't take it back," kind of shy way.

CHAPTER 4

Nia

The moment that I hear the small thump confirming the door has been shut, I rush to secure the metal chain. No more surprises. God, that was embarrassing, and it, of course, couldn't have happened with someone less attractive. It had to happen with a candidate who'd leave anyone else in the dust in the auditions for my G.I. Joe fantasy, my favorite one. The one that always does the job, exceedingly well.

Wrapping my knee-length beige cardigan around me, I tuck my legs under me and pour a cup of tea from the Jasmine infusion pot that I ordered in. I lift my notebook's screen up and wait for the programs to load. Clicking on the music folder, I take a sip of the ceramic, white mug. Dragging music files into a new folder for my first lesson, I end up with too many and start eliminating. Thrill fills me at the thought of teaching again. I can't wait to get to know a new group of young girls. I usually teach ages four to six, the age when innocence and sweetness are still at their peak.

Opening a memo, I jot down a list of errands for tomorrow: get accessories for the new apartment, deal with paperwork for the new job. Mainly all things related to settling in a new place. A smile crawls to my lips as I think about a visit to Pottery Barn. I'm on a budget and can't go too wild, but sometimes all it takes is a few items to set the right ambiance. A stream of excitement of everything new makes its way through me briefly, till my eyes are drawn to the new message flickering at the taskbar.

My mother.

The thought of home doesn't take long to join with the familiar twinge in my heart that never fails to remind me of what I've left behind. I close the screen, leaving my hand on top so it won't somehow lift up. I'm not ready to deal with anything linked to home yet. I leave the threatening device be and walk away, deciding to call it a night.

Night rituals finished, I bring the TV to life and flip through the shows till I land on a movie channel. I watch the credits of a movie that ended with a teary scene. Fluffing my pillows behind me, I wait for the next one to start. When the G.I. Joe theme song starts, I can't help but crack a brief smile.

~ ~ ~

When you sleep in hotels, you can never anticipate the level of morning light you'll be assaulted with. The brightness that I blink my eyes open to is borderline abusive. I'm not exactly a morning person, and that would be putting it in the most minor sense. I do not like mornings. Mornings represent another day to pass, another day to bear.

The first half of the day flies by before I can even notice that I have an hour left until my lesson begins. Fifty-two minutes and thirty seconds to be precise, in which I need to squeeze in buying the stickers that I plan to gift the girls with at the end of the first lesson, pick up my dance clothes from the hotel, and maybe manage to grab a small bite to eat.

~ ~ ~

A soft smile plays on my lips as I watch the girls attempt to perform the few little steps that I taught them for the last thirty-five minutes. The bright studio is full of joyful energy. It's as if pink exploded in here, its sparkly fallout splashed all over the small dancers.

I clap and smile wider at them as they bow in disarrayed unison. "Great job!"

Their elated, adorably flushed faces beam at me. They rapidly take their place, to my hand gesture, sitting on the floor in front of me. I open my palm to reveal colorful, magic unicorn stickers. "You did such an amazing job. I think unicorns are in order." Ten lit-up pairs of eyes eagerly watch me as I move on my knees from girl to girl and press a sticker below their collarbone.

"Miss Nia," a round freckled face with one of those plastic (pink, of course) glasses pips. I shoot her nametag a glance.

"Yes, Michelle?"

She smiles shyly. "Can you dance for us?"

I send the round clock above the door a peek.

"Yes, yes," several sweet voices crackle at once. I nod with a warm beam. They all align to sit with their backs against the studio's mirrored wall, below the wooden rail, as I turn to put a new song on. I go with one of my recent favorites, an energetic summer tune.

I start to get into the rhythm, smiling at the girls. Movements reflected on the mirror before me distract me for a short beat. I nod at the few parents who have gathered to watch us before the lesson ends. The chorus comes and I close my eyes, feeling the music funnel through me, letting it reach my core. For these moments, everything else freezes; it's like I'm in a bubble in which the only thing that matters is the music and my moves.

With the accelerating drum beats, I sway weightless. I add synchronized twirls and subtle Samba moves, floating. The band holding my hair slides to the floor, freeing it to scatter over my face, back, and shoulders. I lose myself in my dance, uniting with the music. As the last notes play, I flicker my eyes open and motion for the girls to join me. They bounce around me giggling, eagerly mimicking my moves. We all bow as the song winds down and I clap enthusiastically.

When I turn around to hug them and show them to the door, I find an army of parents watching us through the glass wall. I get a few raised eyebrows from a group of mothers and some overexcited grins from a couple of fathers. But what catches my attention is the emotion, or lack thereof, on Mrs. Perry's face. She has her arms folded on her chest, her head slightly tilted toward one of the mothers who is talking to her. Is it me, or does she not look pleased at all?

The girls hug me, distracting me from a sudden unbidden worry. I crouch down to hug them back and wave goodbye as they skip toward their parents. Worrying my lips, I turn back to get my memory stick that holds the music and the bottle of water that I left on the floor.

Mrs. Perry is still talking to the parents as I pass by her. The look she throws my way prompts me to stop.

"Could you visit me tomorrow morning for a short chat?" she asks right after excusing herself to a blabbering parent.

"Sure," I say with puckered brows, pulling my hair back in a ponytail grip and letting go. She nods and turns back to the waiting mother. She doesn't mention a specific time and I don't ask, a gut feeling tells me to just let it go.

I swing the locker room door open, cursing under my breath. Whatever happened in there doesn't seem to be in my favor. Did I overdo it with the dance? Shit, I really want this job, and the girls are so sweet. The high I had finishing the class has officially crashed to the floor. Quickly, I change my baggy dance pants to jeans and drape on a cream, knee-length cardigan over a black triple spaghetti strap top. I comb my hair back with my fingers and tie it high in a thin band.

"Mitchell?" I hear someone talk beside me as I continue shoving my stuff to a small duffel bag. My heart makes half a jump at the tap on my shoulder. Startled, I turn back to a pair of smiling, blue eyes. "It's Mitchell, right?" For a brief moment I observe the beaming lady with the bouncy, purplish hairdo, till it registers that here, too, I've filled my application form as Nia Mitchell.

"That's your name, isn't it?" she asks with an air of doubt.

"Yeah, yeah, it is. Sorry, I was just thinking about the lesson."

She sends me a dimple ornamented smile. She extends her hand for a shake, which I mirror. "I'm Alex."

"Hi, Alex. Nia."

"So, Nia, a bunch of us are heading to Jake's. You wanna join?"

She's friendly. Maybe I should go with her; it would be good to talk to people rather than go back to my room and work hard on doing everything but think.

"Um, I guess. Who's Jake?"

She laughs, and it's an ascending, contagious sound. "It's this nearby bar we all go to much too often."

"Sounds good to me."

CHAPTER 5

Reeves

"I heard you turned down The Russian… again." Jake sends his arm forward, straight, landing a dart in the very center of the red pierced dot. "It's a shitload of money…" he mutters, admiring his precise hit. "And you know he doesn't like hearing no."

I take a sip of my water, studying the target board from a distance. "I know," I say.

Jake pivots to look at me. "What's come over you, man?"

I pull the darts from the board.

"Nothing," I say low with my back to him, launching a dart at the target.

"Reeves." His voice is harsh, but even without looking directly at him, I know his eyes hold concern.

"I don't know," I relinquish. "The shit with Katie, and… the usual." I finally turn to look at him with a tapered stare. "It will be the three-year anniversary in a few days." Jake's hard face breaks for a moment. He composes fast enough that an untrained eye wouldn't have even noticed. The pain, however, stays on his face in the form of a clenched jaw muscle. Jake and I don't share a long history, but the one we do share is by far more intimate than any extended one.

"There have been some rumours," he says under his breath, nonetheless it still reaches me and it's enough to draw my attention.

"What rumours?" I ask solemnly. He snaps out of a short reverie and just shakes his head. "Which rumours, Jake?" My voice is as cold as the expression my face has taken. "Is it about A.Z.?"

"Leave it." His eyes mirror mine, and the determination they transmit certainly backs his words. It was just a slip-up; he is not about to elaborate. I know that he won't tell me anything, whatever he has, for the sole purpose of keeping me safe. I break our short stare down and grab a stamp from the table.

"I'm going to work." I slam the door shut, leaving his office. I pass by the toilets and splash cold water on my face. I dry myself with a raspy paper towel and take a deep breath. I need to calm my inner thunderstorm before going outside. In this state, the simplest word out of place and I'll turn into the Terminator himself. Still propped with one hand on the sink, I survey my reflection in the mirror as I run the other over my few days' growth of stubble. Shutting my eyes tight, I take another deep breath that does shit to calm me and push the door open with a flat hand.

Ted, a The Thing double, slaps my back in greeting as I take his place at the stool in front of the main door to Jake's. Lately, I've been taking more shifts at the bar when I'm not on a job. It's not that I need the money, the cash I make here is a joke compared to my real job, but I need the distraction. I don't do laidback. Laidback equals enough time to walk down the deepest tunnels of my mind. I'd rather walk through a nuclear explosion than go there.

Time passes as I stamp wrists and give each individual a short, thorough detection. The flow of patrons is slow but steady, just the right pace to keep me busy. The BS that the bartenders, Dan and Eileen, give one another keeps me entertained as I listen to it through our linked earpieces. Jake has a state of the art internal network communication system we all, including boss man himself, wear while working.

I tap my earpiece and say, "Eileen, give the guy a break, throw him a bone. He is about to drown in his own drool. That tight shirt is cruel, babe. Cruel."

"Reeves, the only one that I'm willing to throw more than a bone to is you," she says in a forced slutty voice. I chuckle in response.

"Don't distract the bouncer," Jake's voice comes over the electronic line. "I need him thinking with his upper head."

"Gotcha, boss."

"Thanks for trying, dude," Dan adds his share.

"Anytime." I release the button that allows them to hear me and reach for the cold bottled water under my chair. Coming up, I'm facing a group of people but see only one. A smug curve pulls up at the edge of my lips as I acknowledge her, thinking how thoroughly I acknowledged her last night while stroking myself in the shower. Just fantasizing about her was better than actually bagging the tails I've had lately.

She is lightly flushed. I'm not sure if it's the evening chilled air or a reaction to seeing me again, but I'm hoping it's the latter. She is as beautiful as the last time that I had the pleasure of seeing her, *and what a pleasure it was.* An absurd thought of whether either of the guys are someone she's seeing jolts to my head as I stamp the wrists of the members of her little group. When I take *her* wrist in my hand, I lightly press with my thumb on the side, where her pulse is and notice it's quickened. I slowly lift my eyes from her delicate wrist to align them with hers.

"We meet again, Nia," I say in a low voice. Though we've met already an abundance of times more, in my head, were she was also flushed, albeit enthusiastically screaming my name.

"We meet again, G.I. Joe."

My brows flash up and I cock my head. Her lips stretch into a smile, a mighty, fucking stunning one. She pulls her hand back, pats my chest once with that smile intact and disappears behind the heavy, black metal door. I look over my shoulder at her leaving back and can't help the stretch my own lips take. If she only knew how close she'd hit... This will be the second time she manages to elevate my mood, in person, and this time she has her clothes on.

I wait the sufficient amount of time one would take to get settled and order a drink before pressing the button on my earpiece, "Dude, straight dark hair, cream sweater, killer bod, with a group, what is she drinking?"

"Oh, *wow.* Wow!" Eileen exclaims. "Mr. I just replaced my bed, there wasn't enough space left on the bedpost shows genuine interest in someone? We are at what she drinks, Reeves? I'm jealous!"

My fellow bar colleagues are familiar with my theory of alcohol and women, the rarer the drink, the rarer the lady. They also full well know that it's about once in a blue moon that I actually care to know what someone drinks.

"Should we tell him?" Eileen teases.

"Oh, you want to hear this one, bro," Dan says, and my lips lift a degree. "Ready...?"

"Shoot."

"Talisker, neat."

Damn, but somehow I knew it would be something along this line. Classy, lots of spice, fresh, smooth, and wild. She's a living, breathing embodiment of my dream girl. Refined, perfect body, clean - stunning face, great taste in scotch. Only I don't chase these kind of dreams anymore...

"I gotta check this one out. What table?" Jake asks. There's a collective snort from both my co-workers at the bar.

"Eight, boss," Eileen sings.

"Fuck you, Jake," I say, amused.

My attention is flung to a higher than the empire state group of trouble that's making its way to where I sit. I stand up to "greet" them, walling their path to the bar.

"Gentlemen, we are at full capacity," I say in a voice that tells them it won't be a smart move to argue with me.

"Hey, Mr. Tough Guy, we won't take long." A guy that smells worse than a distillery stands in my face. I roll my eyes. There's always one idiot to start the festivities. I take half a step back and cross my arms over my chest. "Like I said, I'm sorry, but we are at full capacity tonight."

"Fuck you, pussy," a relatively built guy that I wouldn't peg as intoxicated as the rest says while pushing my chest as though bumping into a wall. Before he can even say, "I'm a fucktwad," I have him in a tight grip, holding his hand backward. I bring my free hand to his throat, pressing just enough to have him gasp for air, but not enough to cause any damage. His friends eye me hesitantly.

"I release you, and you and your friends will turn around and quietly leave, or I'll have to show you what happens if I press harder." And to give him a prelude of the joy I can bring him, I press just a bit harder. He lets out choking stutters as I shove him forward. He wobbles for a few steps and quickly balances while gasping. He sends my way a look coated with poison. I nod at them.

"Have a lovely evening, gentlemen."

"Hey Reeves, I think I'm going for her." Jake's comment brings me back to our earlier conversation. I plop back onto the stool. "Miss Talisker is damn *hot.*"

I tug the button and speak. "We all know you take pride in your masculinity, Jake. But you're still a pussy. Don't let me get back there and kick your ass." I smile at Jake's strained chuckle. My smile swiftly dissolves as I notice a very familiar angelic blonde heading my way. I press the earpiece again. "Jake, get someone to cover for me."

CHAPTER 6

Nia

By the fourth time, Bill, Billy, blargh, or whatever his name is, the guy who's been inching my way, almost pushes me off the chair, I jump up to stand. When he asks me if I'd like to dance, I first take a step back where we don't have to exchange oxygen anymore and politely refuse the tempting offer. What can I say, I'm not the biggest fan of the intoxicated, conceited, and reproducing Horny Trinity.

"Refill anyone?" I ask.

"We can have the waitress bring us refills," says Toni, a wide shouldered brunette with the most delicate voice. She is Alex's roommate, so I've been told. I wonder if it's only a room sharing situation between them, given Alex's constant small gestures toward her "roomie."

"I'm going anyway, I need to stretch my legs." I add a thin smile to my words, sending a stay-back warning glare to the guy who eyes me as if he is about to dry hump my leg.

"Don't take long," says Mr. Horny, sending me what I believe he might think is his best production of a sexy smile. I inwardly shudder.

As I make my way through a maze of tables toward the bar, a handsome, hard-jawed guy, clad in a badass leather jacket, rewards me with a smile after a blatant top to toe scan. He sends his hand to a black device that's peeping from his ear and says something, ending it with a devilish grin. He throws his head back laughing next. Not a beat passes and his demeanour turns severe. I just shrug and move on.

Some alone time is needed, I think to myself as I take a seat on a stool by the bar. I send my original table a peek, waiting to be served. *They are a* bunch of cool people. Alex, Toni, J.D., who's apparently a semi-famous comics illustrator, and Paul, which took me a few moments to make sense of his connection to the artsy gang. With him being the ultimate nerdy programmer type, by look and nature. Nonetheless, he somehow just fits in. I like him; Paul is quiet and polite and intriguingly clever. He is one of those guys who just knows everything but shows it in a humble way. My eyes jolt back once Sir Creepy catches my stare.

I tap my fingers on the hard surface. A disturbing thought nestles in my mind. I might have totally sent to hell the opportunity I've been given at the dance studio. The look in Mrs. Perry's eyes plays in my head and I cringe. I might have taken it a bit too far, letting loose like that in front of the girls and the parents. My chest presses just enough to signal for my gut to clench. Not only do I really want the job, I'm counting on it. I can't afford to lose it. I have some money set aside for emergencies, but that's exactly what it is, emergency dough. Especially with the indulgent apartment I've rented. The only thing I swore I wouldn't cut back on, and I didn't. God, I'm so screwed if I let this job slip through my fingers.

"Another Talisker?" asks the attractive blond server with the impressive showcase under her tight black tee. I frown; wasn't the other bartender serving me before? How would she know what I ordered? She tilts her head to the side, gifting me with an urging smile.

"Um, no thanks. Just ice water, please." She nods. I can't unglue my stare from the word Jake's splattered between the two small peaks her nipples form under the tight shirt. Guess she'd need a Brinks truck to take her tips home. Sliding my drink toward me, Spiky runs her eyes quite openly over me, smiles a little secretive smile, and shifts her stare to the other side of the bar. Mine follow suit. Reaching the point her attention was drawn to, my eyes land on my G.I. Joe. "*My...*" I inwardly roll my eyes.

I get the chance to thoroughly study him as I watch him talk to a real life Tinkerbell. Reeves is handsome in a non-beautiful way. Beautiful constitutes delicacy and flawlessness, even features, but he has none of that. He is attractive in a raw, somewhat fierce, masculine kind of way. Hard, square jaw, sharp planes, high, bristled cheekbones, but it's his smoldering eyes that hold the warning, sexy vibe he exudes. I gaze at them both; his companion appears ridiculously fragile with him towering more than a head above her. It seems as if he might be scolding her. His eyes, some indistinct cyan shade that I hadn't gotten the chance to validate yet, glare at her with a rare blend of irritation and gentleness. She nods, hugging herself, gently rocking back and forth on her pink Mary Jane's while returning his pointed stare. Her soft, golden locks sway, fluttering the middle of her white camisole as she nods again.

The edginess disappears from his tense stare. He runs a hand over his lightly scruffy cheek, ending the rub on his dark buzzed hair. He tells her something, crossing his arms over his chest, causing his curved bicep to bloat proudly. He moves his black jean and heavy boot-clad leg to rest on the foot ring of one of the stools and speaks again to the spectacle of delicate prettiness before him. Her lips twist, and her eyes turn downcast in response. I'm too far to precisely zero in on her eyes, but from where I sit, they seem to have turned glossy. A bolt of alarm crosses *his* face and he inches to envelope her in his arms. Her petite figure is swallowed in his embrace. He crouches for his chin to rest on the crown of her head and closes his eyes. Something streaks through me, a sudden jolt of jealousy which at first I can't make any sense of. I take a sip of my water and look at them out of the corner of my eyes. At second glance, I realize where the envy came from; it's the sense of protectiveness and care his hug emits that causes my heart to tug. I'd do anything to feel secure again, to allow someone to make me feel this way.

But I know that it's not in the stars for me. I gave up on that. Nothing can take away the pain I've been harboring, and the rooted guilt I nurture. I inhale deeply, shake away the thoughts that cloud my mind, and signal to the bartender for another drink. Scotch this time.

I place the bulky goblet on the table I left earlier, returning the smiles that greet my return. Luckily, my persistent suitor found another victim with whom he now occupies the dance floor and I get a chance to enjoy a light conversation with J.D. and Paul.

CHAPTER 7

Reeves

I run by a 7-Eleven for eggs and a gallon of O.J. before getting to the new apartment to wait for the movers, knowing full well how in about an hour my stomach will cause riots if I don't eat a sufficient amount of food. I maintain my body like the oiled machine that it is. I treat sport like a religion, training six days a week. Healthy food is a subsidiary creed. Keeping in shape is a prerequisite in my line of work, together with alertness and strength. I can't let myself slip in either of them.

Having about twenty minutes before the moving bedlam starts, I turn to make breakfast. While the six egg omelet sizzles in a pan, I down half a gallon of O.J. and read the news online. The little talk I had with Katie yesterday intrudes my news skimming. I halt and look out the window. It feels like a rock the size of the moon has been lifted off my chest after ironing out our misunderstanding. I was so glad that she agreed with my resolve on the subject that we could never have anything physical between us. She swore it was a one-time mistake on her part and she'd never pull something like that again. Even if hell froze over, I wouldn't look at Katie any other way but as family, a little sister. I don't know what came over her the other day, but I sure hope it would never happen again.

My thoughts wander to the keen spectator that we had last night.

Nia.

She didn't notice me observing her for a while after Katie and her friends hit the dance floor. I was leaning on the wall behind the bar, behind my laboring colleagues, watching her. There's something about her eyes, I couldn't get *my* eyes off her. My lips twitch at the corner remembering

Dan's smirk when I poured myself a finger of Talisker once I'd decided I was done working for the night. He shook his head at me with a shit-eating grin.

"You don't want to pull any crap with me tonight," I told him above the rim of the glass.

"That I know," he said. "I saw you talking to Katie…"

I narrowed my eyes at him, stressing the fact that he shouldn't even imply anything about Katie and me.

He just sighed in surrender and murmured, "I just wish that for once you weren't as blind as you are where she is concerned." Well, that he got downright straight; when it comes to *her,* I'm blind, and I will without a doubt forever be. No matter what Katie pulls out of her hat, I'd always be there for her, day or night.

When the movers finally spread into several rooms and start getting the apartment in shape, I get a message that makes my blood freeze in my veins on the spot.

Jake: Hunter is here, he wants to see you.

Seven point five minutes is the exact amount of time that it takes me to show up at Jake's office.

~ ~ ~

"Take a seat, Agent Mitchell." No one has called me *that* for a while, at least not since I left the Bureau. But, then again, I wouldn't expect any less from the Big Kahuna. Although it's been a while, almost three years, since I've been under his command. I study him for a long moment, reverentially, the man was, and still is, a mortal god.

"I prefer standing," I answer sharply. Jake eyes me with warning. The clean-cut, elder gentleman with the piercing blue eyes and a suit sitting in Jake's ragged chair, curtly gestures at the chair before him.

"Please sit," he deadpans, and I follow his request.

"How are you doing?" he asks, his voice heavy with years of smoke trailing through his vocal cords. I sigh, not sure what to tell him. This man knows me almost better than I know myself. Whatever I choose to say should be nothing but truth.

"Better," I say, impassive.

"I read the last report on you. You quit therapy," he states. His voice wears a pinch of disappointment, and I wince. He is the last person who I'd ever want to disappoint. We trade pointed stares for an additional moment. "I'll cut to the chase," he says, and I can feel Jake's eyes assessing my reaction. "There's a reliable tip on A.Z.'s recent activity."

I jolt to a stand but Hunter doesn't ask me to sit again. The air gets stuck in my lungs and my palms roll into two tight fists with hearing this name. Hunter, nor either of us, will ever use suspects' full names. Even though Jake's office is checked daily for bugs. "He was spotted on U.S. soil a couple of days ago."

"Will you be collaborating with Jake's people for the investigation? I'd like to be a part of the team if that's possible, sir," I say, looking at him square in the eyes. He slowly shakes his head, and for a brief moment, I see a glimpse of pain in *his* measured stare. "I can do it."

He rubs a hand over his goatee and his blue eyes look up my way. "Reeves, son, I trained you. I know what you're capable of. I know how you function better than anyone."

Jake drops his stare to his busy hand that repeatedly slides his phone in circles over the table.

"Even if I were to collaborate with Jake, I wouldn't assign you to the team. I'm not sending *you* after him. It's not that you are not capable of executing the job. Hell, you are one of the best I've ever had." He lights a cigar, sucking thick smoke in, twice. He raises his eyes back to mine. "We both know it'll be a suicidal mission, and I want *you*, and everyone involved, *including the target,* alive."

I clasp my teeth tighter as I keep listening to him. My heart is beating wildly, rage is streaming through my veins at the thought of the motherfucker who killed Ben, free and within reach. Jake crosses his leg over his thigh, leaning back in his chair, waiting for either of us to speak.

Tense, I wait for Hunter to go on.

"I'll keep you in the intel loop." He offers the best settlement he can, and it's a mighty huge one. That, I know.

"Sir, I appreciate it. Thank you."

"I might need you to work with the investigation team, though. Brief them on the old case." He sucks his cigar again and speaks through the smoke cloud.

My brows knit together. "I don't mean to be disrespectful, but why aren't you using agent Blithe for that? *She's* still in the Bureau as far as I know." I'm not sure why he wouldn't just use my former handler, Agent Daria Blithe. She knows the old case inside out, if not better than I do.

"She still is," he answers curtly. "You lived the case, it was a part of you for over a year. No one can provide details better than you could, or anticipate A.Z.'s moves…"

I nod.

Hunter taps his cigar to a deserted coffee cup. "Don't even think about doing any private investigation." His eyes lift to mine. "Don't you dare pull anything crazy that will force me to put you under arrest." Another smoke puff hazes his face. "Because I will. I want him no less than you do. Ben was under my command. Losing an agent is like losing a son."

My eyes sting and that burning feeling in my chest each time Ben is mentioned shows its painful signs. I take a deep breath. "I'll be at your service whenever you need me."

Hunter gives me a soft blink while Jake clears his throat.

"Reeves, I think that for the time being, till Hunter needs your assistance, you might want to go on a job. A simple one." They both regard me, each with his own evaluating stare.

"I'll see, let me think about it," I answer, leaving no room for further discussion. "If that would be all." Not more than a short goodbye later, I close the door behind me.

CHAPTER 8

Nia

I stop by the little coffee shop around the corner from the studio. It's barely ten a.m. and I'm already dead tired. It's not that I usually enjoy a good night's sleep; I'm used to being woken up from time to time, shaking, crying, sweating, all the lovely perks that follow nightmares. But last night had a new kick to it. My mind was spinning. It would be upsetting on so many levels to lose my new job. Obviously the money is an important factor, but also the sense of tranquility, the ability to let go for just a short period of time, is something I can't easily dismiss. Being able to put smiles on little girls' faces helps somehow to make my self-contempt weaken, sometimes even vanish for a few rare moments.

"Good morning," a young barista with about a pound of metal donning her face, welcomes me. We both stifle our yawns.

"Double espresso and a skinny cinnamon dolce latte to go, please." I flip through a magazine as I wait for my coffee. I down the espresso as if it were a cure for a fatal disease and grab the tall paper cup before heading to meet Mrs. Perry to be given my sentence.

I gulp the last of the drink, discard the cup in a nearby trashcan, and push open the door below the elegant soft pink "Tutu" sign in cursive letters. As I expected, Mrs. Perry is by her desk. Gold, wire rim glasses rest mid-nose, her head slightly inclined toward her screen. I open the glass door to her clean-cut, elegance oozing office, prompting her to raise her eyes at the interruption. She straightens back in her chair and signals for me to take a seat with a gentle wave of her hand.

"Good morning," I say quietly as I take my seat, trying to breathe free the knot in my stomach. She runs a subtle gaze over me.

"Good morning, Miss Mitchell." She pinches the temple of her delicate glasses with two fingers, removes them and sets them to the table. Her powder-blue eyes return my wary stare. "Do you have any idea why I've asked you to come here this morning?"

The knot twists tighter. I decide to go with honesty. She doesn't seem like someone who could be fooled easily.

"Um, frankly, no. I could only assume it has to do with yesterday's class." She watches me quietly. "I sure hope it's not one of the worse scenarios I've envisioned in the last twenty-four hours," I say, not doing such a good job in covering the depressed undertone. Her blue eyes crinkle at the sides. She's smiling?

"Yesterday's class was quite interesting, especially the end," she begins, and I realize I've been choking my bag's strap with my grip for the last few moments. "Some of the parents were very pleased with it." Her lips join the crinkle in her eyes. "Especially the fathers." I feel my face go up in flames. "The girls were enthralled." The expression on her face takes a kind tone.

"However, it has nothing to do with the reason that I've requested to speak to you, Miss Mitchell. The reason I've asked you to come in is, in your application you've noted that you'd be interested in working as many hours as possible. There aren't any other spots left beside your current classes that I could offer you at this point. Thankfully we are fully staffed."

My eyebrows pull in as I wait for her to go on.

"There's a..." she halts for a short pause, considering her next words, "sweet young girl that needs some extra attention. Her parents would like her to have a few private lessons, and I thought you'd be the perfect person for the job."

"Oh, this is good news," I say, surprise lacing my words. "What made you think I was the right person for the job?"

Her lips pull into a small, cheeky curve. "Call it a hunch, dear."

~ ~ ~

Late evening finds me slumped on my new, soft grey sofa, feet on the small glass coffee table above a furry cream rug. I'm bathed, exhausted, and to a degree, content. I spent the entire day organizing my new home. I literally stormed through the two-bedroom apartment, putting to place everything in my path with not a moment of rest. The grumble coming from my stomach reminds me that the coffees in the morning were the only "food" I've had today.

Heading toward the kitchen, I freeze in place when a loud sound cracks the silence of my home, a sound of something shuttering coming from upstairs. Another thud that sounds like an object crashing to the floor above me makes me flinch. At the third one, the hair on the back of my neck rises in tandem to a wave of panic that washes over me. I wait with my breath held for a few moments and another crush booms my quiet apartment. Disregarding the many warning sirens hollering inside my head, I slide into my red flats, and rush out the door.

The hint of violence, the fear of someone being in danger or threat, is stronger than any survival instincts I might possess. My heart bangs in wild beats as I stand before the door of the apartment located just above mine: 3012-B. I knock on the door and wait. When no answer comes, I knock again, persistent, resilient knocks.

CHAPTER 9

Reeves

The knock on the door makes me halt with a piece of an honorary ornament at midair, another reward that was on its way to crash with the floor, courtesy of my recent frustration tantrum. I put the silver-glass object back on the shelf and cover my face with both hands. I raise my head to the ceiling, inhale deeply, and with closed eyes under the shield of my palms, wait.

No one even knows I moved in, at least not anyone who would drop by for a "friendly" visit, unannounced. Fragments of sentences and words from the conversation with Hunter earlier today spinning through my head add fuel to my colossal mindfuck. The thought about sitting this operation out drives me up the wall. I'd never dream of defying Hunter, though I must admit, the idea is way too tempting. The knocks on the door start anew, yanking me back from my contemplative state. This time they are heavier and much more determined, urging me to check who it might be.

I'm not sure what startles me more, the person at my doorstep, her appearance, or the look in her eyes. For a stretched, stunned moment, we just stare at each other, confused. Our odd silence is broken by a collision of our voices as in unison we blurt one another's names.

"Nia."

"Reeves."

Her name on my lips is a firm utterance, holding a mildly rough edge. My name coming out of her mouth is but a soft, muddled breath. My brows sink in and I'm still shaking off the boiling anger her knocks pulled me out of while she studies me carefully, in silence.

"Yes...?" I question. She seems to be weighing her next words.

"Uh... I heard some noises coming from... um... your apartment." She heaves an audible breath. "I just wanted to make sure no one was in trouble."

I can literally feel my constricted features melt. It's the look in her eyes or the hesitation in her beautiful features, I'm not sure what exactly— maybe it's just her presence that calms me down a few notches. I deliberately disregard her inquiry. The chances that I'll address the reason that brought her here are nonexistent.

I open the door wider, taking a step back into the apartment and ask, "Wanna come in?"

"Sure." Surprising me, she walks in. I can tell by the expression that she tries to mask, her own response to my invitation staggers her no less than it does me. She takes one look at the vast, opulent open plan that is the first floor of my duplex, and her stare ricochets back to me.

"You can afford rent for *this* place working as a bouncer?"

My lips pull up at the edge to the two pink spots that blossom on her cheeks. It's quite obvious the words involuntarily just flew out of her mouth. Her pretty hazel eyes fall to the floor.

"It's actually mine. I own this place."

"Oh." Her reply is barely a coherent word, nonetheless it still emits blatant disbelief.

"The gig at the bar is just a side job, mainly to pass my time, or as a favor to Jake."

"Jake?" Her silky hair sways along with the slant of her head as our stares square.

"Jake's..." I say with a bite of ridicule. Another slow smile crawls to my lips at her reply.

"Oh, yeah..." She twists her mouth into a semi-embarrassed smile and rolls her eyes.

My eyes run over her, beginning at her lean legs deliciously wrapped under black yoga pants that reach just above her delicate ankles. Her face is naturally and exquisitely bare. She has on a shirt that resembles the one that she wore after the naked parade, dropped to expose her shoulder.

"Would you like anything to drink?" I ask. Her stare reaches to my eyes after she, not so stealthily, gives me the same visual examination I just gave her. The stretch on my lips broadens with the knowledge. She nods, surprising me yet again. I shake my head with a faint smile as I signal for her to follow me to the kitchen. She has some balls on her, walking into a stranger's apartment after hearing noises that should have actually made her lock her own door instead.

I open a cabinet to a variety of high-end liquors. She studies the loot appreciatively, sending another smile to tug on my lips. I don't wait for her to choose her drink and just pour two servings from a sixteen-year-old Lagavulin. Gazing at me, her lips curve into a grin that ends trapped by her teeth.

"Neat," I state. She nods. I hand her a glass, my stare directed at hers. She has such captivating eyes. A sudden epiphany clicks in, when I was watching her at the bar there was something about her eyes that affected me, something I couldn't translate. Her eyes are indeed strikingly beautiful, but they seem to be in some perpetual mourning, even when she smiles. Ironically so, just like mine.

"Cheers." She lifts her drink. I mirror her and take a generous taste. I watch her over the rim of the sturdy glass as she savors the liquor; her lips twist to the rich heat trailing down her flawless, delicate throat.

"Do you have a death wish?" I ask next. I'm not sure what comes over me but the fact that she put herself in danger coming over here pisses me off. If she were my girlfriend... *What the fuck?* If she were my sister, if she were Katie, she'd never hear the end of it.

"Pardon?" Her eyes rip open.

"Do... You... Have... a... Death... Wish?" I slowly accentuate each word as though speaking to a child. A slow one, that is.

"No, I don't think so...?" she says tentatively, her brows knitted. She takes another sip of her drink, doing that wrinkling thing with her nose.

"So *why in the hell* would you show up at a complete stranger's door, after hearing noises that could only insinuate trouble?" I don't intend for my words to come out with such a harsh bite, but they do.

She puts her glass down to the breakfast bar, slowly lifting her stare to mine. "*Because* I thought someone might be in trouble." The flatness of her tone doesn't go unnoticed; it actually contributes to my mild exasperation.

"You never know who might be behind the door, or what they could do to you." I don't fully comprehend the sudden urge, but I need her to promise me that she won't pull such a stunt again.

"Yes, you can never really know what goes on behind closed doors..." Her eyes drift to the sharp shards on the floor. The muscle above my jaw clasps as my eyes follow hers.

"You can never know," I mutter. She slowly pivots her eyes back to mine. Our stares lock in such intensity that it reaches all the way deep inside of me. "Nia, don't do it again," I say firmly and lose her for a brief moment to her thoughts.

"That's something I can't promise." Her voice is a soft murmur, as though it wasn't event meant for me to hear. We both leave the evidence of my anger and frustration undiscussed and meet for a short, hard stare-off.

"So, *what is it* that you do to put food on the table in this shack?" Nia breaks the silence, obviously trying to lighten the tension we've got ourselves into. I gesture for her to sit at one of the stools while I settle in front of her, bracing my elbows on the counter.

"I'm a bodyguard." *And then some...*

Her eyes fling to me. Unexpectedly, she lets out a short bout of laughter. Glee climbs to my eyes as I gaze at her, waiting for some kind of elaboration.

"What, like 'I'll Always Love You' kind of bodyguard?" My face scrunches in question. Noticing my query, she adds, "The famous movie with the bodyguard and the singer where they eventually fall in love?"

It's my turn to release a short chuckle. "I guess you can say that... Though my clients are mostly middle-aged, balding gentlemen. I usually try not to get involved with them and definitely don't allow myself to fall for them." She laughs freely now, and I like the sound of it more than I care to admit. "Okay, maybe just once." I feign solemnity. "He was kind and made me feel beautiful," I add with a dramatic accord. Her light laughter rolls higher, triggering my lips to rise at the corners. For the first time, I get a glimpse of how beautiful her eyes are when decorated with genuine contentment.

I observe her as she swallows the last of her drink, contemplating what to do next. Maybe work her to willingly bend over my kitchen counter? Just the thought of it makes my blood rage toward my groin. I kill the idea faster than I can say, "Don't fuck with, or fuck, thy neighbor." Not a clever thing to do, bag someone whose face you might encounter on a daily basis. But there's something more to it; there's something else about her that won't let me go with my usual nailing routine. For the life of me, something about her, about what she transmits, just makes me take a step back.

"So, we're neighbors." I down my drink, drowning my previous thoughts in it.

"We are…" Her hand moves to brush her heavy fall of hair over her bare shoulder. I watch the dark silk caress her flawless, olive skin and need to hold my own hand from touching it.

"Where are you originally from?"

Her posture lightly stiffens as she starts rubbing a nonexistent spot on the dark mahogany surface. With her eyes focused on her agitated finger, she says, "Brazil."

My eyebrows rise and I tilt my head in question. I was expecting a neighboring town or maybe another state. "*You're* a bit far from home," I say, and the memory of catching some faint accent in her voice when she screamed at me at the stark-naked incident lands in my mind.

Her eyes that lift to mine throw me back a little. They are two deep mirrors of hazel muddle. "I am."

She turns to bore at her empty glass. The sigh slowly whistling out of her mouth sounds like defeat. Mine is a heavy one that tries to release something that her expression twisted within me. As I'm about to try and return the smile to her face, I'm stopped by the chime of my phone. Our united attentions move to the black device vibrating and ringing between us. I snatch it before the next string of tunes comes as I notice the letters "KT" flickering on the display.

"Hey," my voice morphs suppler. Nia, in an appreciated act of politeness, turns to observe the room. At first there's silence at the other end of the line, a silence that's followed by sniffling and some broken words. A shudder of concern runs through me. "What is it, where are you?"

"Reeves, I… I feel so bad about everything. Can… I… can, I come over?"

"Where are you?" Reflexively, my palm fists into a tight ball.

"In the street, below your apartment."

I take a deep breath. "Come up," I say curtly and throw the phone to the counter, troubled. Nia, turning my way, pulls me back to the present. For a brief moment I've forgotten she was next to me. She opens her mouth to speak and I cut her off.

"You need to leave now." Confusion dominates her features as she studies me for a fleeting moment. We both keep silent as I see her to the door. I'm too caught up with the call. Why in *the hell* was Katie crying?

CHAPTER 10

Nia

I slam the door to my apartment shut, still in a state of confusion spiked with irritation. *Talk about a sudden blow off.* My exasperation momentarily eases as I run toward my phone that's screaming from the direction of my bedroom. I reach the hollering device just as the flickering light dies. My lips disappear behind a flat line as I check the display.

25 missed calls.

I've been away for less than an hour...

The whirlwind of thoughts led by "what in the hell was I just subjected to" vanishes as I scroll through the missed calls list. All from one, single number—my mom. A stab of pain slashes through me with the thought of calling home. I sprawl on the bed, sigh in surrender, and dial the number that I've avoided thus far.

When she picks up the phone at the other side of the globe, my mother sounds uncontrollably emotional. My heart instinctively lodges in my throat. Futilely, I try to thread a question through her frenetic blabber.

"Nia. God. I was so worried." Finally, she calms a degree, speaking clear enough for me to actually understand what she is saying. "Why haven't you called us?" There's a long sigh, but not long enough to allow a response. "I was going crazy. Not only do you have to move so far away, but now you don't even answer our calls? And you don't bother calling back?" I close my eyes, allowing her to let it all out. I take a deep calming breath, drawing circles with the pad of my finger over my plump, white blanket.

"I'm fine," I finally manage to squeeze in.

"Well, you don't sound fine to me!"

"I said I was fine," I repeat. "Everything is okay. I'm in my new apartment. It's beautiful. I'll send you photos. I got a job at a dance studio. Everything is good." I blurt out anything that I can to maintain the conversation as shallowly as possible.

"We are worried about you, honey. You are the only thing that matters." Though her words are a declaration of how much they care and should make me feel loved, they draw the farthest possible reaction. The sense of suffocation starts. My palms feel clammy. The clog in my throat expands, followed by welling eyes.

"I got to go, Ma. I'll call you guys soon. I promise." I sag onto the bed, ending the call. On autopilot, I lumber toward the bathroom. I turn on the hot water and wait for heavy vapor to fog the small space. Peeling off my clothes, I step inside. With my feet curled below me, I let the water soak me up with scalding heat to the point my skin is glowing red. I cover my face with both hands, slightly rocking. My tears trail down, dissolving with the warm water. *You are the only thing that matters...*

And like each time before, images start flashing before my closed eyes.

Eyes the same color as mine, blazing with manic fury.

Pain, sharp pain.

Darkness.

Clinically white room.

A twisted white sheet dangling from a showerhead.

Nurses in white robes.

My parents towering above me.

You are the only thing that matters now...

～～～

"Three, two, one! Drink up, crazies!" Toni, Alex's colorful, to be putting it mildly, roommate orders, already charmingly buzzed. Alex takes her shot glass and throws it back like a pro. Her spiked hair falls into a greater purple mess as she does. I nod and lift mine in salute, downing the sharp, clear liquid. They both grin at me as I set the glass facing down on the table, with a little thud for good measure, and raise my eyebrow.

"So, are you coming with us to that new club that I told you about?" Alex, seated at a chair beside me, asks while tapping my thigh. We came to Jake's directly after our evening lessons to meet up with Toni who was waiting for us already with two empty glasses by her side.

"Nah, I think I'll pass this time. I didn't get much sleep last night. I'm too tired." An involuntary yawn that escapes my mouth backs up my excuse. The wicked stretch on Alex's glossed lips grows, and she winks and pokes my ribs with her elbow. The same one that was broken less than three years ago.

"Definitely *not* that kind of tired," I add flatly, thinking about how my little visit to G.I. Moody ended. She squints her eyes at me with clear doubt.

"Eileen, did you guys hear from Reeves today?" the bar's owner, Jake, asks Miss Tight Shirt, tonight's bartender. Hearing Reeves' name, my attention immediately shifts sideways to covertly, or maybe not so much, eavesdrop on their conversation.

"No... but hey, Boss, who really ever hears from Reeves, right? He just appears..." Jake sends her a crooked smile. He is quite hot, in a non-law-abiding kind of way. He's got the bad boy look to a T. Wicked brown eyes, scruffy, ragged, down to a badass, kickass leather jacket.

"C'mon, talk about exaggerating," the brunette with a small white apron covering an almost nonexistent skirt, holding a small tray, says.

"'Cause you'd know him," says Eileen with thick derision. Jake's stare ping-pongs between the two attractive ladies, his lips holding a hint of a smile.

"I do happen to know him," huffs Miss Miniskirt. Maybe it's just me, but I could swear there's a hint of debauchery in the way she just said that. "And anyway, no man is an island." She eyes her blond colleague, looking utterly smug with her out of context idiom.

My eyes basically roll up by themselves. I can't stand it when people do that, just utter random crap to try to sound intelligent. Eileen sends Jake a wicked glance, which he mirrors. "Well, Erin, hun," she says, adding an exaggerated Southern twang. "In that case, I'd say that our Mr. Mitchell is damn Alcatraz." Jake snorts, scratching his bristled cheek with his thumb. His straight, bourbon hair falls to cover his eyes as he nods next.

"Oh, lookie, lookie, here's the man and the legend himself." Everyone's heads shift to where Eileen's eyes are directed, including mine. *Good Lord.* If I had playful thoughts before about how Reeves could fulfill the hero role in my X-rated military themed fantasy, he just gave a new meaning to the idea. Holy Gods of living, talking porny dreams. The guy looks steamy in a your-body-bends-voluntarily-over-the-first-available-surface kind of way.

He sports khaki, baggy cargos, and a tight white tee that illegally, and very sinfully, accentuates his toned pecs. His short crew-cut stands in spikes at the front and two black rimmed dog tags hang on his molded chest. His green eyes stare back in liquid fire at the people watching him.

As absurd as it may sound, a warm, needy feeling spreads through me, not anywhere specific, just… everywhere. It takes more than an embarrassedly awkward moment for me to realize I'm gawking at him. I jerk my stare back to my cheerful drinking companions as I register his eyes challenging mine, while a twist dominates the edge of his lips.

"Quite the delicious feast, that one." Toni's glossed eyes dance with mirth, squinting Reeves' way. Aiming for nonchalance, I take a sip from my empty glass, adding just the necessary touch to looking like an idiot. Alex smirks around the nail she's biting.

"Well… I'd totally be drooling all over him, but I'm into ladies," concludes Toni with a too transparent wink at Alex.

"And the combination of those two together…" Alex points toward where Jake and Reeves have fallen into deep conversation. They both halt for a short moment to stare back at us and I have a sudden urge to kill Alex, bare hands and all. "But don't worry, girl." She grins widely at me. "You can have them both, I'm doing this one these days." She jerks her thumb toward an elated Toni.

"Good for you," I add flatly. "Do you think I could ask Mrs. Perry to practice at the studio in the evenings?" I ask, looking to change the subject.

"You mean when it's not occupied?" Not waiting for my confirmation, Alex adds, "I don't think she'll mind; we all do it all the time." I make a mental note to address the matter with Mrs. Perry before my class tomorrow. For the sake of my sanity, I need more dance time. If there's something that sets my mind at ease…

I'm not sure whether it is due to the looseness alcohol induces, or perhaps they are always like that, but when my new friends start an exaggeratedly blatant make-out session, I feel less than inclined to stick around and watch.

"I'm going to get more drinks," I mumble to myself, pretty sure no one really listens to me. Deliberately, I approach the bar at the furthest possible spot from where Trooper and Desperado are chatting.

"Another round of shots?" Eileen's breasts reach me seconds before her voice. I force my straying eyes to stop squinting toward Reeves and focus on the friendly face before me.

"Oh, no. I think we've had enough." I shake my head and send the amorous couple a peek. Eileen follows my gaze and beams.

"Well, the more they go at it, the more drinks the guys around here will need. I'll be making a fortune tonight." She grins and I echo her, glad she starts a light conversation that diverts my attention from the liquid exchanging display and my mortal, soldier fantasy. She asks me how I know Alex and Toni, and I tell her about teaching dance at the same studio as Alex.

"So, you're a dancer?" she asks in an oddly loud voice given that I'm right in front of her. Saying that, her eyes stray for a quick moment to focus at something behind me. I nod. "You sure look like one," she adds, her attention back at me.

"Thanks, I guess…" The sides of her eyes crinkle and her smile grows in parallel to a soft squeeze that's felt on my waist. I flinch in surprise and my eyes fling to look over my shoulder to find out who might be touching me. They meet a wide, semi-bristled neck. Trailing upward, they short-circuit with a pair of deep green ones. I take a step sideways so his grip will ease off my waist. Reeves moves to lean with his hip at the bar and studies me.

"Hi neighbor," he says.

I casually blink in response.

Without asking, Eileen slides a sparkling water glass toward him. He rewards her with a thankful side smile.

"So, Dancer, what's for you?" she asks next. Reeves' stare turns to scrutiny, his eyes don't seem to miss any bit as they sway over me.

"Nothing for me, thanks. I'm heading home. But a cold water pitcher for my friends there would be great."

Eileen smiles knowingly and turns her back to us, making, or pretending, to be busy.

"Already leaving?" Reeves asks. I return his profound gaze with a pointed one, and hold it for a stretched beat.

I just shrug in a nonchalant confirmation, "Yeah," and turn on my heels.

CHAPTER 11

Reeves

"Tomorrow, huh?" Ben says, his head stuck inside his fridge.

"Seems like it," I say, absorbed in the gazillion inch TV.

He closes the door, leans with one hand on the stainless steel refrigerator, and gazes at me somewhat troubled. "Eight months... it feels like forever. I can't wait for it to be over," Ben says, referring to the case we've been investigating.

"He is going to reveal the location tomorrow, I'm sure he is. I can feel it," I respond, raising my eyes to square with my best friend's.

"I can't wait to arrest these sick fucks. If I could only shoot this son of a bitch in the head," says Ben.

I let out a deep heave. So do I. But that's something we'll never do. We'll get the location and time for when the attack is planned, wait for the day, and arrest them. And finally get our lives back, at least till the next case. We've been so invested in this investigation that we've almost forgotten how real life feels.

"I'm going to disappear for a while after we're done. I seriously need some time off," I say, and Ben nods. "Trekking in South America or something, I need a change of scenery. I need to shut my mind off."

"You'll upset Katie." He grins with his perpetual wicked smile.

"Why's that?" I frown.

He rolls his eyes and snorts. "You're blind, dude, baby sis has a major crush on you."

It's my turn to roll my eyes. With a headshake, I dismiss the ridiculous observation and add, "Maybe Brazil for a couple of months."

"Brazil does sound good," he says, and his stare turns solemn. "I'm going to propose to Casey when we're done."

My eyes dart to his, and he nods in confirmation. Wow, Ben is going to really start his "grown-up" life. I take two steps toward him and slap his back.
 "That's great, bro."

I pace the vast landing of my living room for God knows how long. Same as always, whenever I don't work or have my hands full with something, anything, I feel like a trapped animal in my own damn head. I step out to the balcony, place my forearms on the railing, and watch the evening as it slowly darkens. Inhaling deeply, I try to push out the thoughts that are threatening to infiltrate my mind any moment now. Of the day both Ben and I were so anxious about. The day that turned out to be his last, and my last as my old self. The driven, content, and peaceful person I used to be. I need a distraction.

Perhaps I should call up one of my "friends," those helpful ones who are always more than eager to let me release my temper in them. I run a mental list of candidates but no one really picks my attention, not enough for me to even bother to get my phone and call them. And with a thought of sex comes a very distracting one:

Nia.

Without over-thinking my next steps, I grab one of my most cherished scotch bottles and shove my keys and a condom in my cargos' thigh pocket, ready to pay a neighborly visit. Not that I expect any warm welcome, or for her to even answer the door, but hell if it'll stop me from trying. I'm more than ready to deal with whatever she'll put out.

Standing before the door that's exactly below mine, I knock and wait. It takes a substantial amount of time for a simple checking of who's at the door to take place, which leads me to think she might be considering if she should open it at all. I grin at the peephole. Finally, a double click of a lock is heard. I'm not even remotely surprised that it's not a smile I'm greeted with. I tilt my head and watch her frown at me for a suspended moment.

Damn, she is hot.

Majorly. Smoking. Hot.

She has a light pink tank top on that looks more like second skin. Her tits, palm-size, full and perky, teasing under the almost see-through garment. And yoga pants that do an artful job of accentuating her sublime body. My lips tip at the edge as my grateful eyes meet hers. She reciprocates with an even colder glare. Yep, she definitely didn't appreciate my brush-off when Katie called. Nonetheless, there's nothing much that I could have done because Katie was just moments from coming in. Explaining having female company after our last talk wasn't something that I wished to subject her to. I'd never upset Katie, at least not deliberately.

Nia is nothing but hostile. Seems like the odds aren't exactly playing in my favor. I slide my hand to my pocket, playing with the aluminium foil, reassuring we'll get there. I bring the bottle of Mortlach, a rare existence, from behind my back in a peace offering and smile suggestively.

"Can I come in?" I ask to her silence, shifting my stare behind her to look inside the apartment.

"Ehm… I'm not sure." Her eyes narrow at me. "The thing is, I'm not so familiar with the assholery protocol…" Her smile is so exaggeratedly sweet, it scrunches her entire face to a ridiculous squinty-eye expression. "So, I'm not sure, you see." In one sentence, and one idiotic expression, she made me want in more than I wished for moments ago. I inwardly chuckle at the insane urge that she just prompted in me to suck, bite, and kiss her lips senseless.

"Okay, I totally deserved that," I say.

"Right." The crinkles between her brows multiply.

"An intoxicating olive branch?" I bring the bottle forward, her eyes round in surprise as I pass her by and walk right into the apartment.

"Excuse me!" Her delicate voice climbs an octave.

"You're excused." I grin with my back to her, almost cracking up as I run a scenario in my head where I ask her next, "Where's the bedroom, babe?"

"God, you are a smug, condescending…" I turn back to flaring nostrils and mildly flushed cheeks.

"Listen, it was one of those bad news situations. I guess I was too quickly sucked into it. I apologize for the brush-off." To my utter surprise, her irritation seems to deflate at once, and instead of asking me to get the hell out of her apartment or give me the lecture of the century about being an asshole, she gestures with half a shrug for me to follow her to the open kitchen. With a content pull on my lips, I follow. My gaze on her ass could easily set it on fire. She has a small, toned, bouncy ass. Seductively perfect. My thoughts spontaneously conjure a scene in which I'm holding this same piece of supreme plumpness, naked though, from both sides as I poun...

"Ice?" She turns to lean her hip on the sink, catching me with my stare still fixated where the object of my brief fantasy was a second ago, licking my bottom lip. I raise my eyes, which are crinkled at the corners, trying to swallow my sexually enthralled smirk. Yeah, plenty of that, *ice*, inside my boxer briefs, please. I shake my head as a response, biting inside my lips.

As Nia pours our drinks, I take the chance to inventory the place around me. I look for anything that will help me gather info on her while instinctively checking the best alternatives for an escape. Sick, yet entrenched. This place is half the size of mine. It's small, but unique; somehow everything about the space says: Nia. Like her, the room oozes clean-cut, subtle, ease inducing, quiet beauty.

"Here." She hands me a glass, still assessing me. I take the drink and nod.

"Nice place."

She glances around, timidly smiles, and hums an agreement.

"Cheers." I raise my glass.

"Cheers." She brings her drink near her naturally reddish lips. In unison, we sip back the amber liquid with our eyes firmly locked. Our stare is so powerful that it brings a light color to Nia's cheeks, causing her to cast her eyes down. I assume it's her attempt to break the tension that in a blink of an eye became so thick between us. She starts toward the plush grey sofa. I follow suit.

I lean back into the sofa after setting my glass on the reclaimed wood coffee table that's standing on a cream shaggy rug. I part my legs, slouching, my arms crossed behind my head. I watch her as she settles next to me with an unwelcomed guarded distance. She crosses her legs and covers them with a light blue, patterned throw pillow. Resting her hands on the pillow, she brings her eyes to meet mine. I smile at her and her lips quirk up... not enough, to my tasting.

"What are you doing here?" she asks next, her pointy nose slightly wrinkled.

My immediate response is a grin. Talk about straightforwardness, I like that. "Paying a friendly visit?" Her eyes narrow in blunt doubt. I raise my hands from behind my head in surrender. "I come in peace." She huffs a short giggle.

"What if I told you that I needed some company and decided you'd be perfect?" I lean forward to take my glass and swig it back, intentionally not looking at her.

"I don't sleep with random guys." The words practically gush out of her mouth. Her brows pucker, cheeks slightly flushed, but the determination in her eyes can't be mistaken. I almost spit the contents of my mouth.

"Whoa." I can't help but let out a healthy chuckle. All of a sudden the condom in my pocket becomes more of an exciting challenge.

"Just making sure we're on the same page." She shrugs again, her eyes still hard.

I, on the other hand, can't seem to calm my grin down. "Got it. I promise to try and get you to know me before..." I shake my head amused. She just rolls her eyes.

"You don't have any personal knickknacks around," I state, both really wishing to learn more about her and trying to steer the conversation away from awkward zone. Nia takes a short validating visual tour of the room and looks back at me.

"I guess. The only things that matter sit next to my bed." I cock an eyebrow. "Which are none of your business," she adds too quickly. I could happily live without the stay-back vibe she is emitting.

"Nia." I scratch my bottom lip with my thumb. Her hazel eyes grow as they trail to mine. "Can you just stop this thing you are trying so hard to pull off?" Her brows almost meet. "I said I'm sorry about how I ended things last time. I'm here to just spend time with a person who I think is pretty cool. I don't have any hidden agendas." I captivate her stare. Foil in pocket better kept undiscussed... "If I make you uncomfortable in any way and you don't want me here, just say the word and I'll leave, no hard feelings." She heaves a long breath and finally her edgy demeanour mellows.

"Sorry for that. I want you to stay." Her eyes coyly counter my solid ones.

I release a silent breath of relief. Just for the record, if she would have had asked me to leave, I would have had to convince her why it would have been a crime against her own wellbeing to not let me stay.

To lighten up the atmosphere I say, "So we stopped at where I was telling you how I fell for one of my clients." I bring back our conversation where I made her laugh, just before Katie interrupted.

Her full lips instantly stretch, releasing a rolling sweet laugh. "Did you just continue from where we left off two days ago?"

My answer is an affirming side smile.

"God, you're weird," she says with an animated expression.

"Guess, I am..."

"How did you become a bodyguard anyway, it's not exactly the most common job." Her finger moves to trace the patterns on the pillow resting on her thighs.

"It was the natural course after I was done serving," I say, my eyes wandering to line her gentle curves.

"Oh, so *you were* a soldier?" Her entire face lights up in curiosity and... excitement?

"Yes, one of the greatest honors of my young-ish life... I was a platoon leader in combat."

"What made you decide to enlist in the first place?"

"It was a condition of my parole," I deadpan. A healthy chuckle rolls off my mouth at her big eyes and "o" shaped mouth. I shake my head, my eyes still dancing. She counters with a brief snicker.

"It was something that I always wanted. I guess the challenge, everything it stands for…" And moronic as it may sound, I thought it would have made the mother I never knew proud.

"What was it like?" Nia asks. I lift my eyes to her thoughtful hazel ones. "Being a solider?"

I slouch back onto the sofa, parting my legs wider. "Well, for the first half year you feel like a kid dressed up in uniform, following whatever everyone else is doing. Getting your ass scolded into submission." My lips slightly quirk. "This was the hardest part for me; I wasn't a following the rules kind of guy before." Unconsciously, my finger moves over the little metal balls of the fine chain holding the dog tags that rest under my shirt.

"Were you scared being in a combat zone?"

"Scared? No. It's just changes you, when it becomes… your reality."

"I can't even imagine being in a situation where I am shot at. It sounds surreal," she says pensively.

"Once you've faced live fire, when you've been in the field in the most chaotic situation, it feels real, very real. The moment that you realize other people's lives depend on you, and yours on them, that's when it all starts to make sense. It's as if you mature overnight. You bond with these people, and they become your brothers."

I grip the chain and breathe through the wrench in my chest as it compresses. "When you understand that you'd die for them, and they'll do the same for you." My voice fades out, my eyes cloud and with causal pretence move to look out the wide windows. A familiar smolder clots my throat, too quickly I drift to dark places. Places I never want to forget, yet fight to stay away from. My stare drifts to look at where warmness radiates to my skin, to Nia's hand on my thigh. I slowly raise my eyes to hers.

"Reeves," my name is a gentle whisper, "are you okay?" She leans toward me, her eyes soft and caressing. My brows pull in and I slightly cock my head, swallowed by her hazel softness. My gaze drifts south to her pouty lips and watch her tongue moisten her bottom lip. My stare deepens at the erotic motion. Every other thought evaporates from my mind as I inch forward, my eyes moving from her stare that had slightly darkened to her lips and back. Her eyes take an anxious tone as my face reaches closer. In unison, our lips slightly part. The small space between us fills with tension. I'm close enough for her subtle honey scent to reach me. I take a lung full to have it reach all the way through. We both slowly inch closer, and when her breath mingles with mine, I airily touch my lips to hers.

There's a second of charged surprise between us, but quickly gears are shifted and the soft, brief connection turns into hasted conquering. Flesh to flesh, teeth to teeth, any control has left us as the barrier has been lifted. The first encounter of my tongue with hers can only be described as an overall feeling of being washed by sensual, electric rain. My fingers thread through her smooth hair, pushing her deeper into the trance our tongues have taken. We don't kiss, we fight for more. To get deeper. To graze tighter. To consume the new territory. Wild attraction detonates all over us. Her hands rest on my bristled cheeks and for a long moment we both disappear into another dimension in which the only thing that matters is our physical connection.

A warning invades my enthralled pleasure: this is not just a carnal kiss, there's something more. With every taste of the sweetness that's her mouth, I know I should pull back and stop it. After a few more stolen moments, I reluctantly, slowly, inch back with my hand still holding her delicate neck. I lean my forehead to hers and inhale deeply, doing an immense job not to lunge my tongue back into her mouth and lay her back on the sofa. I leave a chaste kiss on her pointy nose instead, and stand up, heading to where I assume the bathroom is. Nia doesn't speak, nor makes any effort to stop me.

I close the door behind me, find the sink, and splash cold water on my face. I prop my arms on the vanity and drop my head. There's something about her that just makes me feel good, something I'm not willing to fuck up before I even have the time to explore. And I know, very well, that if I bed her, I'll screw it up. Like I always do. I adjust the swell inside my cargos, close my eyes, and take a few long mending breaths.

Nia is putting our empty glasses in the dishwasher as I reach the great room. She turns back to the sound of my advancing steps.

"Thanks for stopping it," she says, catching me off guard. She has a tendency of doing that, surprising me. "Let's just not mention it again, okay? Do you want to watch a movie?"

For a short moment, I look at her mildly startled. After inwardly determining that she's the coolest chick I've ever met, I nod with a small crooked smile.

"So, you never told me what made you end up here?" I ask as Nia, beside me on the sofa, scrolls between movies tittles.

"I wanted to teach dance." She makes a great deal of studying the screen. I take the remote from her hand, forcing her to grace me with a look.

"No studios in Brazil? You had to move to another continent for that?" The scepticism echoing from my voice can't be disregarded.

"I needed a change, okay? And I wanted to teach dance... Since my mother is originally from here and I have a couple of relatives in the city, it was the simplest destination." My eyes run across her face, assessing her sincerity. Gradually, her expression takes on a softer air. "I love teaching young girls to dance. It makes me calm."

I can't ignore the odd word choice. It calms her. Not happy, content, fulfilled, but *calm.*

Before I'm able to further pry, she snaps out of a short lapse and almost squeals, "*The Piano.*"

I snort. "No chance in fucking hell, not even for you." We both stop short at the latter part of my reply. "I don't do whiny drama."

We end up settling on a comedy after some more lame drama films she tries to sell me and I disqualify for the sake of my short crap tolerance.

Nia brings a light taupe throw and snuggles under it as I stretch my legs, resting them on the coffee table. She extends her hand to release a ponytail she tied earlier, and I watch her silky, dark hair fall in heavy strands around her blanket wrapped shoulders. She gives me a short soft peek. As our eyes meet, we exchange thin smiles and in unison turn to the mounted TV.

Not long after the first scene ends with an idiotic "misunderstanding" that makes me throw my eyes to the ceiling, I turn to ask my movie companion to maybe change the film. I crane sideways to look at her, her long, dark lashes caress her high cheekbones as faint breathing sounds part her lips. She is burrowed inside the throw, her head dropped, almost leaning on my shoulder. I take the remote in one hand, and scoot over to sit closer next to her. Unconsciously, she rests her head on my shoulder. I breathe her in, and turn the TV to the news. As I lean back, Nia's head slightly falls from my shoulder to my chest, and when I lean further back, her head gradually ends up on my thighs. The news become nothing of interest when I find myself admiring the curves and lines of her delicate features. I brush back a couple of thin hairs that cling to her cheek. I can't unglue my eyes. One thing is sure, I'm in a hell of a different situation now, so far from the one I've envisioned coming here tonight. Nevertheless, I like it more than I can even admit to myself. *I* feel calm.

CHAPTER 12

Nia

I flicker my eyes open with a confused haste; it feels like I've slept forever. And the most puzzling part is that I don't remember waking up in the middle of the night, not even once. I can't even remember the last time that happened. I bring my hands from under the blanket to rub my eyes, adjusting my sight to the illuminated room. When I comb my fingers through my hair, a startled cry flits my mouth when I touch a hand that's resting at the side of my head. My eyes rip open and I look up to see Reeves blinking away sleep.

"Morning," he greets me gruffly. I gaze at him with a mix of confusion and curiosity until the moments before I drifted off last night come back to me. I fell asleep... next to him. "Sleep well?" he asks, scrubbing his hands over his face, ending it with a short sigh.

Too embarrassed to admit just how well, I just go with, "I was very tired."

"You looked too comfortable and serene... I didn't have the heart to wake you up."

"Thank you." I smile at him. He reciprocates with a thin curve of his lips, his green eyes swallowing me in. My own eyes run over his face, not even trying to be subtle about it. The stubble decorating his cheeks is denser, adding a tougher edge to his raw, delectable appearance. As ridiculous as it may be, I'm less than thrilled to leave this position, but for the sake of not appearing clingy, needy, or pathetic, I slowly inch up.

"Coffee," I mutter, standing up. I stretch my neck from side to side and head to the bathroom.

"I'll make some," his husky morning voice returns. I inwardly mock myself about how much I enjoy the little domestic morning exchange. Sad.

Scrutinizing my face in the mirror while brushing my teeth, I decide that I look like a fresher version of myself. A version that's finally had a good night's sleep.

There's something about Reeves that puts me at ease, that just makes me want to, well, be next to him. His presence seems to distract me from… me. I can't deny the serious attraction that I have for him. If he hadn't stopped that kiss last night, I would have probably embarrassed myself by climbing him faster than I could say, "slut."

I can't overlook the sting of his elegant rejection. Subtle or not, it was still a rejection. *Ouch.* I guess I'm just not his type. Note to self, in order to prevent appearing pathetic don't go at him, again.

It's been a while since I let anyone stay for a night, sleep while someone is next to me. It actually bewilders me that I let myself fall asleep next to him at all. I haven't done that for a very long time.

Reeves presses the last digit of his number into my phone as I see him to the door, after we have an easy talk over coffees, plural. Each. When his stomach started protesting and we checked my refrigerator for food, or more precisely the lack thereof, he asked if I wanted to join him for breakfast at his place. Just because I did, very much, I declined the invite with an excuse of grabbing something to eat on the way to the studio.

"So, see you at Jake's tonight?" he asks, as if we've discussed it before. I swallow the smile threatening to stretch my lips, too excited to learn that he wants to see me later, again.

"I guess." I go for utterly-fake indifference. "We'll probably be there anyway after the last class." He cocks his head.

"Alex and her gang." The query becomes more evident in his features and I elaborate. "Alex, she's also an instructor at the studio, and her friends. They go to Jake's almost every night. I guess you'll recognize them once you see them. Alex has purplish, spiky hair." A smile crawls to his lips and stretches his prickly cheek. I notice that the green hue of his eyes is lighter, even brighter in morning daylight, and for a short moment, I space out, fixated on it.

"The girls who gave the adult show last night?" I'm pulled back to the present by his question. *Busted.* He grins, noticing my ogling. I twist my mouth with a hint of a smile.

"Yep, them." His face lights up. I shake my head and push him out the door.

"Bye…" Turning on my heels, I head to get started for the day, beaming.

~ ~ ~

I rummage through my bag for the third time, starting to lose my patience. Exasperated, I turn the damn thing upside-down and let the content spill to the floor. No, not in here. I send a glance to the watch above the studios' glass door, I won't make it home and back in time for my class. Crap. My entire lesson is based on a new song that I was planning to teach the girls. I worry my lips, searching my mind for some creative enlightenment, and it marches in… in the most alluring form… Reeves.

Hey, at home? Busy? I text him, more than grateful that he added his number to my phone earlier.

My favorite neighbor. Am here, s'up? My lips immediately pull up with his reply.

Can I ask for the biggest favor?

Shoot.

Any chance you could bring me something I forgot at home? Pretty please.

I'm not breaking into your apartment.

Key under the rug (

R U FUCKING KIDDING ME?????

Disregarding the bold, capital animosity, I ask him to bring me the memory stick I've apparently left on my kitchen table.

Waiting for Reeves, I tidy up the room, putting away shiny balls and colorful hoops, then start my stretching routine. I lift my leg to rest on the wooden railing, holding the point of my dance shoes, I bend my body as far as I possibly can until it starts to feel far from comfortable. While changing legs, I catch a glimpse of someone watching me through the mirrored wall. I'm not sure what makes me slightly warm, perhaps it's the weight of the stare boring into me, because I do, in parallel to a small flutter in my belly.

CHAPTER 13

Reeves

I'm staring, but there's nothing that I can really do to stop it. I'm staring and the emotions that the vision in front of me brings are new, surprising, and powerful. It's a combination of lust and something else which I honestly can't decode. Nia's motions are hot, as in making my dick throb, hot. And her gracefulness and the delicacy of her moves cause a completely opposite reaction—it prompts an urge to take her in my arms and kiss her softly, run my fingers through her hair, caress every inch of her. *Outrageous.* She sends me a timid look, adorably smiling.

I bring the thumb drive from my pocket and put it on display in my open palm. She beams and makes my way in quick steps.

Nia grabs the small item and says, "You're a lifesaver, I owe you big time." Inching on her tiptoes, she pecks me near the edge of my lips. It's a small flutter, but it feels as though she just pressed hard with an iron. My hand on its own accord homes in to where her lips have just touched my skin. I watch her as she runs back inside the wall mirrored, illuminated room, thinking about the many ways she could repay me.

She fumbles with a laptop on a small, high table at the furthest side of the room. As I watch Nia, not yet even remotely ready to leave, the room starts littering in many shades of pink. Little ballerinas, looking alike, hover over Nia, wrapping their arms around her while she's still crouched near the computer. Nia laughs, almost losing her balance. She claps next, and all the mini pink troopers align in front of her. They all mimic her moves as she goes through some more stretching.

Holy fuck! She spreads herself widely on the floor in an insane split. I'm just a second away from salivating. Perverted as it is, getting uncontrollably turned on while watching someone teach little girls dance steps, there's still no going away. Enthusiastically, I remain cemented to my spot. The vision of Nia in the same position only with me under her is way too vivid and captivating to let vanish. My thoughts keep on bouncing from one pole to the opposite, from snapshots of wild sex to warm hugs. The way her eyes gleam as she watches the girls imitate her moves, the way her body slightly bends to the rhythm. The way her hair sways from side to side, gleaming in dark silkiness. I lean back on the wall and keep watching, enthralled.

One thing is more than clear—I want, or more precisely *need,* her under me *soon.* That righteous thought which made me stop that kiss last night can garb its fellow moralities friends and get lost. I'll have to be shot first, twice, with missiles before stopping anything with her again. When I check my watch, I realize more than twenty minutes have passed since I started ogling. I try to catch Nia's eyes to let her know I'm leaving, but my attempt is futile; she's too caught up with her class.

~~~

"Are you working tonight?" Jake asks, slamming his palm on the top of a beer bottle he holds tilted against the table. A small tap is heard with the cap dropping to the floor. A wave of froth trails down the bottle's narrow neck as he hands me the cold beverage.

He proceeds to open the next bottle in the same fashion as I answer, "I'm not sure yet."

Still with the bottle held against the table's side he cranes his neck to look my way. "And that would mean?" His auburn hair falls sideways with the slant of his face.

I return his gaze. Today is one of the rare times Jake is not wearing his leather jacket. You'd think it would somehow lessen his ragged appearance, but it doesn't. The man oozes badass warning, something that gets him more ass than he can tap.

"Do you need me to work?" I ask and he shakes his head, tipping back to take a long swig of his drink. "So the answer is no."

"Do you have any plans for tonight?" He leans back onto his wide, worn chair. He combs his fingers through his hair to remove the strands that have landed on his forehead, waiting for my answer.

"Is that a pick-up line?" I ask. I'm rewarded with a snort. Not even a beat later, his expression morphs serious. "I'll know soon," I answer, well aware of his concern for me. He knows that it's better I have my hands full. He knows that lately my thoughts are tearing at my seams. If I was a recovering alcoholic, I'd say Jake was my sponsor. Jake was the one who unofficially took me through my steps of grief after Ben died. Jake shoots me a querying glance. "I might have plans later… with someone," I elaborate.

"Lady plans?" His lips twitch at the side.

"Yeah."

"Do I know her?"

"You kind of met her before." His brows sink together, deepening his gaze at me.

"Talisker girl." My answer is reciprocated with a reputable nod. We trade an appreciative silent assent in the form of a stare for the lady in subject. There's no denying Nia is indeed someone who can be "appreciated" for hours.

"Okay, man, let's talk business." Jake lifts his legs to rest on the table. "The Russian has a major hard on for you, and you only."

"Tell me something I don't know," I deadpan. Somehow, I believe it's more my client's wife who wants me to bodyguard her brains out rather than actually keep her husband safe and sound.

"He offered 30k for a week. Thirty. Large. Ones. Reeves. For a fucking week." I don't even blink. Money means nothing to me—I have more than I can spend. Money that I wish I didn't have. Money that I got in place of parents. My stare bores into the cartons of beer aligned against the dark wall. Without breaking my fixation on the booze, I ask, "Where to this time?"

"Cuba."

I inhale and hold it in for some beats. I let the trapped air out and turn to look at Jake. "Do we know what he has planned there? Or what I'm supposed to be doing?"

"We do. A couple of meetings with local questionable businessmen." I let him brief me, watching him carefully. With his feet crossed at the ankles, still on the table, throwing and catching a baseball with one hand, he adds, "I want you to keep an eye on what's really going on there, though."

This will be what we call a double job. I'll be indeed safeguarding Mikhail Vasileva, aka The Russian, however, I'll also be "collecting intel" for our benefit while at it. The best way to describe the business Jake runs is a one-stop shop for everything investigatory, intelligence, and protection that resides in the grey area of the law. Albeit, kosher enough to collaborate with federal institutions. Better yet, take care of things that fall under grey areas *for* the federal bureaus. That's how we originally met, when Hunter hooked us up after I retired from the FBI. After I lost my best friend.

And the bar? A hobby, cover-up, office. Jake's shady, ragged, misfit baby.

"You can tell him that I'll take the job," I say and release the tension from my neck, craning it from side to side. "When do I leave?" I ask next, taking the last sip of my drink and tossing the empty bottle into a trashcan.

"That's recycle shit." He frowns, eyeing the brown bottle nestled amid a heap of papers. "Next week."

"Okay." I lean over to fish the bottle from the bin.

"Did you hear from Hunter?" Jake asks next. In spontaneous reflex, my body becomes rigid. I shake my head and Jake's stare strays to the monitor at the side of his desk.

"I'm glad you didn't do anything crazy so far and go after A.Z.," he says, still looking at the screen. I don't answer, knowing deep inside I haven't really given up on the idea… yet.

"Oh, you're both here," Eileen says, smiling at us as she steps into Jake's murky office. She tucks her black, tight shirt inside her black mini skirt.

She holds a white apron on her waist and turns, directing her peach shaped ass at me, wordlessly telling me to tie it up for her.

"Did the lime order arrive, Boss?" she asks Jake, lightly giggling when I gently slap her ass once I'm done tying her apron. Jake gestures with his chin at a wooden box that's resting on the floor a few steps from his chair.

"Great," she sings, now tying her shoulder length blond hair into a high ponytail. "Come handsome, help me with my lemons." She winks at me and I chuckle.

"Babe, you don't need me to carry this thing."

"I don't, but I think *you* want to come with me." She grins at me with a secretive sparkle. "Dancer girl is here." Eileen makes a whole show of blinking twice. Jake lets out a mixture of a laugh and a snort when I jump to my feet.

"I'll take care of your lemons," I say. Eileen giggles again and wraps her hand around me in a friendly hug as we step out.

It takes me less than a breath to spot Nia. She's sitting with a group of two women and three men at one of the long tables next to a gigantic, framed black and white Hendrix photo. She has a black sweater on and her beautiful hair is falling in heavy clusters on her shoulders. She lifts her eyes and they meld with mine. A thin smile blossoms on her lips with the deepening of my stare. Although one of the guys is obviously speaking to her, she doesn't tear her eyes from mine. When he nudges her hand, she flinches, looking his way in a mildly confused expression. My lips rise at the edge. As he puts his hand on her shoulder, my smile at once turns into a hard line. I inhale sharply, making my way to get Nia away from him.

CHAPTER 14

Nia

Quicksand. Quicksand would be the most accurate word to describe Reeves' effect on me in general, and on my body in particular. If I stand too close, I'm pulled in, forcefully swallowed, hopelessly. My attraction to him is beyond anything that I can really try to resist. The way that he watched me earlier, so absorbed, had my heart spasming all over my ribcage. While going through my stretching routine, I closed my eyes, savoring the knowledge of him watching me. It added a delicious thrill to the mundane task. Until the girls arrived, I was actually putting on a private show for him. My every motion, every bend, every flex, was slower, lingered, and accentuated just for him. Yes, my mind on its own had renegaded from the initial oath to not come on to Reeves, again.

A stinging recollection of how he stopped our crazy lip-lock less than twenty-four hours ago comes, bursting my little, hopeful bubble with a mocking evil grin. Sadly as it may seem, I guess he'll just have to remain the subject of my embarrassingly way too many, vivid dreams.

Just as I force myself to unglue my eyes from Reeves' molten green gaze, shutdown these horny thoughts of him, and pay attention to Paul who just nudged my hand, I notice out of the corner of my eye that Reeves has taken a few steps toward us.

I ease my face into a smile for Paul, raise my eyebrows, encouraging him to repeat whatever he'd just said that I've apparently missed.

"Are you seeing anyone?" Oh shit. This I didn't expect. He definitely earned my full attention now. I don't want to lie, but on the other hand, I'd feel awful turning Paul down. I really like him.

"Um, no," I say, avoiding his eyes, focusing on the circles my finger traces around the hem of my wine glass. He remains quiet long enough for me to finally lift my eyes, which meet smiling blue ones.

"I think you and my brother would really hit it off."

I return his smiling expression with a mildly baffled one. "Oh." I take a generous sip from my wine. "Um, the thing is, I'm not looking for anything… serious at the moment."

It's his turn to show surprise. He tilts his head and watches me in assessment. "Okay…" He inhales a quick, heavy breath. "His name is Kenneth. He is thirty. He is an accountant in a small but successful firm. He likes sports, and music, and he is real fun." I smile at Paul's stream of basic, far from being luring descriptions. If he ever thought about a career in sales, he should kill the thought right this minute. "And I kind of already told him about you."

"He sounds…um, interesting," I say the closest thing that I manage to come up with to sound remotely intrigued. My eyes involuntary leave him to trail up to the mass of human hotness blocking our view.

"Can I steal her for a while?" Reeves asks, a hint of a smile playing on his lips as our eyes meet. Paul's cajoling expression flattens a degree by the interruption.

I smile back at Reeves and say, "Give me five. I'll come look for you at the bar, okay?"

"Five." The curve of his lip turns into a side smile. I watch him walk away, looking utterly addicting with his all black, heavy boots attire. Coming back from my inwardly salivating pause, I turn to Paul. Paul gazes at me with a careful smile as I search my mind for an answer. Being the nice guy that he is, he offers me a polite way out. "How about I give you Kenneth's number and you call him whenever it'll work for you?"

"I think that would be best." But what I am really saying is *thank you so much for not making it awkward or being pushy.*

"But think about it… You'll get me as a brother-in-law." He snickers in his charmingly geeky way. I wait for Paul to add his brother's number to my phone and head to the bar.

Reeves leans with one elbow on the hardwood surface, holding a tumbler in his hand, watching me with great attention.

"Thank you," I say, taking the glass with the golden liquid from his hand and bringing it to my lips. I close my eyes, letting the smooth drink fill my mouth. I open my eyes to intent green ones that undividedly, slowly, trace the edges of my lips. The way he looks at me makes my breath hitch and a wave of heat swirls just beneath my navel. Without breaking our eye lock, he reaches for the glass in my hand and turns it so that his lips will touch the exact spot mine just left.

"Thank you for earlier today," I say.

"Uh huh." He nods, utterly focused on me.

"It's my turn to return a favor."

The next sip he takes ends up a hard gulp. His eyes dart to mine and slowly his eyebrow rises.

"Do you want to go say goodbye to your friends?" he asks, as he turns to discard the empty glass at the bar behind him. It takes me a long moment to make sense of his question, and as soon as the realization clicks in, I bite my lip, subduing a smile.

"Are we going somewhere?" I ask, radiating the exact same heated vibe he emits and then some.

"Yes," is all I get in return. His hand finds its way to the small of my back, maybe more the small of my butt, gently steering me to the table that I left not long ago.

~ ~ ~

Our short walk home is packed with palpable tension. Despite our mutual try to hold a light conversation, we're both too distracted to even make it remotely interesting. The choppy, forced attempt at dialogue is dismissed by intent stares and short currents as our hands accidently meet. It's the kind of suppressed, boiling energy that could only be detonated in a bed, or against a wall, or on top of a washing machine.

With these thoughts seizing my mind, I miss the first time Reeves asks, "My place?"

I don't even try to play classy and just nod with an easy shrug. Well, it's better than actually uttering the words restlessly fidgeting on the tip of my tongue: "the elevator will be just fine."

The ride up in the small compartment is short, but it's a lifetime in randy years. The force that sparks between us feels like a third being, warping us in a dizzying whirlwind. When the short chime indicates we've reached our floor, our unified loud sigh of relief comes in stereo. We both let out a light chuckle and trade amused stares.

As I follow Reeves into the apartment after he effortlessly unlocks the door, the idea of us about to take a leap into this uncharted territory invades my lustful, impatient thoughts. The idea that maybe taking this step would not be the smartest move marches in, carrying with her a bag full of forthcoming possible awkward moments. It's pretty clear we are on the fast track to become good friends, or we already are. I like him, I enjoy his company, much, and would like to continue having him around. I'm not sure what a hookup would mean to him, as for me it is what it is, a hookup and nothing more.

We reach the open kitchen as I finally decide to speak up and make sure my intentions aren't in any way vague.

"A drink?" Reeves asks, stopping me from actually saying what's on my mind. The way that he watches me as he waits for my answer suddenly unnerves me. I hop back to sit on the counter, taking a needed distance from his impossible pull. Reeves' side smile appears at my action. He slowly takes one step to face me. He props his arms at my sides on the marble surface, caging me between them. Slightly prone toward me, he is close enough for our breaths to mix. I swallow hard.

"You didn't answer my question," he says hoarsely. His eyes are heavy with something that I could only interpret as the same hunger mine mirror.

"No, I'm good." *Very good.* My voice comes out bound by a soft breath. The green in his eyes is so sharp up close. Our eyes collide with intensity and in harmony slowly trail down to our mouths and back. My lips part and I send my tongue to moisten the sudden aridity.

"You're good." He repeats my words, inching even closer. His head slowly descends for his nose to hover next to my pulsating artery. He inhales me in, his lips, feather like, touching, not touching, my skin. I hold my breath in at my body's response to his closeness. My breasts feel heavier, my nipples stretch against the fabric of my lacy bra, together with the heat that spreads from between my parted thighs to the rest of me. Brushing my cheek with his bristled one, he shifts back to look at me.

"I enjoyed watching you dance," he says with a throaty edge. My eyes run over his slightly flushed face, taking in every handsome, masculine feature. His defined, stern brows, almond-green eyes, his straight nose, and firm, high cheekbones. The scent of his breath mixed with alcohol next to me intensifies every sensation of anticipation swirling within me.

"I'm glad you liked the show *I gave you*," I say. And that's all it takes for his mouth to crash into mine. In a matter of seconds, it's as if we continue right where we left off when our mouths met last night. In a matter of seconds, our tongues enthusiastically taste one another. Our crazed pace is followed by pants, moans, and bites. Teeth bumping against teeth. Lips opening wider, desperate for more. Gradually his weight is deliciously heavy on me. His hands travel from my hair, where they are threaded just above my neck, to my ass. He cups my butt from both sides and slides me forward to feel his throbbing heat through his jeans, just where I'm burning for him.

As I start to slowly graze against him, he swallows my groan, and moves to peel my black sweater from me. My tank top follows, unfortunately, forcing us to break the delectable connection that is our kissing. Reeves tips back again to stare at me, and I take the opportunity to rip his long sleeve shirt over his head. The sight of him, all defined and ridged before me, the soft fabric with his body's warmth in my hand, brings me to new levels of want. I send my hand to the back of his neck and pull him toward me. His mouth lands at the hill of my breast, his hand squeezing the other, causing every muscle in my lower body to tighten.

He holds the lacy fabric of my bra between his teeth and gently peels it down. The exposed, sensitive peak hardens and I want to scream for him to cover it with his mouth. Reading my need, he leisurely retraces his way back with a soft scrub of a day-old scruff on my skin till he reaches the point. As he licks and sucks on my hard crest, a moan funnels from my lips. He bites just enough to make it wonderfully painful and then lazily licks it with a caress of his flat tongue. Repeatedly, and ever so gently.

My hands run over his hard, curved chest and down to his defined abs, willing both to take the time to feel every inch and urge him to go further on. Reeves' hand moves to cup my throat, his thumb helping my chin up as his mouth claims mine again. His lips drop down to suck my bottom lip into his mouth, greedily. His teeth join to slightly bite just before his tongue follows in with determination. The erotic dance of our tongues is charged and electrifying, turning my body into a stimulated string of nerves. As we continue consuming each other with kisses that are on the verge of savage, Reeves' hands move to hold my pelvis, his thumbs on my skin just above the hem of my jeans. With his hardness pressed against my middle, and his mass on me, he slowly leans me backward.

A cold bite of marble prickles my back as the heat of Reeves' touch spreads inside of me. One of his hands massages my breast, near aggressively, while the other skims my skin from the side of my neck till it reaches the other. I arch into his touch, sensing the swell and the moisture in my groin intensifying. He is prone above me, watching me with undeniable burning as I bite my swollen lips and direct him a stare that commands him to go on.

Just as he leans in to lick my lips to part while his hand moves from my breast to slide under my jeans, his phone starts to chime and vibrate right beside us. He quietly curses but keeps exploring me urgently. His fingers thread further inside my pants, and ever so slowly graze over my thin, satin panties. He adds pressure, moving his thumb in slow motion up and down over the soaked, delicate fabric. I push my back away from the hard surface as his finger moves the fabric sideways and sinks into me.

Following the sounds of my escalating moans, the phone stubbornly rings again. And again. At the fourth time, the device starts a new session of chimes and shudders, and Reeves flings his engaged stare to check the screen. His sudden stiffness is more than evident. The last thing that I want is for him to stop this heavenly torture, nonetheless, I say in a breathy voice, "Maybe you should get it, it might be urgent."

Reluctantly, he takes a deep, composing inhale. Irritation takes over his features as he picks up the phone. I inch to sit, adjusting my bra, and watch him answer the call.

"Katie, what's up?" He holds the phone with his shoulder next to his ear, and steps to wash his hands, to wash me off, at the sink. A bitter frisson shoots through my stomach, and I turn to shrug my sweater on, cinching it around my waist. He listens to whoever this Katie person is with his back turned to me, the only clue of his state is the flex of his hard jaw.

"Calm down, doll." His voice is the softest I've heard it so far. The tone of his voice and the accolade slits through me. "I can't understand what you're saying. Breathe, Katie." He turns around, his face veiled with worry, his brows sunk together as he heads toward the balcony.

I decide not to jump to any conclusions and instead search for the bathroom to freshen up. I take a step back to lean on the tiled wall. I close my eyes tight and tip my head up against the coldness. Willing to ease my overall erratic high, I take a few lengthened breaths. I stay put for a few moments more just to give Reeves further privacy to end his call. Plastering my game face on, I reach for the doorknob. I'm not even sure how to approach this situation we've gotten ourselves into. What do you say to someone you've just encouraged to feel you, closely, while he might be seeing someone else? Bile starts crawling up my throat thinking he might be in a relationship. It's not that I'm a saint of any sort, far from, but I'd never be unfaithful, nor help someone else be.

And it's not that we owe each other anything, but still, it's not that I find myself too often in such a situation.

Reeves has his back to me when I step back into the kitchen. He rummages through a drawer, before turning back. He shoves a wallet into his back pocket while holding a set of keys in his other hand. Impatience is clearly displayed through his edged features.

"Listen Nia, I'm sorry, but I've got to go, now."

"Is she your girlfriend?" I blurt. "Because I'd never start, or continue anything with you, if you are in a relationship." For sanity's sake and to get his hands on me again, I tense while waiting for his answer.

"No. She is not my girlfriend. But I don't have time for this right now. I have to leave." I cringe at the mild exasperation holding his words. The blend of frustration and humiliation, to a degree, being once again so easily brushed off, stings. I send him a hostile gaze. I'd be okay with this cold halt if some sort of explanation was given, which he is obviously not about to give. I take a few steps toward the main door, passing by him. I shrug off his hand that finds its way to my back. Our short walk to get out couldn't be more in contrast to this same route we took getting in the apartment. I'm not sure who is more eager to get out, me or him.

"I'll call you," he says in a voice that could not sound more contrived.

"Whatever…" I answer, skipping the last couple of stairs. Faster than he can reply, I am at the door to my apartment. His response, whatever it was, is swallowed by the thud of my door as I slam it shut.

I rest with my back to the door, able to hear his steps fade away and the sound of the elevator doors closing. I try to calmly, if possible, replay what just happened in my head. I shy away from being that girl, the overreacting, bitching type. Nevertheless, the simplest elaboration would have been enough. Again, it's not that he owes me anything. But I'd expect him to have the decency to give me some excuse rather than just run off to some other woman with no explanation whatsoever, again… Fool me once shame on you; fool me twice, having me spread my legs for you with the slightest snap of your fingers, shame on me.

CHAPTER 15

Reeves

The chaos running through me is playing at the seams of my loose nerves. The panic in Katie's voice when I finally answered her call. Not having answered the first few times. Having to stop with my goddamn fingers deep inside the subject of my many jerk offs. I press the remote to lock my black Land Rover and jog toward where Katie said she would be, scanning the area under the evening light. When I finally spot her, standing by her car, talking to an elderly lady, seeming unscratched, the breath I had caged inside me gushes out in relief.

"Reeves," she says to my chest, burrowing under my arms. I kiss the crown of her head and give her the comfort that she seeks in a tight embrace.

"Are you hurt?" I pull her back to run a closer inspection over her. She shakes her head.

"She is fine, we both are," says the lanky lady in the oversized pants suit standing next to us.

"What happened?" I ask, returning my attention to Katie. It's more than evident she is making an effort to stay composed. I wonder if it's for my benefit. Strangely enough, she is the one person I'm not able to read. Maybe it's because of what she represents or whom she belongs to, but when it comes to her, I'm almost blind.

"I spaced out and bumped into her car sideways," she answers in a thin voice, her eyes gesturing to the lady beside her. She claps her pink glossed lips together, and her big blue eyes decorated by an apology return my hard stare. She reaches for a lock of her blond, wavy hair and nervously twirls it around her finger. My lips stretch to a grim line.

"Did you exchange papers? Is there anything else you'd need from us?" I ask the lady beside us who eyes me curiously.

"Yes, we did. I am fine," she responds.

I nod. "I'm sorry about your car." My eyes, followed by hers, zero in on the serious scrape to the side of her vehicle. "If there's anything else you might need, Ma'am… Here are my numbers." I fetch a business card from my wallet and hand it to her.

"Let's go get something to drink," I tell Katie who just bobs her head in agreement.

"I'm sorry, Ma'am," she says to the lady who already has her back to us, entering her car. Katie adjusts her purse on her shoulder and threads her fingers through mine. I twist my mouth but let her have it her way. I always do.

"Chamomile tea, and…" Katie turns to me in question while the waitress waits, tapping with a pen on her open notepad. "Coffee?"

"Draft, whatever you have on tap is fine," I say, and the brunette server sends an enthusiastic, inviting smile my way, which I disregard, turning back to Katie. Katie gazes at me carefully, biting her fingernail. I reach for her hand and place it on the table, stopping her anxious self-defiling, and slouch back into the red and white vinyl booth.

"What really happened?" I ask. She swirls a lock of hair around her finger, and when her beautiful eyes gloss over, I cover her palm with mine. She raises her eyes to look at me fleetingly and casts them down.

"I was thinking about tomorrow and got distracted," she says. My heart squeezes viciously in tandem to the tear leaving her left eye. I abandon my side of the booth and move to sit next to her. She leans her head on my shoulder and whispers, "Will you drive me there tomorrow?"

I need to swallow the lump in my throat before answering. "Of course, I will."

"Reeves, it's so hard."

"I know, doll," I say, and wrap my arm around her.

"And it doesn't get any easier. I thought that with time it would but it doesn't. I miss him so much." She can feel my empathy and agreement by the nod of my chin on the center of her head.

"Three years," I say, and futilely attempt to block out the snaps of visions too vividly taking form before my eyes.

The last knowing glance we traded.

The smoke of the gun.

The perpetual pain that follows doesn't take long to show. I release the tight hold that I realize I have on her. She lifts her gloomy eyes to mine, and our stares link in unified pain. For a long beat, our eyes convey sorrow, memories, and loss.

It takes me a moment to grasp what Katie does next, a moment too long. I snap out of my momentary lapse when her lips on my mouth part and her tongue urges mine to gap. I squeeze my eyes tight and gently pull my head back.

"No, Katie." I flicker my hardened eyes into hers that have taken a softer tone. "No." A fresh tear threatens to roll from her eye and I shake my head.

"I'm sorry," she says and seems relieved by the waitress' interruption as she places our drinks before us. I turn to face Katie after thanking the waitress. Her stare is glued to the steaming white pot. I hold her chin between my finger and thumb and bring her to look at me.

"We've been through this, Katie. You promised," I say, willing my determination to funnel through my voice and stare. "This will never happen. I love you very much, *as a sister*. I'd do anything for you, but this. You are beautiful inside and out and I'm sure there are a lot of guys out there who'd do anything if you'd just give them a chance." I crack my lips into a smile and add, "I'd beat the crap out of them if they'll ever lay a finger on you, both on Ben's and my behalf." She lightly giggles though through a dejected grin.

"Why wouldn't you give it a try?" she asks next, composing herself. I reach for the tea pot and pour her a drink. I take a sip of my chilled drink.

"I care about you, but not like this," I say. "You are like a sister to me."

"Because you are stubborn and annoying," she says playfully. I'm more than glad for her mood to shift and that she starts her usual banter.

"How old is Jake, by the way?" she asks as we are about to leave. I sign the bill and throw her a look over my shoulder.

"Too old for you."

She rolls her eyes. "Well, if you don't want me, I need to look for someone else who will." It's my turn to roll my eyes. I tug her hand, pulling her after me toward the exit.

"Why didn't you call Stanley to come help you? Not that I mind you calling me, but I guess he'll be upset to find out you were in trouble and didn't let him know."

Katie leans her hip onto her newly dented Volkswagen Golf. She raises her hand to cover her eyes from the street light as she looks up at me.

"Well, you know how my dad gets when we near the date of the anniversary," she says and her words tear us both up inside. I huff assent. "I didn't want him to have something else upsetting him." Her eyes focus on the metal chain around my neck that holds mine and Ben's dog tags. My thoughts sway to the little shrine of photos and medals the Evans have in their living room. The thought of Ben's family, the guilt, the responsibility, and the self-condemnation that suffocates me each time they shower me with love and a sense of belonging tugs at my heartstrings. That's when I need to leave. That's when I need to get away from Katie, from my thoughts and everything that takes me to the moment where I wish that gun was pointed at me instead.

"Okay, when do you want me to pick you up tomorrow?"

"We plan to be there right after my ECON class. I guess around noon." She beeps her car unlocked.

"You want me to pick you up from campus?"

She nods with a thin smile. She inches to her tiptoes and leaves a soft kiss on my jaw. I cup her cheek and rub my thumb over her soft skin, returning her smile. I watch her until she gets settled in her car and starts to drive away.

~ ~ ~

Reversing the Jeep into one of my parking spots, I contemplate whether I feel like going to the bar, or maybe just sleep or drink the rest of the evening away.

I throw my keys to the kitchen counter and fetch a water bottle from the fridge. I step out onto the balcony and slouch on one of the brown loungers. The apartment is not wide enough to contain my frustration. Drinking the cold water, I stare ahead aimlessly as the sky slowly converts into a darker blanket.

A painful coil strings within me. I close my eyes and shield the world away, resting my arm over my face. Three years. Tomorrow will be the third anniversary of the day my life fell into pieces. The third year in which the closest person to me was taken away. Each time my thoughts bring me back to that day, to his last moments, I cannot find even one damn reason why it should have not been me. As tomorrow becomes almost tangible, the memories that so far I've managed to keep at bay, crawl in. Sounds and voices, fragments of sentences, start funneling into my head, escalating into a beldam of accusations and guilt.

I step back into the apartment and start pacing the space, almost manically looking around for something. I don't even know what, just something that will stop this commotion in my head. My heart drums to the beat of chanting in my mind. I pass room after room, looking, searching, till I find myself sitting at the side of my bed, next to an open drawer of the night table, with my unmarked gun in my hand. I observe the weapon, rotating it from side to side. My eyes roam over every mark, every turning, and every imprint. As I realize what I'm studying so fascinatedly in my hands, a cold shiver runs over me. I toss the weapon into the drawer and slam it shut. I drop back to the mattress and close my eyes under my trembling palms. I shake my head with a need to shout, with a need to shut it all out. I want to be numb. I need to do something to take it all away before I lose it, and either destroy everything around me or take a path that has no return.

The only thing that's strong enough to maybe help sedate this madness would be to bury myself in Nia, continue where we left off just a couple of hours ago. That would surely help me forget, take me to better places. I just know it. And now that I've felt just how heavenly she feels, the want has intensified to levels I can't even deal with. The thought of any other pussy to calm the situation down is not even an option. Not even the twins, Ella and Eva, aka the Sisters of Mercy, that start a threesome party faster than you can roll on a condom, could kill this obsession. Bless their charitable spirits, of course.

Given her far from being tranquil reaction when I left her earlier, I decide to first text Nia before actually showing up at her door.

Hey, are you home?

I watch the phone stay still for five minutes. That turns into ten, and as expected, a reply doesn't arrive. I don't have it in me to go over there and apologize, explain myself, or whatever it is that might appease her. There's only so much I can really deal with right now. I certainly am not in any condition to carefully cull my words or even try to act civilized. While knocking on her door and pinning her to the wall doesn't seem like something she'll go along with. I give the closed drawer a second glance, heave deeply with the aim to keep my sanity intact, and walk out the room.

I throw back the fourth shot of the frozen numbing liquid and embrace the desensitizing effect that doesn't fail to show. As it starts spreading through my body and the light buzz takes over, I fill another glass to overflowing and down it, and the next one, and shortly after, another. When the room starts to blur and my feet begin to lose the ability to hold me, I lumber to my bedroom and crash to the bed. I close my eyes, and let dear oblivion take over.

CHAPTER 16

Nia

For as long as I can avoid the world, I bunker in my apartment. I shove my phone under a pillow and skim Spotify for new songs. I listen to a tune that catches my attention, closing my eyes, thinking of possible dance steps. When five o'clock finally crawls in, I leave my bedroom, throw my duffel bag across my shoulder, and start for the door. I run by the coffee shop for an energy enhancement shot and head to work.

Today will be the first time I give Lily a private lesson. I worry my lips, taking the last few steps into the studio. When I asked Mrs. Perry about using the studio after hours for practice, she took the opportunity to brief me some more about Lily's situation. She thought it would be easier for me to approach her if I knew her delicate state. As Mrs. Perry explained, Lily's parents are going through an ugly divorce, one of those "money is all that matters, kids are but a pawn" kind of disgraceful disunions. She warned me of Lily's vulnerability and tantrum tendencies. It's not that I'm not capable of dealing with the mentioned challenges, on the contrary, if there's anyone who'll be perfect for the job, it would be me. It's true what they say: "practice makes perfect."

Unfortunately, I'd mastered dealing with vulnerability and uncontrollable tantrums before my twentieth birthday. It's actually these same things that brought me to where I am today: far away from home, owning only a part of the whole that used to be my heart. The other half had been buried away over three years ago, together with the remaining of my happiness, and my Patrick.

As Lily's smile blooms on her lips, mine quickly joins. It takes me the better half of the lesson to get her to cooperate, but eventually she does and the glee she radiates warms me all the way to my core. I watch her with a thin smile as she clumsily, yet charmingly, sways to one side and makes a little twirl that ends with a light jump.

As opposed to the majority of my other students, her clothes are less polished. She has a stain at the hem of her short, wavy skirt. Her red braid could use some readjusting, but still, she is as sweet as the rest of them, if not sweeter. I decide to have some fun with her for the remaining ten minutes of the lesson and put some kids techno music on. We swap places, and it's me imitating her moves now. I make a whole show of having a hard time keeping up with her, making her giggles be heard above the music. When I thank her as the music winds out, she hugs me tightly with an embrace that I keenly echo.

Lily helps me tidy up the room, and we both shrug pullovers on, ready to leave. My brows knit as I check the clock again. The lesson ended fifteen minutes ago and there's no sign of Lily's parents.

As Lily notices my concerned expression, her face falls. "Sometimes they need to be reminded." Her voice comes out weak, stretching a chord in my heart along the way. I gently smile at her.

"I'm sure they'll show up soon, the traffic gets busy at these hours. Here, let me re-braid your hair, okay?" I ask and lower to my knees. She comes over and sits with her back to me. I untangle her red curls and comb them with my fingers.

"They are always late," Lily says, and it's her next words that make me want to hug her tight. "They even forget me sometimes."

"Tell you what," I say, turning her by her shoulders to face me. "Let's go to the office and call them."

I try to hold the thin smile on my lips, hearing Lily's mom tell me she had indeed forgotten that she was supposed to pick up her child, and the earliest she could be here is in an hour, not even excusing herself. I keep a light tone while telling her to pick Lily up from the coffee shop around the corner. I turn my head away as a frown veils my face when she just hangs up the phone, no apology, no thank you. Inwardly scowling, I turn back to Lily.

"Your mom is on her way. How about we go get some ice cream while we wait?" The radiating smile that lights the kid's face sends my own lips to stretch in genuine contentment. I zip Lily's pullover to the very top, holding the studio's door open with my rear. "We're good to go," I say. Turning toward the street, I stop short.

"What are you doing here?" I ask Reeves, who's leaning with his shoulder against the wall at Tutu's threshold.

"You didn't answer my text."

"Did you expect me to?" I secure my hold of Lily's hand. Reeves' eyes descend to my hand and wrinkles at the edges as he sees the kid holding it. He pushes himself from the wall.

"Hi there, what's your name, beautiful?" His smile grows and Lily mirrors him.

"I'm Lily."

Reeves squats and shakes Lily's free hand.

"Beautiful name for a beautiful girl. I'm Reeves, Nia's friend."

I glare at him and he winks at me.

"We are going to get ice cream," Lily sings, elated.

"What a coincidence," Reeves' grin broadens. "So am I. Can I join you?" Lily chirps a joyful hum of consent and I narrow my eyes at Reeves' smirk. I start walking, Lily in tow.

"Hey Lily, do you want a piggyback ride?" Lily almost swoons when Reeves sends her another one of his melting smiles. He is good, that I've got to give to him. *Damn Reeves.* He won the little damsel over without so much as a blink.

I ask, "So they all fall for it, this cute smile you put on?"

"You think I have a cute smile?" His smirk my way is accompanied by a teasing glance.

I roll my eyes for the fourth time in five minutes.

"I didn't say that. You think you can just show up here and that's it?"

"No. " The cocky undercurrent is gone. "I really wanted to see you." I can literally hear the crack in my tough exterior. "A good friend had been in an accident and she needed my help," Reeves adds. "I was worried."

"Hope she's okay," I say, and he nods confirmation. "This good friend of yours seems to have quite bad luck, it was her the previous time you ran off, right?" He nods again, his jaw flexing as he focuses his stare at some point ahead. "Is she *really* just a friend?"

"She is much more than a friend." His eyes turn to me, holding great resolve. I'd be lying if I said that didn't turn my stomach upside-down. "But it's nothing romantic, if that's where you are going with it." He runs his stare over my face.

It's my turn to nod. I decide to leave it as is. That's what I wanted to know. Other than that, any additional question might imply I might be seeking for anything more than just his company. And I definitely don't want to go there.

"You know, you could have just said you were leaving to help a friend. It sure would have made me feel better about myself," I say quietly.

"Noted."

Utterly concentrating, Lily digs a spoon into her candy sprinkled, strawberry ice cream. The kid's so captivated by the mound of sweet goodness that for a good ten minutes, Reeves and I become invisible. Out of the blue, she peeks her head above her goodie cup to look at us, more precisely at Reeves. I've kind of became a third wheel after Reeves showered her with his Reeves-charm.

"Have you ever seen Miss Nia dance?" Not waiting for an answer, she goes on, "I love watching her dance. I love how she moves." Reeves gifts her with an encouraging smile and turns to look at me in pure sin.

"I could watch Miss Nia *move,* forever." His voice is low, a husky accord seasoning his words. The heat wave washing over my middle makes me believe that he might have spoken directly to my core. Our eyes latch for a brief moment.

"Are you boyfriend and girlfriend?" Lily asks next, digging a long spoon into her pink ice cream.

Our answer could not come out as synchronized even if we've practiced for years.

"*No.*"

The sweet kid frowns at us. Reeves and I exchange amusement with our eyes.

Breaking her little stare, Lily turns to me, "I need to use the toilet."

"Do you need me to come with you?"

She shakes her head.

"So we'll wait for you here, okay?"

"Do you have any plans for later?" Reeves asks as I watch Lily making her way to the restroom.

"No," I answer and turn to eager green eyes. "Are you working tonight?"

"No, I'm hanging out with you." His lips lightly pull at the side. "You are okay…"

"Oh, wow. I've just totally swooned all over the place." For extra drama, I press my hands to my chest. He tips his head back in a short chuckle. Next, he takes my hands, laces his fingers with mine and tugs me toward him. I end up almost touching his chest. I lift my eyes to meet his and before I'm able to take my next breath, his lips brush mine.

And we kiss.

It's not as desperate and frenetic as the previous times, but nonetheless, it's still drowning us, rapidly. In no time we float into each other's arms, and just like the times before, everything around me completely dissolves. We take turns in dominating our consuming connection, which is a delicious combination of sweet and intense. His fingers lace in my hair, pulling me deeper, and mine trail to hold his cheek that's decorated with light stubble. My other hand finds its way to his warm neck, slowly sliding under the collar of his black undershirt.

"You are eating, Miss Nia!" I hear a sweet voice scold, and flinch back, flames crawling up my cheeks.

"Oh, I wish I was…" Reeves murmurs under his breath, only for me to hear. Having him add his little comment doesn't help my worked up body, nor the flush.

"Um… errr…" I just give up and look back at Lily who's watching me carefully with a thin smile.

"*He is* your boyfriend." She nods her head with utter determination and beams.

"Well, he is a boy and he is my friend." I smile back at her. Reeves, by my side, lightly squeezes my waist, and my smile grows.

"Lily-pie."

We all turn our heads to the woman mummified in tight black, carrying a small Prada bag, looking in our direction from behind enormous Chanel shades.

"Mommy!" Lily waves her way.

"Miss Mitchell?" The woman who looks as though she emerged from a Vogue Runway special edition tilts her head in question.

"Hello, Mrs. Beckman." I stand up, unable to stop my blatant gaze at her. She is skinny in an exists-on-wheatgrass-juice-only kind of thin. Courtesy of the thick layer of makeup she has on, her face looks frozen. Lily inches to hug her mother, and the breeder takes half a step back.

"You don't want to stain Mommy's dress, right, hun?" My heart sinks to Lily's withering smile. I need to work the muscles of my mouth to keep my lips pressed together, keeping my next words in.

"Thank you," she throws my way. Shifting her attention to her spawn, she says, "We need to hurry up. I have to drop you off at Nana's before going out."

Deflated, Lily turns to me and hugs me tightly; I reciprocate in the same manner. She then moves to Reeves and wraps her little arms around his significant bicep.

"Bye, beautiful," Reeves says in a gentle tone, patting her ginger, curly mane. "Poor sweet kid got frosty for a mother," Reeves murmurs. I nod as we both watch them exit the cafe.

"Honestly, I try not to judge, but it seems her kid gets in her way," I say, my eyes still at the door. "I feel sorry for Lily."

Reeves' touch on my chin as he pivots my head his way cuts off my absorbed gape. "We are going," he says, watching me. I counter with as much consent as I can incorporate into a single stare, with a double pacing beat, anticipating what's coming next.

~ ~ ~

My eyes hungrily run over the side of his wide neck as Reeves turns the key to unlock the door to his apartment. It wasn't actually discussed where we were heading, but somehow we've ended up here.

I moisten my lips, very well aware of everything *him*. How his long sleeve, black Henley hugs his ripped, wide, upper body. The way his worn-out jeans hang around his lean waist. The closely shaved hair decorating the nape of his masculine neck. His fresh mixture of sea breeze and citrus scent.

He slides the door open for me to enter. With the tap of the closing door, he turns to me. In parallel, without any warning, his lips land on mine, and I'm lifted up to be pinned against the wall in the most aggressive, yet welcomed, manner. I wrap my legs around his waist. Reeves' left hand cradles my ass, holding me suspended as he leans into me. His other hand moves to cup my cheek while his thumb lightly strokes my parted lips. As he presses against me where our bodies meet, I suck his thumb into my mouth, caressing it with my tongue.

"You drive me insane. I can't stop thinking about this," Reeves says, grazing his thumb against my tongue. Not long after, his tongue takes the place of his thumb. He traces mine, sucking, tasting me slowly and hard. He pulls back just enough to drink me in with heavily heated eyes. "I need to feel you, now," he says next, and a warm pull takes control of every organ beneath my waistline.

"Nothing is stopping you," I breathe. The carnal way he looks at me at this very moment is a vision that I'll never be able to forget. It has so much heat, hunger, and determination that it leaves me breathless. His mouth homes in on my collarbone, starting a delicious attack. He sucks my skin in small little bites that have me whimpering. Still engaged in tasting my skin, Reeves walks us to the living room sofa. Reaching his target, he drops us both with him between my parted legs. He props his arms by my shoulders, distancing just enough to gaze at me.

Still watching me attentively, he sends his right arm to pull his shirt over his head. He throws the cloth over the sofa and his weight is back on me. I close my eyes, indulging in every bit of his warm mass covering me. He presses his thigh to my middle in delicious, torturing pressure. His hand moves to my cheek, and slowly trails all the way to my breast, leaving gentleness aside as he palms me. I fling my arm to the back of his neck and pull him to my mouth. The tips of our tongues short-circuit, sending the sensation all the way down to my throbbing heat. Our kiss gradually, with greater energy, evolves into a battle of strokes, pants, and dominance.

Reeves inches back with one of his hands planted firmly at my back, bringing us together to stand on our knees, to face each other. In no time, we discard of my top and bra. I send my hand to his chest, grazing my way south over smooth skin, ridges, and soft hair. The tension directed from my eyes to his is so intense, it's almost tangible. I trail my hand further down on his hard body and his eyes, for a brief moment, leave mine to follow my hand as it reaches the bulge in his jeans. As I press around the swell, his eyelids flutter and his next breath is sharply sucked in.

Reeves' hand shoots to hold the back of my head, slightly tugging forward for his mouth to hover next to mine. "I need your bare skin around me, Nia," he whispers huskily to my mouth. It's all that's needed for me to slide my hand inside his jeans and wrap it around him. He is hard, yet smooth and warm, and everything that I want in me. Reeves grabs my thigh, wrapping it around his hip. He slowly pushes us back till I'm sprawled on the sofa beneath him. The next moments are dedicated to ripping jeans off heated bodies, heavy, needy breaths and stolen, and urged kisses as we straggle to get rid of any fabric separating us.

Reeves tips my chin, holding it between his fingers and thumb. He bites on my bottom lip while croakily saying, "I'm getting a condom."

One last kiss and he inches up, heading toward the bedroom. I follow him with my stare, headily, savoring the sight: firm, toned back, and curved, sexy ass. I notice that my body is literally emitting heat, my nerve ends at full attention, waiting impatiently for his skin to touch with mine again.

Settling on his knees before me, he nudges my legs to part. His eyes are a liquid, raw green as he hands me the condom. I prop up just enough to reach him. My attempt at ripping the silver packet with my teeth is abruptly stopped. My next breath is heavy, and thick as Reeves cups me, gently spreading me for his thumb to reach closer. I arch my back, my head falling back in tandem to a moan that escapes my mouth. His thumb starts tracing, grazing ever so gently up and down my heated spot.

"I won't be able to put it on you when you do this," I murmur with my eyes still closed and my head still tilted back, utterly high on his touch.

"We have plenty of time," he says, sinking a finger in me.

"Reeves," I breathe and another one joins. "God," and his thumb joins to circle my throbbing peak. I almost scream next when the pressure becomes impossibly heavenly. His other hand sprawled between my breasts pushes me slowly to lay on my back as his fingers continue to deliciously spread me wider. I focus on his consuming stare as I build higher and higher. Still working me to overpowering desire, he inches closer to suck my nipple into his warm mouth. The pressure of his thumb moving in circling motions around where I need him becomes almost unbearable. His mouth joins the sweet torture with painfully sweet bites on my nipple. His name comes out in a string of chants when my body can't take it anymore and I cum around his fingers, hard.

Just when I think I can breathe again, he draws back to kneel between my thighs for his tongue to lick my spasming tissues. I cry again, jerking my body away, but he holds me still, suckling me to the edge of blissful oblivion.

CHAPTER 17

Reeves

I give Nia a moment to come down from her loud and very rewarding orgasm, feasting my eyes on her as I roll on a condom. Her hair is scattered on the sofa in a dark halo around her beautiful face. Her cheeks flushed, her mouth swollen and red from my kisses and bites. She is perfect like that, absorbing the orgasm I just gave her. She is the most stunning sight I've ever seen, spread before me, waiting for me to make her cum once more.

Christ, my cock is so strained and hard it begins to hurt. I need to be inside her. Her hazel eyes watch me in heavy sedation. Returning her stare, I grab her thighs and lift her pelvis to line up with my erection. I tug her forward. Her head sinks deeper onto the sofa and her legs open wider for me. I watch myself sinking ever so slowly inside of her. I shut my eyes, savoring the feeling of her hot walls closing around me, devouring me.

"Fuck," I gush. She feels beyond amazing. Nia purrs a moan as I move inside her and unhurriedly pull back. I hold still for a beat and thrust forcefully. Her lips part and she arches her back.

"Uh." Another moan leaves her mouth. My blood burns inside my veins to the exquisite sound. The noises she makes, the way she feels—soft, warm, and tight—I'm completely lost in her. She feels fucking incredible. I slow down, holding still deep inside of her. I do not move. I don't want this moment to end.

When Nia's fingers move to pinch her nipples, my dick grows harder. I let out a groan as her narrowed eyes lock with mine. Moving my hands to cradle her ass, I jerk her closer to me and start pounding, rocking wildly on my knees. Her moans escalate and she starts chanting my name again. I can't believe anything can ever feel this amazing. I squeeze her ass with both hands, sinking deeper inside of her. She clenches tighter around me, eagerly sucking me in. Fuck, I'm not going to last much longer. If I had to choose a way to die, this is how I'd want to draw my final breath, inside of her.

As her panting hastens and becomes erratic, my thrusts mimic the rhythm, turning forceful and faster. The room fills with the sounds of our rapid breaths, pants, curses, the sound of flesh against flesh, our names on each other's lips. At her final cry, I watch her falling apart in bliss in my hands, her eyes closed, her hair clinging in thin clusters to her sweaty face. She is spent, sedated, and breathtakingly gorgeous. I wet my lips, focusing my eyes on her, pounding harder. As I sink deeper, she opens her eyes to mine, her gaze at me doesn't waver though her entire body jerks with each of my slams into her. She contracts tighter around me with my next thump, and I cum so hard the world spins around me. I empty myself inside her while she watches me heatedly. My sight hazes into blessed darkness as I tip my head back, letting ecstasy wash through every part of me. The high is so hard, it's almost euphoric.

Nia is curled on the sofa, hugging her bent legs, snuggled in my deserted shirt. She is watching me as I make my way back from the bathroom. I pass by the fridge and fetch two water bottles before joining her in the living room. I hand her a bottle and almost empty mine in one long swig. She watches me, a small smile playing on her lips behind her bottle. I mirror her and our smiles grow in unison.

"To doing your neighbors!" She clinks her bottle to mine with a wicked grin, encouraging a chuckle to roll from my mouth. She snickers lightly and takes a sip of her own bottle. *She's just the coolest chick.*

We fall into easy conversation, slouched side by side. I watch her attentively next as she tells me about how beautiful Brazil is. And all I can do is focus on every delicate curve of her face: her big eyes, her pointy nose, her naturally swollen lips. The way her hair falls in heavy masses over her shoulders. My thoughts wander to how peaceful she makes me feel. Her company is so easy, I don't have to fight anything away while with her. Everything that's ill doesn't even attempt to appear.

"Have you ever been to Brazil?"

Her question pulls me back. I nod.

"Yeah, but I didn't have much time to enjoy it. It was a business trip, so it was basically work all the time." She pulls the sleeves of my shirt to her elbows.

"You should definitely visit again," she says returning to hug her bent legs.

"How about you, are you planning to visit home anytime soon?" As soon as the question leaves my mouth, I regret asking it. Smiling Nia disappears behind sad eyes. I say the first thing that jumps to my mind with a need to get her back from whatever made her look this way.

"Where did you learn to dance that way?"

"My mom says I've always danced." Her smile returns as she continues, "She says that I was dancing before I could even walk. I get lost in it, it's the best legal high." Nia elaborates and tells me how she joined any possible dance course before the age of fourteen. Gazing at her, actually interested in what she has to say, a sudden realization lands in my mind: we just had sex and I don't have the urge to have her close the door behind her and leave. I actually want her to stay. I actually want to hear more about her. And mostly, I want to have that little pull on her lips stay for as long as I can make it.

More than an hour of talking passes while we exchange equally insignificant and intriguing information about ourselves, preferences, our jobs, the small part that I can actually share, down to favorite movies and music. Each time we learn of the many similarities we share, we trade soft smiles. It's when Nia asks me about my family that a small debate starts in my head. I contemplate if I want to tell her more about myself. Or, as each time this topic has been raised with everybody else before, do I take a step back and end the conversation. End whatever is starting between us.

"No, I don't have any siblings. The closest thing to a family I have is Katie and her parents." Nia's eyes grow as she takes in my answer. Her demeanour alters, guarded. "Katie is like a sister to me." I feel like I need to clear up the Katie situation, especially after sleeping together.

"She is my best friend's little sister. My best friend, Ben, who passed away a few years ago." Nia's expression turns into a blend of empathy and contemplation.

"I'm sorry about your friend," she says quietly.

I acknowledge her with a gentle blink. "Ben's family took me as their own the first time Ben brought me home, about fifteen years ago." In a way, for them, I sort of stepped into Ben's big shoes. Shoes I could never really fill. Shoes I don't deserve to be filling.

"Where are *your parents*?" Nia asks next.

"My mother died while giving birth to me, and my father is traveling around the world still trying to figure out how to continue living without her," I say flatly. It never stops to amaze me just how easy *these words* come out of my mouth. Quite early, I came to terms with not having a mother. Well, when you're born into such reality and there's nothing else to compare to, it's just what it is. I bring my eyes back to her and can't help just how much I'm liking her reaction. She doesn't have that look of pity in her eyes, the one I get each time I tell someone new about my past.

It's as though she accepts it and instead of giving me a sorry look or some lame response, she just says, "Yeah, life can really suck."

"True," I say, trying not to think about tomorrow, not now, but it still surfaces.

"Hey, where did you go?" Nia's voice penetrates my reverie of Ben's name as it is engraved on a headstone. The next words that come out of my mouth leave me both surprised and muddled. I'm not sure what astounds me more, the fact of actually talking to anyone beside Jake or the Evans about tomorrow, or the ease I feel telling it to *her*.

"I was thinking about tomorrow. We are planning to visit Ben, his family and me."

"How... How long has it been since he...?"

"Three years, tomorrow." My answer is curt. Her face stones over and her surprised eyes dart to mine for a brief moment of silence. It seems like the next breath is a difficult one for her to take. Her stare is empty, sad, and distant. When she comes back to me, she seems distracted.

"Um… Um…" she starts, and frowns at her futile attempt to articulate.

I just look at her and wait as she seems to be having an inner battle. All too familiar with the feeling of failing to share, or communicate at times, I just squeeze her hand. Nia couldn't look more thankful for the sound of my phone ringing next. I give her a short glance before starting toward the kitchen. I wasn't planning on answering, but do so for her sake, to break the tense moment we just had. Let her out of the emotional loop that she too evidently was pulled into.

"Jake," I answer the call.

"Are you coming over?"

"No. Not tonight."

"Where are you?"

"At home, Nia's here."

"Lucky son of a bitch." Amusement lines his words.

"I'll drop by tomorrow."

~ ~ ~

I play with a lock of Nia's hair between my fingers, relishing the feel of it on my skin. I lower my head just enough to inhale it. It smells of honey, pure. I run my eyes over her calm face, watching her sleep. Again, she'd fallen asleep on my shoulder. Not long after we ordered Italian and had it with a couple of wine glasses, she fell asleep. This time I've carried her to my bed and tucked her in. I lie on my side, my head leaning on my propped elbow, watching her. She seems so peaceful, and delicate. But I know better, I've seen glimpses of it many times in the short while we've known each other—she holds something painful deep inside of her. Her sad eyes, the many times she disappears inside her head, it's too familiar. I can't seem to overlook it, even if I tried. I softly run my thumb over her velvety cheek and bend to leave a soft kiss on it. I breathe her in one more time and turn to grab a book before heading to the balcony to read, letting her sleep.

CHAPTER 18

Nia

In utter leisure, I flicker my eyes open to Reeves' dim bedroom. He must have carried me to his bed last night. Once again, I am surprised to find out that I have fallen asleep next to him, and even more staggered at just how easy my sleep was. It's so calm and deep that I'm tempted to ask him to sleep by his side every night.

I pivot my head to rest my cheek on the pillow and watch him for a peaceful while. He is prone on his stomach, his toned arms hugging the pillow his face is planted on. His long lashes caress his fair skin. The sheet barely covering the hem of his boxer briefs.

I send my hand to touch his warm skin, walking my fingers lightly on his wide back and sigh with mixed emotions. I'm not sure how to deal with... him. I thought that after we had sex, this attraction would ease down. But it's not, definitely not, and I know so as I'm holding myself back from waking him up and begging for more.

Silently, I make my way out of the bed and close the door behind me. I rapidly shrug my clothes on, take the key to the apartment, and lockup before heading to get breakfast.

Reeves is still sleeping as I take out a plate and set the six doughnuts I bought on it. I wasn't sure which kind he'd prefer so I just got everything I like. I place the tall cup of coffee that I got him next to the plate, turning it so the note I've written on its side will face Reeves when he sees the little feast that I left him. Inspired by what he has laid in store for today, I wrote:

Hang in there. I'm just a staircase away if you need me...

~~~

"Girls, please continue practicing the moves. I'm going to get something from the office, okay? Who wants to take my place?"

"Me, Miss Nia, me!" Almost all hands rise in unison. My eager little dancers send ten pairs of puppy eyes at me. I choose the ones lacking glee.

"Lily." I smile at her and she shyly smiles back. I gesture for her to stand in my spot and face her friends.

At the office, I get the permission slips from Mrs. Perry. She calmly observes me, asking how I'm doing. We exchange a few words about the girls and the upcoming show we are working on before I return to my lesson.

"Yes, yes. And he is sooooo nice." I come back to an attentive group of girls, listening to a gushing, elated Lily.

"Who is soooo nice?" I smile at them, imitating Lily's chirping tone as I take back my place. I mouth thank you to Lily, and take off from where I left with a one, two step dance.

"Your boyfriend." A chorus of sweet voices replies. *Oh, God.* I friendly frown at Lily and shake my head, facing the girls.

"I don't have a boyfriend," I say.

After a few minutes of honing their movements as they dance, I gesture for them to sit in a semi-circle to discuss the lesson. As I wait for them to get settled around me, snippets of everything Reeves filters through my thoughts. His sweaty, firm body above me as he gave me one of my wildest orgasms ever. The sliver of vulnerability in the undercurrent of his words as he told me about his friend, Ben. The next thought about how he might be feeling right now pulls at my emotions. I make a mental note to text him after class and check how he is doing.

When I greet the parents, saying goodbye to the girls, Alex swifts by. She whispers in my ear while still in motion, "Jake's." I nod confirm with a quiet smile and she winks in response.

"*I am* planning on giving *each* of the girls a little solo part." Inwardly scowling, I answer to a mother who asks me to give *her* daughter *the* solo part.

~ ~ ~

"God, some of the parents can be so controlling," I tell Alex, who's standing by my side as we wait for the bartender to fix our drinks.

"Tell me about it. Sometimes I'm not sure who is more eager, the girls or the parents." We nod in agreement.

"Where's Toni?" I ask, glancing over my shoulder to the table where our group is. It's Alex's usual gang, minus one roommate/lover.

"I think we are over," Alex says too casually to my taste. My brows knit in return.

"You think?"

Alex shrugs. "I haven't seen her for a couple of days, and she hasn't answered my calls."

"Um, aren't you guys living together?"

"I don't know, she just hasn't been around..."

"Aren't you worried?"

She just shrugs it off again. "Toni is kind of strange at times. She should be let be."

The bartender sets two shot glasses, a finger of scotch, and a beer bottle in front of us.

"To crazy-ass lovers!" Alex declares before throwing back her shot glass. I snicker and mirror her.

"Katie!" The bartender, I think Dan, or Danny was his name, grins at someone behind me. Hearing the familiar name, curiosity kicks in and I turn around to the miniature beauty who I saw with Reeves the other night, when I was spying on their somewhat emotional exchange.

"How you doing?" he asks in a gentle voice. Her response is a flit of eyebrow motion, saying "so, so." He extends a hand over the bar to squeeze her shoulder. She is utterly pretty, in a fragile kind of way. Also from up-close, she looks like a human version of Tinkerbell. A group of friends joins her, a fusion of the debate team meets the cheerleading squad. Tinker would be a hybrid of both.

Only when she sends a stare my way do I realize that I've been gaping. I timidly smile and she echoes me. For a brief moment, my heart teeters at the thought of her probably visiting her brother today with Reeves. My next breath is stolen from me, when my own past mixes with the realization. I take a moment to collect myself before getting back to Alex who joined the usual group while I was caught in my musing.

Once it floats to the surface, my past, I can't seem to focus on anything else. I just nod at the people talking to me. I'm too absorbed in my thoughts to even try to pretend to be responsive. Memories of home keep suppressing even after I've emptied the glass with the strong liquor. As the freight train hurtling in my head gathers momentum, my own traumatic past begins to entwine with the thought of the emotional torment Reeves must have gone through today. I text him.

Hey neighbor-friend, how are you doing?

When I check my phone again, for the tenth time in the past half hour, it's still void of a response. Half an hour more is all I can tolerate before I say goodbye and hurry home.

I worry my lips, unlocking the door. I fidget while making my way to the kitchen, contemplating on checking in on Reeves. I get a scotch bottle and hold it in my hands, then put it back in the cupboard. I go to the bedroom next and change into a delicate, almost see-through negligee. I observe myself in the mirror and just shake my head, quickly changing to loose, flowery pajama bottoms and a white tee. I slip into my shoes, grab my key, and climb the stairs to the floor above.

It takes Reeves a few good minutes to answer my persistent knocks. Wearing nothing but black boxers, he squints his liquid green eyes at the light coming from the hallway where I'm standing at his doorstep. Behind him, the vast space of the apartment is dark. It doesn't seem like he's been sleeping much, though. In fact, he couldn't appear more restless.

"Hi," I say softly.

He answers with a silent questioning stare. A look that's a combination of query, fatigue, and weariness. Tentatively, I take a step forward. As he takes one back to allow me inside, with a quicker heart, I take another. I turn to close the door behind me, shutting my eyes and taking a slow breath. I turn back to find Reeves' hand in the quiet dimness. By the softest of moonlight coming from the balcony windows I find his stare and counter it with a gentle, reassuring one, leading him after me in silence. I leave my key at the counter as we pass by the kitchen on our way to the bedroom. I kick my shoes off, still holding Reeves' hand and next, take him with me to bed.

Watching me through the sliver of moonlight with hard eyes, he follows suit. I softly kiss his lips before taking my place, resting my head on the pillow next to his. I watch his silhouette in the dark, placing my hand on his chest and just let him be. He moves his hand to cover mine and we both stay silent with our thoughts for an extent of time that feels as though a few hours have passed.

The sound of sheets crumpling as Reeves turns to face me breaks our prolonged silence. We watch each other intently for a breath as out of the blue he asks, "Why did you call me G.I. Joe the other day?"

Instinctively, my face heats up. I couldn't be more grateful for the obscurity we lie in. I wouldn't dream of letting the next words that leave my mouth in any other circumstances, but even for the mere possibility that what I'm about to tell him might cheer him up, I do.

I shift to lay on my back, cover my flaming face with my hands and blurt, "Because you look like the star of my military themed fantasy." I couldn't be more delighted at the chuckle that escapes his mouth. I pivot my head sideways and peek at him from between my spread fingers. He is grinning, genuinely grinning. I move my hands away and smile back at him, wholeheartedly. He just tugs me to him and cuddles me to his side. Soon after, he strokes my hair ever so gently and I fall asleep, content.

CHAPTER 19

Reeves

I lean with my hand propped on the kitchen cupboard, gulping down half of an O.J. gallon, thinking of last night. My lips lift up with Nia on my mind. I'm still floored by how with the simplest of gestures, she managed to sooth every malady I've been carrying throughout the day. She was right beside me, for me, and apparently that was enough. That was what I needed in order to calm down and eventually even fall asleep.

Her knocks on my door found me sitting in the dark, wishing, like each time I visit Ben, that it was me in his place. Ben was always the better part of our duo. Ben was the poster boy for Most Likely to Succeed, everyone's favorite. He left a loving family, a beautiful, caring girlfriend who was about to become a fiancée, an arsenal of friends, and a promising career, when he died too young.

And what would I have left had I been the one who got caught? A father that still mourns the day I was born? Nameless, faceless sex partners? A few friends? *His* family?

Before these malignant thoughts roll into a snowball of contempt and self-hatred, I close my eyes and bring myself back to last night. To how Nia knew just what to do to reach me. How I didn't want to talk and just be. And she'd let me. Too bad she had already left before I even had a chance to see her pretty face this morning.

As I put the empty gallon to the counter and turn to start the day, I let out a healthy chuckle, having Nia's image before my eyes as she covered her face, and told me I looked like her sexual fantasy. If that isn't the hottest thing to hear from a woman, I'm not sure what is.

Checking the time, I realize I have a few hours to get ready before my flight to Cuba and decide it's enough time to make someone's fantasy come true. I take the quickest shower in history. Thankful I kept my uniform, I smirk all the way to my closet. Still wearing a shit-eating grin, I study myself in the walkthrough closet mirror: ACU jacket, cargo pants, boots. It's been awhile since I wore these... I even went all the way with a close shave.

Humming, I skip every other step to the level below. I knock and wait for Nia to open the door, having a very hard time subduing my smile.

Nia's expression when she opens the door skyrockets my mood. She is the very picture of shocked excitement. Her chin literally drops while her eyes devour the sight of me. *Fuck yeah!*

I scratch my temple with my thumb, squinting at her teasingly. "Hey. I'm the neighbor from upstairs, can I borrow some sex?"

Her lips stretch to the wildest smile, she grabs me by my jacket's lapel, eagerly pulling me inside.

"Whoa..." I gladly cooperate. Our mouths mesh in no time through unified chuckles. She takes a step back to look at me again and shakes her head with a greedy smile before jumping me. I catch her, and she wraps her legs around my waist. Her mouth attacks mine and her needy grazing against me causes me to almost lose balance. I stride with her dry humping me to the nearest wall.

"Get down to business," she orders, biting my lips. I think my dick just turned into rock.

"Fond of the uniform, are we?" I pin her to the wall, pressing against her, my mouth biting at her jaw. With one hand supporting us, I send my other to squeeze her full tits.

She lightly snickers and says, "Oh, shut up and get busy." And raids my mouth.

I gently put her down, kiss her, and spin her to face the wall. One of my hands reaches her breast under her shirt, while the other cups her, tightly. She moans, and leans her forehead to the wall. I send both hands to pull her pants and underwear down. I grab her ass with both hands and graze it against the swell in my pants. I then help her get her shirt off, and lean to trail my tongue slowly from between the two dimples decorating her lower back to her neck. I spread her thighs with my own and cover her bare warmness with my hand, grazing it in slow pressure. She moans again and pushes back into my hand. I slide a finger inside her tight heat. Fuck, she is soaked.

I undo my zipper next and free myself. I grab her by her thighs and prop her ass just where I need it. Nia's hands slide on the wall as she positions herself closer to me. Hastily, I roll on a condom. I hold her tight with one hand and position myself, ready for her. I tease her briefly, till she huskily orders me to fuck her. My blood runs in flames through my veins at her command and I sink into her. *Chrisssst.*

"Hold on to the wall," I rasp as I increase my thrusts to a forceful pace. Nia's pants and screams are all over the place and all over my head. It's the sexiest thing I've ever heard. Still holding her with one hand, I bring my other to her mouth, and slide three finger inside.

"Suck them," I say next to her ear in a husky voice, still steadily thrusting in and out of her. Obediently, she sucks my fingers wet. I lean to press my body into her and change my pace to enter her slower and deeper. My damp fingers end on her clit and I start rubbing in rhythm to my shoves. Nia's moans become needy and stretched. I bring my mouth to her shoulder and kiss, bite the silky skin, driving wildly in her.

"God, Reeves... God!" And I sink deeper and more powerfully till she starts spasming around me. I'm so close. She cries a strained moan enlaced with my name and I let go.

～～～

"Can you stop being such a chick and just shove that spoon in?"

"Correct me if I'm wrong, but I don't think you thought I was a chick ten minutes ago when you were screaming my name." Nia just rolls her eyes, her lips in a side smile. "I try not to eat junk."

"Ice cream is not junk. Don't you dare call it that," she mutters with a feigned scowl and brings her spoon to my mouth. "Open up now, you know you want to…" She wriggles her brows. I chuckle and obey.

Nia covers her bent legs with the large sweatshirt she put on after we got our heart rates back to normal. She rests her hand on her knees and sends the other to the family size ice cream container on the sofa between us. I slouch back and dig another spoon in. Nia gazes at me for a long moment, holding the spoon's tip next to her lips, thinking.

"Um…" She draws my attention. "What do the roman numbers stand for?" I open my arm sideways, looking at the ink on the inner side of my bicep. "And the initials?" She loads a small mound to her spoon.

"It's a date," I say, her eyes focus on mine, waiting for me to go on. "It's the date we lost Ben. And the initials B.E. are for Ben Evans." I sigh deeply. Nia worries her lip while I bring another spoonful to my mouth. "Since we were about fifteen, we thought about getting matching tattoos, Ben and me, lame huh?" I snort, and Nia lightly laughs in assent. "We were looking for either the coolest thing or the most ridiculous one." I chuckle, thinking about the idiotic ideas we had throughout the years to mark our bodies with. "But we never found anything that we both agreed on. Not something monumental, nor something really dumb." Nia lips stretch wider.

"It sounds like you were really close."

"We were, he was my family." There's a twinge in my heart, but it's not the usual one. Somehow, talking to Nia about Ben is not as depressing as it always is. Surprisingly so, it has an undercurrent of a fond memory of my best friend rather than grief.

"You should have a happy date. We both should," she says, the last part coming out softer. My eyes come up empty in the search for hers. She seems lost inside her mind, once again.

"You want to talk about it?" I ask quietly. She turns to look at me somewhat startled. It takes a short beat before my question sinks in. She shakes her head from side to side and I just send my hand to cover hers, blinking in understanding.

"We need a happy date. A date that won't erase the past but will let us remember it with acceptance." She goes back to her previous point. "A date that will make my happy beat my sad."

I don't let her sink back into whatever she had in her past that upsets her. Desperately needing her smiling again, I say, "Maybe the date that your sexual fantasy was finally fulfilled?"

She grins at me widely. "That could be it."

"I hope that by having a date you don't mean you want to get a tattoo."

"Why not?" Her brows lift in question.

"If I were your boyfriend, I'd never let you defile your perfect skin by marking it." Her response comes as an involuntary grimace. I'm not sure that I'm able to read what she thinks, it appears to be as though she's making an immense effort to look casual. I let it go and pat her thigh.

"Okay, it was more than a pleasure but I have to…" My phone stops me from saying goodbye and heading to pack before my flight. I check the screen and read the text from The Russian, excusing himself for postponing the trip at the last minute. I can't calm the beam illuminating my face. After a short text exchange in which he tells me a family matter came up and that he'd probably need me only next week, I tuck the phone in my pocket. I level my eyes with Nia who's watching me with a hint of a smile.

"What are you grinning about?" Her own smile broadens.

"I just got some good news."

"What good news?"

I set the melting ice cream can to the table and inch closer to her. I pull her bent legs and spread them at my sides. She squeaks and her eyes take a devilish glee. I hold her thighs and hover above her.

"I have more time to play soldier with you."

～～～

I make my way to Jake's, thinking it's been one of the best weeks that I've had in a long while. There's nothing special that I could put my finger on that made this week as great. It just was. Between my training routine, doing some "office work," as far as reading reports on people can be called office work, working some shifts at the bar and hanging out with Nia. Somehow we've found ourselves, unplanned, evening after evening, having sex, talking, watching late night shows, and sleeping in my bed. Seems like these evenings we're spending together just make everything... better. Hunter hasn't contacted me for a while, but I'm sure that he'll let me know if there are any developments.

Dan tips his chin in greeting, and Eileen blows me a kiss when I pass by the bar on my way to see Jake. The moment my foot steps into the office, I regret coming in. Jake is on the phone, more precisely barking into the phone. He paces the room and curses under his breath while listening to the person on the other end of the line. Instantly, I manage to scrape up who he might be speaking to... his ex-wife.

Jake married his high school sweetheart at a relatively young age. They were both very much in love and even much more reckless. At eighteen and a few days, Carmie and Jake became parents. Dylan, named after the singer and the legend, of course, was raised in an unusual environment, to say the least. By the age of three and a half, he was able to name every motorcycle on sight and sing heavy metal ballads like any other kid his age would croon Old Macdonald. Still very much in love, but with careers and goals that collided with being parents or even living together, they got a divorce not long after Dylan's fifth birthday.

As a product of their crazy-ass loins, just like his parents, Dylan had also developed one hell of a personality. One hell of a personality that came to bite both Carmie and Jake in the ass when at sixteen he filed for emancipation. Which he claimed was not for any lack of love for his parents, but only for the sole reason that he believed he could do a better job of taking care of himself than either of them, together or alone, could ever do.

Even now when Jake runs his fingers through his hair and yells, "You cannot fucking do that to me again, Carm," I know he still cares for her. I think she was, and still is, his one and only. Albeit, this one and only drives him crazy like no one else can. I turn on my heels after grabbing an apron from a freshly ironed stack. *I might as well make myself useful...*

Jake says to the phone, "Hold on, Carm, it's Reeves." He listens to something she says and rolls his eyes with a hint of a smile.

Jake swipes a finger over the phone's screen and a husky, sexy feminine voice bursts into the room, "Hey, Mitchell, miss me?"

I chuckle and say, directed at the phone that's now resting on the table, "More than I can bear, Mrs. Rey." I intentionally call her by her married name. Jake flips me off while Carmie's laugh fills the room.

"Not for much longer, I'm coming over soon to strangle your friend." She laughs again. "You know what, come for dinner tomorrow." I give Jake a questioning look, he nods with a shrug that says just how much he can't control the Carmie situation.

"I'll be there. Can I bring someone, though?" I ask with Nia on my mind. Jake's eyebrow rises together with a jerk his lips take. I'm not sure what that expression insinuates and I'm not willing to even give it a chance to be elaborated.

"Oh, please do. Is she a hottie?" Carmie asks with a hint of amusement.

"She's just a good friend…"

"Mmm, hmm," they hum in stereo.

CHAPTER 20

Nia

I give myself one last check in the mirror, waiting for Reeves to pick me up. He asked me if I wanted to join him for dinner at Jake's house last night, just before I fell asleep, once again, in his bed. I agreed immediately, just as I've agreed to almost everything he'd suggested this past week. The thought of him leaving tomorrow morning is not something I'm thrilled of entertaining. I like having him around. He tends to make me smile, a lot. He tends to keep everything that's bad at bay.

I smooth the slim, cornflower-blue cotton dress I have on and apply mascara. I slide my feet into beige, suede, ballet-flats, and hastily wrap a taupe pashmina around my shoulders as I hear the knock on the door.

Reeves, wearing a pinstriped, black button-down and fitted jeans, smiles broadly as he sees me.

"You don't look bad yourself," I answer the silent compliment. His lips twitch together with the move of his hand to the small of my back to guide us to the elevator.

"You look great," he says next to my ear, and my smile almost splits my face in half.

~ ~ ~

"You are not moving in," Jake mutters, cutting a chunk of steak that he brings next to his mouth.

"I'm not asking you, love. I'm telling you." Carmie smiles over-sweetly, seeming unfazed by his harsh rejection.

108

I covertly watch her, pretending to be engaged with the contents of my plate.

Her straight, blond hair is almost waist length. She is slim and tall, mere inches shy of Jake and Reeves. She's sporting rock chick attire: black skinny jeans, a loose Rolling Stones tank top, and dark, but subtle makeup around her powder-blue eyes. She seems like the kind of woman you'd never want to cross.

"Carm, the only way for you to move back in is for an indefinite time. You want to come back, then stay, goddamn it." Jake gives her a look that makes me want to hide under the table and wait for the storm in his eyes to pass.

"A. I'm staying. B. I'll be sleeping in your bed." She pops a cherry tomato in her mouth and winks at Reeves who fondly snorts.

"Would you pass on the greatest sex ever if he slept in the next room? No, right? You'd just make yourself comfortable in his bed. No?"

I blush. Reeves smirks and Jake shakes his head as if saying "unbelievable."

When Reeves makes a move to get up and asks, "More beer?" Carmie jumps from her seat, orders him to stay put, and heads to the kitchen. Coming back, she gives each one of us a cold bottle and to my discomfort, straddles Jake's thighs.

"I'm staying over, and we'll just deal with shit," she says, her lips close to his. Her voice is soft but still loud enough for us to clearly hear her.

"No." He brushes his mouth to hers. His hand moves to grip her thigh. She threads her fingers through his straight, messy hair and licks his lips. Their mouths meld in one hell of a sizzling kiss, making me dart my eyes to Reeves who seems to be less than bothered by the erotic exhibition we're subjected to.

"I'm used to it." He gifts me with a side smile.

When the door opens and a young fusion of Jake and Carmie enters, we all turn our heads his way. "Fuck, really? Can't you guys ever be normal?" says the new addition to our group.

"My handsome baby." Carmie leaves Jake's thighs and takes a few steps to almost squeeze to death the epitome of cool grunge.

"You'll scar him more than we both already did with this fondling..." Jake's husky voice follows Carmie kissing her spawn on the lips. "Hey, kid." Jake tilts a bottle in greeting at his son.

"God, Carmie," the son says to his mother.

"Oh, shush!" she responds and takes a step back to admire the mildly annoyed twenty something. "What an incredible production you are, eh? Each time I see you, you get more and more handsome." The production in subject grimaces and grabs the untouched beer bottle Carmie left by Jake's side when she attacked him moments before.

Jake and his son dap greet.

"What's up, Dylan?" Reeves asks.

Dylan nods in response, his lips slightly pull up as he notices me.

"Well, well, well. What have we got here?" Dark brown eyes blatantly run over me. An eyebrow raises, his head slowly bobbing while the smile on his lips expands.

"My friend, Nia," Reeves says in a firm tone and moves his hand to cradle the back of my chair.

"Nia." Dylan takes my hand and plants a lengthy kiss on it.

"Nice to, ahem, meet you," I say, pulling back my trapped limb.

"It is nice. Very nice," Dylan replies. He takes a swig of his bottle.

"I wouldn't even try if I were you," Jake says with a hint of humor. He gets all of our attention as Dylan, Reeves, Carmie, and I turn his way. "She's *with* him." Jake nods at Reeves and turns to wink at me.

"He just declared her a friend. In bro code that means she's free for anyone else to take a shot at..."

Good Lord.

"Believe me, son. Don't."

My eyes squint, looking for Reeves' reaction. At that very moment he turns to look at me and something happens. I'm not sure what, but it's like a charged frisson, some unexplainable vibe that loops between us.

"Oh, c'mon. They are so together. Can't you see sex written all over the halo they share?" Carmie says, waving her blond clusters back.

I want to die.

"We're right here," I murmur. Reeves sends me a small smile which, yet again, I can't even begin to translate. Dylan tucks his hand into the front pocket of his ripped jeans, studying us with his bottle frozen next to his lips in midair.

"Now, seriously, you guys totally have this 'we're so deep in each other's souls' thing," Carmie adds and turns to Jake. "Just like we do, huh, my handsome baby daddy."

"We do; the problem is that only one of us is clever enough to want to make something of it."

Carmie and Jake's instant stare-off is a sixth presence in the room.

"Damn, you're right, Carmie," Dylan says, breaking whatever his parents just put on the table. "When you're done with him," he adds, winking at me. My face lightly warms and my eyes move to the set of white tee and plaid shirt he has on. I can't look him in the eyes right now. Frankly, I wish I could disappear for a few moments till the odd ambiance takes a hike.

"Dylan." Reeves' warning comes low and firm. He leans over so his lips reach my ear and whispers, "Don't look at them straight in the eyes, they're all crazy. They'll turn you into one of them."

I beam back at him, and everything clears off. We're back to normal, for less than a second, that is. Abruptly it's tension zone again, only this time it's hard core. It starts with two phones beeping. With brows knitted and lips partly gaped, I watch as both Reeves and Jake produce two pairs of phones from their pockets. Both men observe the devices they have in their hands. Jake's face instantly edges, while Reeves' eyes turn from green to scary.

Jake's next words are spoken as soon as Reeves' stare darts to the door. "Don't even think about it. I'll tie you up if I'll have to."

Reeves' jaw edges. He slowly turns to Jake. They have a short, wordless conversation till Jake inches up, gesturing with his hand for Reeves to follow. He clutches Reeves' shoulder. "Let's go visit the lady's room, shall we?" They disappear in the wide corridor. "Mother Fuck has bigger balls than brain," we hear Jake say as they duck behind a closed door.

Unfazed, Carmie shrugs. "Work…" To my surprise, she suggests the three of us go have dessert on the balcony.

~ ~ ~

Reeves is not with me when we drive home. He might be the one steering the wheel, but his mind is elsewhere, a territory I seem to temporarily be banned from visiting. After the fourth time my attempt at starting a line of communication is dismissed by a curt answer, I let it go.

And yet, somehow, I find myself turning to sleep next to him. I watch Reeves through the moon's halo softly illuminating the dark room. Hard features, head rested on his hand over a pillow, staring, burning a hole in the ceiling. As my eyes become heavy, I feel the warmth of his hand covering mine. I turn my hand so we're palm to palm and lace our fingers together. The last thought before falling asleep is of Reeves leaving for Cuba tomorrow, for a whole week, for work. The idea of not being able to sleep next to him for a whole week drops my mood even lower. Funny enough, I already miss him though he is right next to me.

~ ~ ~

Sunday evening finds me curled up under a woollen throw blanket with my skin burning and red, swollen eyes, damp cheeks, and the meanest knot causing havoc in my stomach. I look at the open card box on the table and saw my teeth through my lip. My mother thought I'd be happy to receive the last items I'd forgotten back home. Little did she know, these are the items I actually made sure to "forget."

A small photo album of happier times.

Unused, two open return date tickets to Vienna.

The last note from Patrick. A note that I made sure to hide away in the cover of the family photo album. The one I take out with shaky hands and an even shakier stomach. A note that makes my heart bleed.

Nia,
> **If there was anything I could have changed, take it back...**
> **I've never meant to hurt you.**
> **I'm so sorry for everything.**
> **I love you.**
Patrick

The box has been standing, accusingly, tauntingly, on the living room table since I got it on Monday, the beginning of a week that could easily be named a week crafted in hell. It's been a week of odd numbers and plagued moods.

1 was the new friend/lover I was missing and needing like I've never thought I would.

3 were the times I've sobbed under a burning shower.

5 were the number of meals I've existed upon. If a small bag of Oreos can be considered a meal.

7 were the times I cried myself to sleep.

999 were the times I checked if I got my period.

CHAPTER 21

Reeves

For the umpteenth time, my eyes run between the small thumb peeping from The Russian's notebook to the slightly ajar door. I chew my gum in agitated tempo, tapping my fingers on the table, waiting for the message to appear and confirm all the data has been successfully copied.

Shit. Unmistakeable heels patter my way. I raise my eyes to the vision of an advancing Mrs. Vasileva, who besides being my client's wife, is also known for her distinguished, opulent taste and her love for her husband's young human shields. Jake once said that the lady has a hard time differentiating between fidelity and promiscuity as they kinda rhyme. I check the screen again, willing the damn process to complete.

It should be done any minute now, like the meeting being held in the next room. The last thing I need right now is company, of any sort. I can't get caught hacking his hard drive. This guy doesn't do slap on the wrist, it's more in the vein of a body parts search across the damn Atlantic. I can't even have him see the screen up.

"Mr. Mitchell." The fine-looking wife of my client sways her hourglass, expensively clad body, into the room. A vision of beautiful affluence haloed by a cloud of heavy, sweet perfume. I send the notebook another glance before standing up to meet her, making sure I'm blocking her line of sight from the incriminating device.

"I think someone broke into the suite, can you come up with me to check it out?"

If I had a nickel for every time she used this excuse before…

She licks her perfectly painted red lips and runs a hand through her ass length, golden hair.

"Ma'am, your husband's orders were very clear. I should stay here till he is done." In other words *ma'am:* your husband would much rather not have anyone, accidently or not, interrupting the illegal weapons deal he is about to shake hands on, nor does he wish for his wife to fuck the staff.

"Mihkil will be very upset if I told him you disobeyed me." She pulls a cigarette from a golden, thin case. *Disobey.* I'll give her the benefit of the doubt that it's a language barrier thing...

"Ma'am, you can't smoke in here," I say, well aware my time is dwindling. "I'll check the room right after Mr. Vasileva is through. Why don't you wait at the reception, just in case there was an entry?" I need her gone, right now. Her stare narrows at me. She twists her mouth and swings her curves toward me in slow steps. Shit.

She rests a red manicured hand on my chest, and my eyes drop to follow her action. I shake my head. As she runs her milky hand over my navy-blue tie, I murmur through gritted teeth, "Your husband is in the next room."

The Mrs. falls into two of my hardest limits, never to be crossed.

1. I'd never fuck anyone in a relationship.
2. I'd never fuck business for pleasure.

Last, she's not Nia.

What. The. Fuck?!

"He is busy..." A thick Russian accent engulfs her whisper. The muscle above my jaw tightens. I rest a heavy hand on the small of her back. Silent but determined, I turn her to face the direction she came from and lead her to the door.

She gives me a hostile look over her shoulder and spits, "I can have you fired."

"Do as you think fit, ma'am," I say in a cold tone, prompting a flush of anger to cover her cheeks. Once Mrs. Cougar is out of the room, I'm back at the table. Just as the last of her steps fades, heavier steps echo from the corridor, where my client's voice is heard way too close. Shit, shit, shit.

As The Russian's silhouette crosses the room's threshold, the confirming message pops: Files Copied Successfully.

"Here you go, sir." I hand him his laptop and phone while discreetly pulling the thumb out of the device with a pull of two fingers. Fuck, that was close. Inwardly, I beam. I love these adrenaline rush moments. Color me reckless, hell, I do.

I leave The Russian and his beloved wifey to pack and go get my stuff from the connecting room. Behind the closed door I pull out my burner and text Jake.

Done. I got it all. And then some.

Jake's immediate reply makes me snort a laugh.

Honey, you just got me hard.

I leave the room, my carry-on in tow.

~ ~ ~

I finally let myself unwind, melding my back to the luxurious, leather chair, looking out the circular window. We're scheduled to land in a couple of hours. This trip can't end soon enough. I can't wait to be home. However, I've promised Jake to run by the office, first thing.

"Can I get you anything?" asks one of the two polished flight attendants for the third time.

"Water, please," I say and try to seal out the high tones my client and his wife's argument has taken. For the second time today, I regret not flying back commercial. The Russian insisted I join them on his private jet, and I didn't have it in me to argue the generous offer.

I adjust the ear buds and press play on my phone, listening to Fink until the last text from Hunter conjures before my closed eyes. Apparently there's been quite a development with the A.Z. case. Once we, Jake and I, called Hunter back, he briefed us, as much as he could, about a possibility of the sleeper cell—the one Ben, me, and our former unit dismantled and arrested most of its members—reforming to avenge the fall of the original cell.

I'm not sure how I'll react if I ever find out where their operation takes place this time. Who am I kidding? I know perfectly well how I'll react and so do Hunter and Jake. That's the crux of the reason that I don't get to have the full details. My fingers start to feel numb by my death grip on the sofa's arm. I inhale slowly and exhale even slower for some moments. It's the thought of seeing Nia later tonight that finally helps loosen my tension.

It's been radio silence for Nia and me this week. Between being too busy, to hardly having a few moments a day to myself, to feeling it would be weird to call her, I just went with easy. I didn't. She's obviously a friend. A friend with whom I've been sleeping with, literally and figuratively, for a while now. Somehow calling her just felt strange, maybe too involved. But still, trying to keep it casual or not, I can't wait to see her.

~ ~ ~

"Son of a..." Jake mutters, his eyes wide open, looking at the thin screen standing amid debris of empty takeout boxes, papers, and cups on his cluttered table. He rubs his scruff, huffs, and turns to look at me. I nod with a hint of an annoyed twist on my lips.

"What are you going to do with it?" I ask Jake about the evidence I brought back, of The Russian's illegal, to put it mildly, affairs. Let's just say, the guy has his hands "full". Full with everything that could possibly reek illicit.

"With his money and connections, this one is way out of my territory. I'll pass it forward," he says, clicking the mouse he holds, his face still glued to the monitor.

"He doesn't spare on anything, eh?"

I pull out my buzzing phone from my pocket and check the screen. Nia.

Are you back?

A smile takes form on my face, a wide one, that is.

Am here.

Can you come down for a few?

"Do you still need me here?" I ask Jake. He shakes his head, not wavering his stare from the screen. "So, I'm out of here." He nods to the monitor.

On my way, be there in 10.

~ ~ ~

I'm not sure what drops faster, my smile or my heart, to Nia's expression as she opens the door. Happy to see me would be the last thing that jumps to my mind when she barely manages to pull her smile further than an inch to one side.

"Hey, what's up?" I take a step forward to wrap her in my arms. She doesn't answer and just burrows her head into my chest. My breath hitches at the enormous contentment that washes over me at finally having her in my arms.

"Not much," she says to my tie, her voice entwined with a light shudder.

"Nia, what's wrong?" I ask softly and hold her tighter. She sinks into me and my heart flutters. "Do you want to talk about it?" Her head gently bobs under my chin. I just hold her for a few beats more and then suggest we go for a walk.

"How was your trip?" she asks while we wait for the elevator.

"It was good," I say, studying her face. She seems lost and tired. Worry creeps in, spreading slowly.

"How was your week?" I ask as we head toward the park, walking distance from our apartment complex.

"Could have been better." She cinches her knee length, white cardigan around her slim waist. She doesn't elaborate on her vague answer. We take a seat on a bench facing the duck pond. We both stare ahead at the water, the trees, the endless green. I turn sideway to face her.

"Nia, what's wrong?"

She huffs and buries her face in her hands, "I don't want to drop this on you. But..."

"You can drop anything on me. Talk to me," I say, watching her squirm, still shielding her eyes from the world, from me.

"I feel so stupid... how could I let it happen... I actually didn't do anything wrong. I just..." She sighs. "I'm so sorry Reeves, really, I never intended for anything to." Another sigh. The escalating drumming sound in my ears is coming from my ribcage. I remove her hands from her face and hold each in mine.

"Look at me," I say firmer but still with a soft edge. "Whatever it is, just tell me."

She lifts her eyes to mine, a thin watery layer had glossed them over. She worries her lips. My breath is held until she finally speaks.

"I'm late."

Instinctively, my eyes dart to my watch. Late? Late? LATE! F...U...C...K! I nod calmly, still holding her hands, while a nauseating burning grows at the pit of my stomach.

"How late?"

"More than a week. It's never happened before, I'm never late."

"We were careful..." I think, unintentionally uttering the words out loud.

"We were," she confirms softly, her eyes filled with concern.

"Did you... uh... have a test?"

She shakes her head.

"I didn't. I didn't have the courage to..."

"I see." I frame her face with my hands and inch closer with mine. "Let's do it together. Don't worry. Whatever it is, we'll deal with it together." She blinks and I caress her face with my eyes. "Okay?"

"Yes." Her eyes soften and I lean even closer and softly press my lips to hers.

"Everything will be okay," I say, even though a hurricane of worry is causing mayhem inside of me.

She quietly says my name as I inch to stand. My eyes link with hers. "I think I've just fallen deeper in friendship with you."

My lips crook up, and the storm inside me calms a degree to her timid smile. "You've been *in friendship* with me?"

"Hopelessly..." She grins and my lips pull higher.

I think my heart just melted. I offer her my hand. "C'mere." When she stands next to me, I tuck her under my arm and kiss the crown of her head. "I adore the shit out of you, friend." I do, I really do.

"You're a true poet." She laughs. Unfortunately, it's a short and agitated sound.

~ ~ ~

"Let's see. We've got blue, we've got grey, we've got red, we've got purple..." I wiggle my eyebrows, setting the arsenal of home pregnancy tests that I got at the pharmacy on our way home, on my en suite vanity. "Oh, and we've also got pink. This one might look innocent, but I kid you not, this motherfucker claims 99.9 percent accuracy. It's badass pink!"

Nia, by my side, watches me with a smile, the under seams of anxiety are still very much evident behind that gorgeous smile. I wink at her.

"You think you got enough tests?" she teases. I swat her ass and she squeals, jerking forward. "I don't think I've got enough liquid in me for all these sticks..."

"Try to fill up a cup and just stick them all there."

"God, I can't believe we're having this conversation." She shakes her head.

"Pee away, milady." I bend to a full-blown curtsy before stepping out of the bathroom. Nia laughs it off, waves, and closes the door behind me.

My smile crashes down as soon as I lean against the wall. Gone is my breath. I gently bang my head back while whispering, "Fuck, fuck, fuck." I do something I haven't done since I can remember: I pray. Not sure to whom, but I do.

I compose myself and call out, "Hey Nia, come out, let's wait together."

She slowly opens the door and looks at me, seeming completely freaked out. I inwardly grimace at the worry she radiates. She took off her cardigan and she is down to a long sleeve, white shirt and jeans. Needless to say, anxious or not, she's still incredibly attractive. I can't get enough of how beautiful she is. I offer her my hand and she fills it with hers.

"Dance for me," I say. Her eyes flash open.

"Are you for real? I'm about to hurl here, and you want me to dance?"

"Wasn't it you who said dancing calms you down?" My eyebrow rises. "You know what, we both will." I pull her after me to the bedroom. She frowns, yet follows.

I put the wackiest song that I can find in my playlist on and turn up the volume. Nia observes me with knitted brows, a smile slowly creeping into her lips.

When I start swaying and jumping to the crazy tune, Nia bursts into laughter and joins me. The rowdier the vibe gets, the goofier our moves become. I hold her hips and fling her to straddle me. We move together, totally out of control. When Nia starts to shake her sweet ass too excitedly, I lose balance and fall to the bed with her on top of me. Our stares unite for a long beat, and we both smile softly.

"Are you ready?" I ask, breaking our silent bubble. She saws her lips and nods. All color leaves her face. I push out an exhale before entering the improvised field lab in my bathroom.

"It'll be okay," I say, rubbing her arm, not convincing either of us. Nia hides behind my back as I turn to check experiment number one: white and purple stick. My sigh of relief followed by a breathy, "Fuck," prompts her to peek from behind me. Nia looks up at me and our stares catch with glee. We both let out a brief snicker of relief and high five. Same reaction goes to the second, third, and fourth sticks.

"Oh, shit." I exclaim at 99.9 percent accuracy, exhibit pink.

"What?" Nia swallows the word in a sharp intake.

"What was it, two lines, or one?"

"Two?" she asks wearily, and I beam. I shove a finger through the knot of my tie, releasing it in a long pull.

"Oh God, thank you. Thank you!" Nia drops her head. I can only relate to her massive relief. Finally, the twisted string in my stomach unties. "I wanted a happy date… Here's a happy date for us." It's her turn to wink, and mine to chuckle.

~ ~ ~

I lie in bed, wide awake, although I couldn't be more beaten. This week in which I was about twenty-four seven in alert mode, the flight back, and the pregnancy threat situation that literally scared the living shit out of me, all mesh in my head. I think I've reached the point where I'm too exhausted to even begin to unwind. I sink my head deeper into my clutched hands on my pillow. As I process the potential colossal mess we've just dodged, everything Nia takes over my mind.

Random thoughts flit by, and they all end with one beautiful girl with stunning, sad eyes who took up residence inside my heart. They run from our goodbye earlier when Nia said she needed alone time to process everything, to the fact that I've never, so far, been to her bedroom, to having her occupy my mind all the time while I was away. Together with a strong feeling of how I should take a step back, comes the thought of how little I really know about her. About her family, friends, about her life before she moved here. I've managed to glean from everything she's said, and not, so far, that she must have had some hell of a past.

Just like I know how involved I'm becoming with her, I know that for her sake and my heart's that maybe at this point we should just stop. Perhaps it was a wakeup call in the form of a false alarm to stop whatever is taking over me, strongly and steadily.

The short chime of my phone breaks into my mulling. It's after one a.m., who on earth would be calling me now? In complete contradiction to my momentary emotional retreat, my heart makes half a summersault when I see Nia's name on the display.

"Are you awake?"

"Why are whispering?" I ask with a smile that I'm not exactly controlling.

"I thought you might be sleeping."

"And you expected me to answer and continue sleeping?" Her soft snicker reaches me and my smile grows. "How can I help you after one a.m., Miss Mitchell?"

"Ehmm, any chance I could join you?" Her voice over the line is supple and somewhat hesitant.

"You want to sleep over?"

"Yes," she answers and my previous thoughts are locked into a provisional drawer right after I flip them off.

"I'm waiting for you…"

Not more than five minutes later, she's spooned in my arms with her back pressed to my chest. No more than a soft, "Goodnight," whisper later, and her breathing becomes steady and calm. I inhale her subtle honey scent, and with every sweet intake, the idea of taking a step back crumbles down piece by piece. By the time I kiss her silky hair, that idea turns into dust that's carried away by the light night breeze.

~ ~ ~

The next few days post False-Alarmgate, is an awkward zone between Nia and me. Somehow, we are either too busy to meet, or just make a hell of an effort to be. We don't see each other during the days, but we fuck each other to sleep every night. There's a lot of raw, rough sex going on and not much talking. Not that I'll ever complain, but it's too odd not to make me wonder if we managed to screw up our friendship. It's a thought I'm not even willing to bear.

CHAPTER 22

Nia

"Lovely, these are just lovely sounds," Alex mocks the rumbles my stomach produces. Growls that color the silence in the locker-room where we both change into jeans after our classes. It feels like I haven't eaten for a week, which in a way is kind of true. Only after last night's deep sleep did my appetite return from its long hibernation.

"Coming to Jake's?"

"I'm not sure. I'll check with Reeves, he is picking me up for dinner."

Alex's gaze narrows at me, and she threads her fingers through her crazy, purple hair, making it even messier.

"You guys are together now?"

I give her a head shake. "We're just friends." To be honest, I'm not sure what we are anymore. Finally, we'll meet in broad daylight, something we haven't done for some days now.

"Cool, so he is out there for grabs?" An overly plucked eyebrow is cocked at me. I dismiss the flare in my stomach as a side effect of my hunger.

"I guess."

"Oh, I hope you guys join us even more now ... He. Is. Fine!" I smile at her, and what a hard effort that smile takes.

"Aren't you with Toni? Didn't you get back together?"

"Nah, we're back to just sharing an apartment, nothing more."

After Alex leaves, I take a few moments to apply eye shadow, blush, mascara, and a thin layer of nude lipstick. My fresh flush is courtesy of a sudden realization: I've just applied makeup, which I do only when I go out on dates, and I did it thinking of the person waiting for me outside. Immediately, I yank a tissue paper from the Kleenex box rested on the wide, illuminated vanity, and wipe my lips clear somewhat brutally. I leave the mascara on. It's one thing to try and look as though you'd made no effort, but it's a totally different one to look like a rabid raccoon.

I'm not looking to impress him. We're just friends, good friends, with a whole lot of fantastic benefits. Benefits in his bed, benefits on the counter, benefits on the sofa, horizontal, vertical, and my favorite, wild, rough benefits. Wild, rough benefits in uniform… Every possible damn mind-blowing benefit. But benefits do remain in friends' territory for us.

This is how it should be. I cannot allow myself to put my barely held together heart out there. I'm not sure that either my heart or I would survive as much as even a tiny seam tearing out. And anyhow, his messages, Reeves', verbal and silent ones, on where he'd like to take this friendship of ours were received loud, rather bitter, and very much clear.

"*If I were your boyfriend*, I'd never let you defile your perfect skin by marking it." Read: I'm not your boyfriend, take note of that, don't get any hopes up. His brush-off of the subject when Dylan asked if we were dating was quite illuminating. How about the last few days? It's been the worst case of odd vibe. I must admit, though, it was mostly my doing, this growing apart we've got going on. It was me making all possible excuses not to meet during the daytime. I wanted to meet him, very much, but somehow it felt as if I needed to give him some space after the bomb I dropped on him, on us.

Hypocritically so, at nights I've ended up in his bed, every night. That was my doing, too. During the days I've been keeping myself busy, but the nights are a whole different story. At night I need him. But I should really stop dwelling on a non-issue, it couldn't be better this way. We are of the same mind: just friends.

So why does it still hurt?

~~~

"I missed your face," Reeves says, watching me attentively above a lit candle as I lean in for a bread stick.

"You've seen my face every day," I murmur, nibbling on the crispy delight.

Yes, we didn't go to Jake's after all. I might or might have not persuaded Reeves that we must have Italian tonight. It might have to do with Alex's recent zeal with Reeves, but even tortured, I'll never admit to that. Reeves keeps silent long enough to draw my look up.

"You meant to say, *every night.*" He twists his mouth, running a finger on the red and white checkered tablecloth. I lower my stare to follow his finger as it moves from side to side next to a white plate.

"More wine?" I ask, reaching for the open bottle between us, but his nimble hand gets to it before me. He holds it firmly, gazing at me in edgy silence. He then tilts the bottle toward my glass and starts pouring the rich red liquid.

"Why are you acting so weird?" he finally asks, setting the bottle back and raising his eyes to mine. His jaw is tense as he observes me, waiting for my reply.

He's wearing a long sleeve, bottle-green shirt. The fabric accentuates his wide, sturdy pecs, while the color does wonders in emphasizing his striking eyes.

Reeves insisted we go out tonight and now I know why he wouldn't succumb to any of my lame excuses to just a sleepover. He apparently has his mind set on not allowing me to ruin whatever we have going on. *Thank God.*

"I thought you needed some space," I say, and my stare drops to my nervous hands on my thighs.

"I needed some space?" he repeats. "Only in the daytime?"

My breath catches as I lift my eyes into scrutinizing greens.

"I thought you might want a break after the little bomb I dropped on you."

His brows sink in. "But you still come over *every night*…"

"I sleep better when you're around," I say in a low voice, watching his edginess soften.

"Why's that?"

I shrug and reach for another bread stick.

"One of these days you'll have to tell me what's really going on inside your mind," he says in a way that tells me that he is letting go of whatever we've just discussed. It's more than evident that we both know there's so much more lying under our brief exchange. I couldn't be more grateful to him for changing the subject to a lighter one. He tells me about the persistent attempts of Dan to get Eileen to finally agree to go out with him. Poor guy apparently has it bad.

"Oooh, I love this song." I interrupt our easy conversation, as the first tunes of "Lemon Tree" fill the small restaurant. Reeves eyes light up.

"I like you smiling," he says, and I beam.

Between delicious bites of artichoke, pine nuts, and parmesan fresh pasta, we tell each other about the week we had. The wine slowly but consistently keeps flowing as the time pleasantly flies by.

"That's it, I can't breathe!" I drop my fork and slump back onto the wooden chair.

Reeves smiles.

"You didn't even eat half of your dish."

I frown and he shakes his head with a hint of amusement.

He takes a long sip of his tall glass and says, "Okay, let's pay and run by Jake's." Catching the waitress' stare, he signs for the check.

"Nah… Let's just go home."

He cocks his head in question.

"I'm not much into socializing tonight."

"You're socializing with me."

"It's different with you."

"How is it different with me?" he asks.

"It's the best kind of escapism." His smile causes butterflies to flutter in my stomach. Strike that, these are not butterflies and they are not fluttering, it's more akin to gigantic eagles, winging in ferocity.

~ ~ ~

As I unlock the door to my apartment, before actually stepping in, I look over my shoulder at Reeves. "Can we not, f…ahem…k… tonight?"

"Come again?" He snorts a laugh.

I fling the door open, having him follow me. Mid-way inside the living room I turn to him, "We can do something else, can't we?"

His recent snort turns into a wide smile as he watches me squirm, both humored and undecided. Reeves sends a hand to my forehead.

"Feeling good, love?"

"We can do other things, can't we? We don't have to… Oh, I know, let's play…"

Reeves folds his arms over his chest, watching me with a touch of mock.

"What? I was just saying that we can do other things."

"Honestly, Nia, I have no idea what's gotten into you."

"Yes, let's play. Ooh, I know, let's play Scrabble. We can play Scrabble and not each other, right?"

"Scrabble and not each other?" Reeves bursts into guttural laughter. "You're all kinds of crazy today, but it's damn cute. Okay, playing it is… not each other."

I smirk and head to get the board game.

We sit on the rug next to my living room table with the game board between us. Reeves is crossed legged with a ghost of a smile and I'm on bent legs to his left, arranging my vowels on one side of the rack.

I check my letters one more time, wrinkling my nose, catching Reeves' lips crooking higher. I go first, my "B" totally kicked his "E's" ass. I place an "R" on the star at the center of the playing board and add the rest of the letters.

"Ready…?" Reeves utters the word that I've just placed with the most suggesting smile. I roll my eyes. "Nine points…" He notes the number down on a piece of paper and turns to use my "Y," for his word: "yours."

"If you are ready… I'm yours." He grins and I roll my eyes again, amused. "Always," he murmurs. We both beam at each other.

I bite my lip, holding a smile while placing my next word. Oh, he'll love this one. When I'm done I blink at Reeves twice.

His grin doubles. "I like where you are going with this," he says somewhat huskily at my "swallow."

He winks at me after setting his word: "lick."

"We're at twenty-two to eighteen," he says, utterly amused.

"I'm getting soda, get you anything?" I ask, inching to stand. He shakes his head slowly, but by the way he looks at me, I know exactly what he'd like to drink: me. A heat wave swirls inside my tummy and continues south. I close my parted lips, unglue my eyes from him, as hard as it is to do, and turn to the kitchen.

I place the can on the table, settling in the space that I've just vacated. I take a long sip, studying the board again. Once my word "come" is arranged on the board, I take another swig. Reeves watches me keenly, green heated eyes tearing off each piece of clothing that I have on. I smile into the can, beyond enjoying his attention. He shakes his head, clearing his mind and turns to observe his rack. His eyes crinkle as he places his word.

"Pound," he says, popping the P. He grins and I twist my mouth, trying to ease my own smiling. "Your 'O' helped my pound," he says, and I can't help my giggle.

"Umm…" I move my lips from side to side, checking the board and my letters again. "Rock," I say while placing the tiles slowly, one after the other.

"Hard," Reeves says the word before setting his letters on the board. Involuntarily, my eyes fling to his crotch. He smirks. I bite my lip and feel my cheeks heat up. He bobs his head and mouths, "hard." The looks we trade next are a combination of humor and fire. Fire that I've grown to know so well, a fire that could only be extinguished with him, *hard*, between my legs.

I make a whole show of thinking, as I pretend to choose my next word. *Oh, I've chosen it, carefully…* I feel like throwing my pompoms to the air in victory. With the tip of my finger between my lips, I bend to the table, making sure my cleavage is on display. As soon as I place the "L" that concludes "anal," I watch the tiles fly into my white shaggy rug. The innocent board follows suit as it is swiped away in one swift movement, and it's me that's next on the table.

I'm on my knees, breasts pressed to the wooden surface, and a hard body melds into mine from behind. I can feel him pressing against my rear and his breath next to my ear.

"You were saying…" My earlobe is in Reeves' mouth, and a very distinctive excitement thrusts slowly against me. The only thing I'm capable of getting out of my mouth is a moan.

"Umm, don't get too excited, we are not touching *that* word," I say as his tongue starts to slowly trail from behind my ear down my neck. I tilt my head back, giving him better access. I slightly move into him, take his hand in mine, and slide it under my shirt, guiding him to my breasts. "But you can touch anything else you want." He pushes down the lace of my bra to get my nipple between his fingers.

"I am." His low voice wraps me with want. His other hand slides down over my shirt, halting next to my fly. Easily, he unbuttons my jeans and his fingers slide between the rough fabric and my satin panties. Rubbing his palm over me, ever so slowly, his hand on my breast moves to give the other the same delectable treatment.

"Tease," he says as he rhythmically and blissfully instigates every one of my nerve endings. I send my hand to reach between us, sliding it inside his jeans. He pulls back just enough for it to get inside his boxers. I palm him, grazing over the warm and smooth skin. He lets out a low groan and pushes into my hold. We stroke each other, my hand around him, *his* ardently exploring me, till we're both panting with desire.

"Reeves." His name comes out of my mouth on a moan, and he sinks his finger deeper.

"Say it," his voice is rough and hoarse. "Tell me what you want."

"I want you," another finger joins and I pant mid-sentence, "inside of me."

Before I know it, my jeans and panties are ripped off me. He positions me back at the table and props my ass up before him, reverently caressing it.

"Hold tight to the table," he says, and the sound of his zipper freeing him is like a sweet promise. I feel his body's heat back behind me, then he nudges my legs to spread. Right after, he directs himself to where I'm eagerly waiting for him. He teases me first, and I lean back against him. As he sinks just one inch more, I drop my head between my spread arms. One of his hands moves to hold me by my shoulder and the other by my waist. He pulls back just a little, and then in one fierce slam, he causes the wildest delightful cry to fly from my mouth.

There's nothing subtle nor poised about our need for release as I lean into him while Reeves thrusts into me, repeatedly and with strength. He pulls back and pounds into me again and again. I grip the edge of the table, absorbing his raw, blessed attack. He grows thicker, and I become slicker and greedier. He slows to leave hungry kisses on my back, from the middle of my spine to the nape of my neck. I press back against him and he picks back the pace and continues playing on each of my aroused strings.

"Yes, yes," I pant, begging for him to go even faster. He does. And he reaches deeper. The sound of our bodies colliding fills the room. He releases his hold on my shoulder and brings his hand between my legs to start circling, pressing just enough to make me explode into millions of particles of ecstasy.

Still landing from my mind-shuttering orgasm, spasming around him, I feel him increase his already wild pace. Not long after, just before reaching his own relief, he freezes for a short breath, pinned deep into me.

"God, you feel amazing," he rasps. With his next forceful thrust, "Fuck, Nia," is uttered through a strained breath, just before he falls on top of me. Satiated, we even our heartbeats.

"And just for the record... I won," I say, and we both lightly chuckle in unison.

"And just for the record, Scrabble is officially my new favorite game." Reeves watches me, his eyes light with amusement as I shimmy into my panties while reaching for my jeans.

"Uh," his low, clear voice prompts me to meet his eyes. He rubs the back of his neck. "You kind of have...a..." He points to my legs. I tip my gaze to search for-I'm not even sure what. He drops to his knees beneath me, his jeans still unbuttoned. Reeves extends his hand toward my knee and peels a little tile that had glued to my skin while *I* was on my knees.

He softly hovers the pad of his finger on the indentation the small letter piece has left. His face tilts up to look at me while donning the most gigantic grin. My lips stretch in reflex. I slightly bow to check the new imprint. I let out a giggle as I see a red-ish "R" marking my skin.

"Maybe I should add a trademark symbol above it," Reeves says, and we exchange elated stares.

"Am I yours?" I playfully tease.

"In a way," he says and turns to put his clothes on.

What is that supposed to mean? When I open my mouth to comment, he already has one foot inside the bathroom. I snap my mouth shut and resume shrugging my jeans on, obsessing over the three words he just uttered.

~~~

As night falls, once again, we turn in at Reeves' apartment. When he asked if I ever ate, ransacking through my perpetually empty fridge, I took the opportunity to coax him to go to his place instead where food can be found in abundance. Food, I learned quite quickly, is a good way to his heart. It's not that I don't want him at home, it's my bedroom that I rather he wouldn't visit. There are too many mementos in there that I rather not share with anyone.

We lie side by side in Reeves' wide bed, indulging in the fresh scented, navy linen. Reeves is in his boxers, leaning high on a pillow against the headboard. I'm on my side, facing him with the soft comforter threaded between my thighs. Raptly, I watch his lips move as he tells me funny stories from his travels as a bodyguard. I lightly laugh when he tells me about one of his client's man-eater of a wife and the excuses she uses to get her husband's security people to her room while dear hubby labors nearby.

My eyes independently start to crawl down the length of his tall and firm body while I listen to his calming voice. His tight, fair skin, the ridges and rims of his chest, his defined abs, the soft dark trail between his shaped V that leads to his boxers. For a span of a minute I'm lost, drinking the sight of him. My eyes return to leisurely feast on his handsome face, his sharp nose, his plump lips, hard cheekbones and the little crinkles now decorating his eyes. He cranes his neck my way, locking our stares.

"I don't know much about you," he says in a soft voice. It's more a genuine interest, rather than any sort of accusation. "I've told you things about me that I've never shared with anyone else, and yet you've told me nothing about yourself."

"What would you like to know about me?" My stomach begins to twist in a knot.

"Whatever you are willing to tell me." He sends his hand to cover mine. He rubs his thumb in circles over my skin. "You can start by telling me the real reason you decided to leave home. Why am I an escape?" My chest tightens viciously both at the way he looks at me at this very moment, and because I know it's time I should tell him something about my past.

"I moved away because it was too hard to be at home." Reeves turns to mimic my position, laying on his side, his eyes owning mine. "I lost someone dear to me about three years ago." I swallow over the lump forming in my throat. Reeves' cringe of pain and empathy sends my heart to pang. His stare next prompts me to go on, saying I have his full attention and so much more. "It changed everything for me, *it changed me.*" My eyes roam to focus on a spot on the wall behind him. "It changed the way I felt about myself, the way I saw... life." My lips twist in a bitter smile. "Reeves, I'm sorry but this is too hard and... I... had a part in losing this person... I'm sorry, I need more time. I know you've opened up to me, and you'd like me to do the same to you. That's what friends do. I want that, too, maybe I just need more time."

Reeves' hold on my hand tightens. He doesn't push me. His silence lets me know I'm the one in control.

With a far-off stare I resume. "The way people acted around me, my friends, my family, it felt like no one really understood what I was going through. I had to have a break, a fresh start. Everyone tried to help me out of my shell." I take a deep breath. "But it didn't help much. Maybe I wanted to be in that shell." I hold a tear back. "It felt like I didn't belong there anymore. I still feel like I don't belong anywhere."

I turn to look at him and our eyes catch for a strained beat. Reeves brings his hand to cup my cheek and I lean into it. He inches toward me and presses his lips to my forehead before sending his hand to his nightstand drawer to produce a black marker. I watch him as he removes the cap with his teeth. He then turns to the wall, just above the headboard and writes:

You Belong Here

He draws an arrow that points to the pillow I've been resting my head on every night for the last few months. My heart starts to beat double-time. Emotions bubble up inside of me. Scared, I laugh it off. With the greatest pretence in history of nonchalance, I roll my eyes and say, "It's always about sex, huh? 'You' is pretty general, you know. You can just use it to woo anyone you get in here." I let out another titter, trying to mask the storm inside of me, and wink.

It isn't a laugh, or any sort of amusement for that matter, that he reciprocates with. On the contrary, his lips turn into a hard line and his eyes fire up. I watch him as he takes the cap and fists it in his hand forcefully till his knuckles whiten.

His chest lifts with his next inhale. His eyes turn soft as he watches me profoundly while bringing the marker to point at his bare chest. With his stare penetrating mine he slowly writes on his skin, just mere inches above his heart:

Nia

"You are right, you belong in here." Reeves places his hand over my name.

He just tore me apart, savagely, in the best of ways, and I'm left petrified. Tears choke me and my next breath is a hard one to take in. I turn my head sideways, making an immense job of collecting myself, of holding my tears back. I'm scared to even allow myself to admit what I'm feeling right now. I cannot.

"Shh, listen carefully, if you're quiet enough you'll be able to hear my heart telling you that." He smiles at me gently. My own heart is about to overflow.

Reeves' hand finds my chin and tilts my head for our eyes to level. He brushes my hair over my shoulder. He leans lower to lay on his stomach with his face inches from mine. He slowly tilts his head.

And he kisses me.

Everything he is trying to tell me lands in the very core of me with the way his lips touch mine. It's soft, and gentle, and warm, and airy, and I mirror him with the same suppleness. Dissolving into him. It is our kiss that explicitly puts out there what I'm not willing to acknowledge. I slowly flatter my eyes into his and everything just feels so much better.

When I meet his mouth again and press harder, he rests his palm spread on the center of my stomach and eases me back. He tilts his head, looking at me in a way that makes me shiver inside. Soulful greens caressing every inch of me. He leans back and resumes kissing me, with a slow, feathery touch. Repeatedly. When we slowly ease off, my heart is filled with so much more; it's saturated with emotion. An instant panic takes over me as the need to tell him how much I care for him takes over.

I couldn't be more thankful for Reeves' phone to ring, relieved that he takes the call. I need a moment. I need a moment to process what has taken over me so forcefully. I need to calm my damn speeding heart and mind down.

CHAPTER 23

Reeves

It takes me a moment to decide whether to take the call, given I'm about to say something to Nia I might regret later. I can feel it in my bones. My emotional stability just left me, she tore me apart, I'm not even sure I know how to deal with it. Taking this call would be the best way to break the intensity we've once again fallen into. I couldn't be more positive Nia felt it, too. It can't be any other way when it's as strong.

I inwardly shake off the spell and answer. Just like any other time before, as soon as I see Beth's name across my phone, a pull between warmth and care, guilt and deception, starts to cause riots within me.

"Hey, Beth."

"How have you been, my dear?"

"Fine, busy. Same ol'." I pause for a beat. "How are you guys doing?"

"We've missed you, Reeves. We haven't seen you for a while."

I turn to look at Nia who's watching me. I'm not sure if that glee in her eyes is due to her feasting on my looks, or just watching me, trying to gather who I'm talking to. Frankly, I don't really care. Whichever it is, the fact that her eyes are *on me*, is what really matters.

"Perhaps you could come for dinner on Friday?"

"Beth, can I call you later, I have someone over."

I'm not too keen on turning this into a long chat, having Nia beside me, especially after the moment we just had.

"Oh, sure. Sure. Anyone I know?"

I return Nia's gaze and our lips crook up in unison.

"No. She is a new friend of mine. My neighbor." I add the neighbor part to make sure Nia remains in neutral territory. Why in the hell do I keep doing this? Nia's grimace doesn't escape me. *What's wrong with me?*

"A new friend? Perhaps you could bring her on Friday?" Beth takes on the mother part too well. She always does. Both in the caring and in the nosy departments.

The next words seem to just fly out of my mouth, not much thinking it over. "Nia, would you like to join me for dinner with friends on Friday?"

Nia's brows furrow for a short pause. She shrugs and mouths, "Okay."

My smile expands. Yes, I want her with me there. I want her with me everywhere.

"We'll both be there," I say to the phone, watching Nia as she turns to lie on my bed with her olive, lean legs propped on the wall.

"Oh, that's great. I'm looking forward to seeing you both." Beth's soft voice jubilates. "How about seven-ish?"

"Sounds good," I say before ending the call.

"So, who are the friends we are visiting this time?" Nia asks, tilting her head backward to catch my eyes.

"The Evans. Ben's family." I slump back on my pillow.

Nia's look trails to the ceiling above us. "Are you sure you want me there?"

"I wouldn't have asked you if I didn't want you with me." She drops her head to the side, gazing at me.

"Do you visit them often?"

I nod.

"I have family here, but I haven't visited them," she says as though to herself.

"Why's that?" I ask, shaking her out of her musing.

She scratches her collarbone, pensive. "I'm not sure." Her nose wrinkles. "The last time I spoke to my aunt was right before leaving home. She told me that I should start putting the past in the past and that it's about time I started to let it go." She frowns. "Then she gave me a whole lecture about how three years have passed, and that three years is a long time to still be mourning." She runs her fingers through her hair, brushing away a lock that clings to her cheek. "How can anyone decide what you should, or should not feel, only because a certain timeframe has passed?"

"No one can, or should." I keep quiet even though there's so much more I could say. She's opening up to me, and I don't want to do or say anything to draw her back. I'm eager to learn as much as I can about her.

"I think that for the entire first year, I was in shock. It felt like I was slipping away from everything I knew. I felt caged in my own head. Somehow, I carried myself through the pain." I send my hand to thread my fingers with hers. "Throughout the second and third year, I went through most of the commonly known stages of loss. And here I am, almost three years after I lost one of the people I loved and probably will ever love the most."

Her last words strike right through my gut. For so many reasons they leave a burn. Starting from the many similarities we share to hearing her say she loved someone as much. I'm embarrassed to admit to myself that the sting I just felt was a product of jealousy of a dead person.

"Three years and there's still the last stage, the one I can't seem to embrace. I could never accept it," she says. "I can't. I feel so guil—" Her words break. Quicker than I can react, she flings a hand to her mouth and she's out of the bed. Out of the room. Back to her shell. Shit.

I give her a moment and then follow her. She's leaning with one hand propped on the kitchen's marble surface, a glass of water in the other. I take a few steps toward her, stopping when her back is lightly touching my chest. She puts the glass to the counter, sighing. I wrap one hand above her shoulder and pull her back into me. My breath is held until she drops her head to rest on my chest.

"Uh…" she murmurs.

I wrap my other hand around her waist, holding her tight. I kiss the crown of her head. "You don't have to say anything else if you don't want to. Thank you for everything you shared with me today." A frisson of relief and gratification filters through me as I feel her relax in my arms. We stand in silence, each in our own thoughts for some moments.

"*Thank you.*" Her quiet voice interrupts our pensive silence. She twirls in my arms to face me. "Thank you for listening, and thank you for not pushing me any further." She inches up on her toes and gently presses her lips to mine.

I tip my head lower, my hand moves to the nape of her neck and I bring her closer. Her tongue meets my lips, stroking, coaxing its entrance. When she kisses me next, it's nothing sexual, nonetheless, it's our very first kiss that seeps all the way to my bloodstream. I lightly graze my thumb over the delicate skin of her neck, slowly tasting her sweet mouth. Feelings I've never felt before emerge within me, stirring my stomach with warmth. Her hands trace to my shoulders, caressing me with gentle strokes.

I lift her to straddle me and carry her to my bed.

We lie in silence, Nia still in my arms, her head on my chest. I thread my fingers through her soft, silky hair, thinking about things I want to tell her but can't really let out of my lips. She roams her hand over my stomach leisurely, stopping above my heart.

"I love being in here," she says, and I swallow the emotions that multiply to the power of ten at the very place her name is still inscribed in black marker. It's *her* - *my* best source of escapism, in all possible ways.

~ ~ ~

"Think about it before you answer, man. It could do you good, especially with the new developments," Jake concludes the last ten minutes of our conversation, suggesting I'd go on a new job now that the A.Z. case has taken on full velocity. Elbow leaning on the kitchen counter, dipping my forehead into the heel of my palm, I think about Jake's offer. A half-drunk coffee cup waits beside me. I'm mulling over being away for such a long time.

"Two months?" I ask again, not sure what it is that makes me feel ambivalent about Jake's proposal.

"Two, or more, I'll know for sure later today. Being away right now is the best thing for you." I hear the sound of the keyboard clicking at the other end. I scrub my morning scuff, more precisely late afternoon stubble, with my head still bowed.

"I'll think about it."

"You guys coming later?"

"We wouldn't miss Carmie on stage for anything."

"You bet your sweet ass you won't. She'll castrate you if you dare."

"Speaking of emasculating... So the missus eventually moved in, huh?"

"What can I say?" Jake grunts. "She's my baby momma after all... And she's fucking crazy... Who can really deal with her?" He sighs in amused surrender. Oh, how the mighty have fallen. Hard.

"See ya tonight."

Pushing myself to the extreme lifting weights, and a long steamy shower later, I head to get ready before picking Nia up from her lesson. She is not expecting me to, but the thought of watching her dance hasn't left my head since the moment she left this morning.

Tucking my hands inside my camel cargo pockets, I watch Nia smiling at her little people squad's performance. She seems pleased, calm, and proud. And damn she's pretty. My eyes trace every inch of her stunning self. She's wearing one of those black bra look-alike tops and knee length grey sweats. When her eyes pull to me, sensing I'm watching her, her smile widens enough to make my heart jump. A few pigtailed heads turn back to check where their instructor's attention has diverted. A familiar little redhead sees me and immediately splits class.

Seconds later, when Lily's small arms circle my thigh in a tight hug, I dip my head to send her a wide smile.

"Hey beautiful." I lift her into a hug.

"Hi, Reeves," she counters with the widest grin.

"I think Miss Nia will be upset if you don't get back to your friends."

She nods. Nia shakes her head with crinkled eyes when Lily takes her place back in the pink troopers circle.

"Hi, you." Nia kisses my cheek as she comes out of the studio, a quarter of an hour later in tight jeans, killer heels, and white, loose halter-top that almost reveals her perky breasts from the sides. I need to hold myself from dropping to my knees at her feet.

"Hi back." I plant a kiss on the center of her forehead. Why didn't I kiss her lips? 'Cause I wouldn't be able to stop at that. Simple. I help her into her jacket.

"This is a nice surprise." She hugs my side. I wrap my arm around her shoulder and squeeze her into me.

"Let's get going, I want to grab something to eat before the show."

"Hey, Nia, wait."

We both turn to see a chick with purple hair. Quickly, I recognize her. She's Nia's friend. I've seen her a couple of times at Jake's. Oh… yeah. My lips jerk up, she's the one who made out with another chick the other night. Sweet.

"You guys going to Jake's?" She is short of breath and adjusts her bag's strap over her shoulder.

Nia stiffens before answering. "Yeah. Want to join us?" I can swear the last part of her sentence has a reluctant air to it.

Purple-hair chick offers me her hand and a smile. An NC-17 rated smile. "I'm Alex. And you are Reeves."

I gift her with a friendly nod and return her shake.

"I've been meaning to talk to you for a while now, but you always seem so busy at the bar."

My brows pull in, both at her inviting stance, and more at Nia's sudden rigidity. "Well, you can talk to me now."

The way she's checking me out doesn't go unnoticed. Wasn't she playing for the other team? We keep walking, my hand lightly at the small of Nia's back and Alex on my other side.

"Are you seeing anyone?" Alex casually asks. Talk about balls. My eyes squint toward Nia who all of a sudden seems very captivated by the streetlamps ahead. I guess it takes me a bit too long to answer, because it ends with Nia answering for me.

"He is not dating anyone if that's what you're asking."

The annoyance her words emit throws me back. *And…* it's Nia's turn to verbally extinguish anything serious happening between us. We are both doing a mighty damn good job in this game of avoiding commitment we are playing. When she does it, it fucking burns.

"I guess I'm not." I can't even try to mask my irritation. Alex is either oblivious of the tense exchange, or totally indifferent, as her smile grows wider.

"So can I ask you out?"

Nia accelerates her steps till my hand drops from her back. I take a step forward and grab her hand, tugging her back beside me.

"We can all hang out together. I might not be dating anyone but *there's someone*," I say in a clear, iced accord. Nia's eyes flicker my way, the look we trade next screams volumes.

Alex shrugs. "Well, you can't blame a girl for trying." I reward her with a side smile.

～～～

Carmie doesn't just perform, she dominates the stage. She rips her audience's hearts out of their ribcages and collects them in a jar, one by one. Singing a Poison cover with her strong, husky voice, her band dissolves into the background and all eyes are on her.

We are crammed around the closest table to the stage, Nia and some of her friends, Jake, and me. Dylan is somewhere in the back, probably attached to a bottle or a hot chick, or both.

"Wow, she's amazing," Nia says next to my ear, eyes wide at Carmie.

"She is," I confirm, leaning toward her. Our mouths almost touch as she turns my way. We both gasp. In a span of a second, everything including Carmie's alluring voice fades away. Our eyes run in duet to each other's mouths and back, with each loud thud of my heart we move an inch closer. I tip my head to align with Nia's lightly quivering, parted lips. Our breaths mix and I can almost feel her soft touch.

"Reeves." A pair of slim hands wrap around my neck. Both Nia and I flinch back, dumbstruck. A cloud of sweet scent engulfs me while soft lips press onto my cheek. I cast a short glance at Nia before moving to give Katie a warm hug.

"Hey," I say over the music, ruffling up her golden waves with my hand. Katie tips back to look at me and then burrows her entire petite figure under my arm.

"Let's go grab a drink and catch up," she shouts above Carmie's lingering song.

Nia is watching the show on stage as I tap her shoulder, bending to ask her if she wants a refill. She shakes her head and freezes when her stare falls on Katie by my side.

"I'll be right back," I say to Nia and let Katie lead me to the bar. I don't miss Jake's disapproving head shake as I do.

"What?" I mouth, spreading my arms in question. He shakes his head again and pivots his stare back to his ex.

"Mom said you're bringing someone on Friday," Katie says, dropping to a stool next to where I'm leaning with my hip on the bar.

"Yeah, my friend, Nia." I tip my beer back for a generous swig.

"Friend?" Katie repeats, eyes fixated on me.

"Friend and neighbor," I say casually. I'm not willing to discuss who I'm seeing or sleeping with. It's too soon after she told me she has a crush on me. The last thing I'd ever do is hurt Katie in any way.

"We're taking five, you guys are awesome. Thank you," Carmie says to her insta-fans. Not long after, Carmie charms the pants off Dan, asking for a drink. Katie excuses herself to go talk to a friend and I find myself alone with the star of the evening.

"God, I love you so much Reeves, but you're the world's biggest dickhead." Carmie fans her black tank top, trying to cool down. I let out a light, confused chuckle.

"What have I done now?"

She shakes her head in the same manner her ex did just moments ago. "You didn't, that's the problem." Another headshake. "You should be with that one over there." She gestures with her bottle Nia's way. "Not with this one who doesn't understand no as an answer."

My jaw instantly ticks. "Don't say that about Katie. And it's not like *that* with Nia."

Carmie's lips twist with annoyance. "Oh, it's not? So, how is it with Nia, then? Tell me?"

My eyes roam to where Nia is sitting, and I catch her curiously looking my way. As our eyes hold, she winces and breaks the connection faster than I can send her a smile.

"Exactly!" Carmie nods. She pushes herself from the bar and pats my chest. "Okay, I'm on. Please stop being an ass, okay kid? Man up and do what you really want to do," she says before striding between noisy tables toward the stage.

I place Nia's drink before her as I take back my seat next to her.

"Thanks," she murmurs, and continues talking to one of the guys at the table, Paul.

"You still owe me an answer." Jake leans back to talk to me behind Nia's chair, reminding me of his job offer from earlier today. I nod into my bottle.

"Let me sleep on it." *Maybe I should just leave for a while.*

Everyone stops talking at once, including us, when Carmie and the band start playing "Total Eclipse of the Heart." Before the chorus comes, Carmie's performance turns into a private one, for her ex-husband.

Carmie sings. Her and Jake's stares spark as Carmie slowly sways her curves, parting her way toward him. Once she faces Jake with an expression that screams desire, haloed by misty light and smoke, whistles and shouts come from the excited crowed. She holds the mic, absorbed in Jake, putting everything she's got into the song. Her voice is strong and rough, emitting electricity, emotions, and sex. She sings about how they could never be wrong together, how his love is like a shadow on her all the time. The way they stare at each other makes me think that even if the world blows away right now they won't even notice.

I gaze at Nia as she watches them with a wishful flare, having the urge to spin her around and kiss the life out of her. But I don't. Maybe showing affection outside our homes would give our relationship a classification, an acknowledgment that we're both not willing to confront.

A few drinks and a couple of songs later, our table is engrossed in a heated discussion about the dramatic football season that just started.

"Reeves," Katie interrupts, resting her hand on my shoulder. I crane my neck back to look at her. "Any chance you are taking me home? My friends are going to an afterparty and I'm not in the mood."

"Sure." When it comes to Katie's safety… "Give me a minute, okay?" Katie nods but stays standing next to me.

I tap Nia's thigh and lean closer. "I'm taking Katie home and coming back." Nia looks at me, then at Katie. She stands up and smiles at Katie.

"We haven't been introduced." She sends an inscrutable glance my way. "I'm Nia, Reeves'…" She halts for a moment. "Reeves' friend."

"Oh right, Nia." Katie mirrors Nia's smile. "I guess we'll have plenty of time to get to know each other on Friday, though." Another sweet smile. "You don't mind me stealing him from you for a while, right?"

Nia shakes her head.

"It was nice finally meeting you, Katie." She turns my way. "You don't need to come back for me, I'm not sure how long we'll stay here."

I squat to level our eyes. "I don't want you going home by yourself."

"Reeves, just go, okay?" She takes her seat, resuming her chat with her friends.

I text Nia as we leave, asking her to ping me when she gets home.

CHAPTER 24

Nia

The coffee tastes bitter, or maybe the coffee is good and it's my thoughts that leave the foul taste in my mouth. Repeatedly, I run phrases and snippets from last night in my head, which leave me restless and mostly… upset. It's been a while since I've slept by myself. I didn't want to sleep in Reeves' bed last night, I was too railed up. For a couple of hours I held up from even answering his message, but I knew he'd worry and probably come looking for me, and truth be told, I wasn't so inclined to see him.

How can someone tell you with the sincerest of stares that you're in his heart and the next day make sure the entire world knows there's nothing remotely serious between the two of you. I much rather he'd choose one approach and stick to it, the combination of warm and cold wears me out and drives me up the wall.

But to be honest, how can I even say anything to him, demand anything other than what we've got going on? And really, who am I to complain while not even sharing a nugget of my past with him? I can't deny that it was me who jumped in to tell Alex that he was not dating anyone. I had to, it took him too much time to respond. He hesitated. In my book of "falling hard for someone," hesitation is definitely a glaring warning sign. And then there was Katie… Without even a blink of an eye he chose her. He chose to take *her* home. I'm torn on this one, too. Yes, I wanted him to ask me, I wanted him to make sure that I was okay first. Yet, I couldn't say anything, it's Katie. She is practically his family. How could he not chose her? I'm definitely not feeling any adoration for the mess that I've become.

I shut my eyes as tight as I can. I can't concentrate. Urgh!

I take a calming breath and the special moments Reeves and I shared last night swirl in. When he pulled me next to him saying, "there is someone," it was more than obvious who that someone was. Our almost kiss before Katie showed up, that one said so much. Maybe it's for the best that she interrupted us, I was about to blurt out something about emotions, again. I wouldn't know how to deal with him not feeling the same way. It's better left unsaid.

I hug the cup in front of me with both hands. Even though I'm trying to deny it, he's gotten under my skin—deep, deep under. When I'm with him, there are no nightmares, there aren't burning showers, crying, or the constant self-contempt. When I'm with him, I'm simply happy. At this point, I can't even imagine losing him as my friend.

I'll take whatever he offers. It's better than not having him at all.

Knocks on the door shake me out of my web of confusion. I drop my eyes to my boy-shorts and white tank top, which showcases my lack of bra to the max, and shrug. I peek through the peephole and open the door to the subject of my turbulence. I need to locate my jaw back to its natural place with Reeves standing before me wearing nothing but black boxers.

"Did you at least use the elevator?"

He squints his eyes, scratching his defined abs. I need to kill the urge to jump him, as I run my eyes over him. I can only imagine how warm and delectable his skin must feel right now, given it's more than obvious that he just rolled out of bed.

"No, the stairs," he says mildly irritated and very much sexy. He even has a sleep mark near his nose, sexy and adorable. "Why?"

"Your attire…" I gesture with my hand to his lack of cover. Oh, mighty God in heaven, he might even be sporting a semi by the look of those puffed shorts. Reeves' stare drops to where my eyes are zeroed in and he lets out a short, husky chuckle.

"My eyes are up here, Nia," he murmurs. I can only imagine the color my cheeks have turned. Somewhat ill at ease, I lift my eyes to his that take a solemn expression. "Why are you acting weird again?"

"What do you mean?" I ask.

He twists his mouth, wordlessly saying: "Stop playing games."

"You totally weirded out on me, *again,* last night."

"Is that even a word?"

"It is now."

"I have no idea what you're talking about." I turn on my heel, taking a few steps to reach one of the kitchen's stools.

Reeves sends his hand to the door and shuts it. "Oh, I think you do. I'm not sure what's going on with you lately." He plops on a stool across the table from me, leaning his elbows on the surface, linking his fingers together, gazing at me. "Ever since that pregnancy shit you've started acting different." He stares at me with concern and displeasure. "I don't want to lose you as a friend."

Here we go, that word again… I think it officially became my least favorite word in the English language.

"You got me as a friend," I say quietly. Quietly and disappointed.

"Good." His stare tapers at me. "If there's any issue. If there's anything you want to tell me, you can tell me. You know that, right?"

I gaze at my linked hands, avoiding his eyes. Tell you that I'm falling for you and have you running out the door? Newsflash "friend," it's me not wanting to lose *you*… With some effort, I produce a smile and nod.

"You want coffee?" I untangle my hands, jump off the stool, and head over to the coffeemaker. "I really don't get why Jake and Carmie aren't together," I say, fixing our warm drinks. Better to have someone else in the spotlight. If we discuss friendship one more time, I might go for the knives in the first drawer.

"They are a special kind of dumb?" Reeves responds, ending his words in a sigh. He covers his face with his palms, stifling a yawn.

"It's so sad, I've never seen anyone more infatuated with each other than these two." I place our cups in front of us.

"Well, some people just don't see what's good for them even if it's shoved in their face."

I choke on my next sip. I have an urge to shove a mirror in his face and force him to repeat his wise statement.

Another coffee, cornflakes (the very best my kitchen has to offer) and a short, easy conversation later, Reeves leaves to get ready for a meeting with Jake. As soon as he closes the door behind him, I send him a text.

LURVED your outfit, it's the new dress code for visiting me ;)

Some minutes later a response arrives.

Dare you to top it ...

I did top it, later that night, by showing up at his doorstep wearing nothing but my birthday suit. I think that at that moment I became his favorite person on the entire planet.

We're back to being us.

~ ~ ~

"Why are you so fidgety?" Reeves asks outsides the Evans' threshold, tugging on my hand.

"It feels like I'm meeting your family for the first time."

His lips twitch before he dips to leave an airy kiss on my temple. "*They are* my family, and you don't have to be nervous. They're pretty cool." His eyes enfold me with fondness. "Thank you for coming with me, and," he shakes his head, lips in a delighted arch, "you look great."

He squeezes my hand and I send him a light smile, looking at him from under my lashes. Funny, I've noticed that the more casually I'm dressed, the more he seems to appreciate my looks. I went with a neutral-colored blouse, black capris, and nude flats.

Reeves knocks on the door which quickly opens to reveal an elegant, curvy lady with the kindest blue eyes. Mrs. Evans' smile at Reeves warms my heart. It's motherly and genuine.

"I missed you." She folds her arms around his waist, closing her eyes in pleasure. He reciprocates, letting her hug him for as long as she wishes. I watch them till Mrs. Evans lets go of him and turns to look at me kindly and with unmasked curiosity.

"This is Nia," Reeves says, and to my surprise, rests his arm around my shoulder. The lady in the asymmetrical, green-pastel dress, apron, and a high updo casts a quick glance over to Reeves' hand on my shoulder before her eyes return to me.

"Nia, nice to meet you. I'm Beth." She takes my hand in both of hers. "I wish I could say I have heard much about you, but well, it's Reeves. You'd have to torture information out of this one." She sends him a playful, feigned scowl. "So now it's all on you to tell me about yourself."

"Sure, though there's nothing much to tell," I say as she gestures for us to go inside a cozy living room. On a textured, L-shape, tan couch, between a wooden rocking chair and a fireplace, sits who I assume is Beth's husband. The wide-shouldered man rises to stand as we come in. The first thing that I notice about him is the graveness that he radiates. His soulful dark eyes, trimmed beard, and lanky physique register next.

"Stanley." Reeves takes a step forward to meet Stanley in a pat-on-back greeting.

"Son," the older man says.

With my stare trained on Reeves, I'm able to notice the twitch in the side of his face as he takes the accolade. In an uncharacteristically timid air, Reeves introduces me to Ben's father.

"Pleased to meet you." The man's rigidness softens. "You must be very special, it's the first time we get to meet Reeves' girlfriend."

"I'm not sure about the special part, but it's nice to meet you, too." I can feel my cheeks cover in light warmness.

"Oh dad, she's not his girlfriend."

I can't help the glare darted Katie's way.

Katie smiles, taking a few steps to reach us. "Don't embarrass her." She sends me a friendly smile.

It's like labelling has become a new religion. What's everyone's obsession with classifications these days?

"Hi again, Nia." She gives me a brief hug and turns to give Reeves the same treatment. Katie and Reeves share a private joke that ends with Katie pushing his chest and Reeves ruffling her blond locks.

"You can take a seat, we'll get the food," Stanley says, sending his hand to the small of his wife's back, guiding her to the kitchen.

Reeves' hand finds mine as we make our way to the dining room. My eyes instinctively fall to our linked hands. I slowly bring them up to look at him, finding him gently smiling. The thuds in my chest seem to get louder. As we settle next to the table, three things I can't seem to overlook happen in quick succession:

Reeves eyes constantly escape to some point at the opposite side of the room.

Katie's eyes burn into our joined hands.

Katie's friendly pushing of Reeves aside to sit next to me, between us, saying he gets to spend enough time with me and it's her turn now.

When Stanley sets the roast chicken and potato dish on the table, Katie and I are already deep in conversation. Katie shows much interest in my job, asking about dancing and the girls. She tells me in return about her studies and college life. Without much effort, her easy and friendly charm makes me feel welcomed. I can see why Reeves is fond of her. She is just sweet.

Standing behind Reeves, Beth lays her hand on his shoulder and says, "I made your favorite dish." Reeves brings his hand to cover hers and thanks her. "Okay now, I'm just getting the salads, you can start eating." She unties the apron from around her full waist.

"So, how did you two meet?" Beth smiles my way after making sure everyone has piled enough food on their plates. I chance a glance at Reeves whose face is lit with wicked glee.

"Go ahead, you tell them," he tells me through a smirk. I narrow my eyes at him.

"Um, it was one of those accidental encounters... Due to some mix-up we both ended up with the same hotel room, and Reeves kind of walked in on me."

"She nearly jumped out of her skin," Reeves adds in a tone that makes me blush all over.

"Bet it was a memorable encounter," Stanley says in his heavy drawl.

"Oh, *it was*. Epic. I'll never be able to forget it." Reeves almost illuminates the room with the amusement glowing off him. I pin him with a warning stare which he counters with a wink.

"How's work?" Stanley asks Reeves next, thankfully letting me out of the spotlight. Reeves tells him about his recent trip to Cuba, which leads to the both of them falling into a private conversation. Listening to Katie and Beth talk about Katie's upcoming exams, I still manage to hear Reeves tell Stanley about an offer he got for a job that might have him traveling for a few months.

My heart sinks to the floor.

By dessert, I'm already half in love with the Evans. It's a combination of their pleasant personalities, how welcome they make me feel, and mostly, the obvious love they all share for Reeves.

Beth pats her lips with a napkin, smiling at me. "I hope we'll get to see more of you, Nia."

I smile in response, not sure how to answer.

"It's so kind of you to offer to teach Katie some dance moves."

"I'll be more than glad to do both. I think Katie and I will have a great time." A warm, fuzzy feeling washes over me when Reeves smiles at me next. It's a supple smile, a wholehearted one.

"Reeves, would you like to show Nia around while we take care of the dishes?" Beth asks.

"We should help, it'll be quicker," Reeves answers, and Beth dismisses it with a shake of her head.

"Katie will help us, you show Nia the place, go." She beams at him. The Evans start clearing the table as Reeves pulls back my chair for me.

Reeves jaw stones over as we halt by what I can only describe as a shrine. Pictures, many of them, in all ages. Trophies from sports competitions, Army medals, and many more mementos featuring a blond, brown-eyed twenty-something. I study the young, handsome guy, a spitting image of his dad, smiling at me from the many pictures as Reeves softly says, "Ben."

My heart squeezes at the undercurrent in his voice. He doesn't give me enough time to get into the details in the cabinet and pulls me away to see the rest of the ample home.

He closes the door behind us once we are in a plaid style room, one that cannot be mistaken as to whom it may belong. My eyes run from wall to wall, collecting the memorabilia that tells of Reeves' best friend. I learn that Ben was an Indians and Anime fan by the large, framed posters decorating the walls. Reeves spins me to face him.

"I'm so glad you are here with me." He grabs my face from both sides and kisses me, hard, urgent, pressing. Between sucking my lips and delicately attacking my mouth, he says my name, "Nia." Another kiss. "I…" He pulls me closer, reverently exploring my mouth. Anxious to hear what he's trying to tell me, I shift every control over to him, dissolving into his hold. Alert, I wait to hear what he is about to tell me. "I," he pulls back to look at me, but then kisses me again. This time with greater intent.

At a knock on the door, Reeves freezes and the magic instantly dies. Just as quickly as he was kissing me, he lets me go. He jerks back so rapidly that I almost lose my balance. Katie's blond halo pops into the room.

I can feel it deep inside, I've felt it moments ago in his touch, in his kiss, whatever was about to leave his mouth was something I really wanted to hear.

"Here you are. Can I steal her for a few?" Katie asks with an easy grin.

"Sure." Reeves coughs and shoves a hand to his front pocket. My cheeks flush at his response, to the not so covert way he just adjusted himself.

My blood still pumps through my veins and Reeves is all over my mind as Katie hands me a vanilla ice cream container. Her eyes scrutinize me, her lips pulled up with a gentle grin. Her warm smile manages to calm me down a bit after the emotional whirlwind Reeves just put me through. Katie sprinkles roasted coconut flakes into the bowl.

"Are you in love with him?" She turns to me, sucking on a vanilla covered finger. My eyes jump from the container to her.

"Whah? No!" I blurt. "We're just friends," I say, ice cream scoop held frozen in my hand.

She blinks at me, takes one step to stand at the very rim of my personal space. Her voice next is low, tinted with an irate undercurrent.

"Good." Her eyes slice mine. The way her mouth twists into a threatening smile makes me think that the angelic looking girl facing me is about to grow red horns.

"Good. Very good. Because he doesn't love you. Nor sees you as anything more than a friend." Her eyes crinkle. "*Friend*," she lightly chuckles. "Excuse me," she puts a hand on her chest, her mouth curved in malice. "By friend, I mean fuck buddy, of course." My jaw drops at the hundred and eighty degree turn in her act. Drops of melted ice cream fall from the utensil in my hand as I gape at her in shock.

"Let me just make it crystal clear for you, so we won't have any misunderstandings. Okay?" I put the scoop to the container, railed up and utterly muddled. "Reeves and I have always loved each other. Unfortunately, the time was never right for us to be together. I was too young, then we lost Ben, my studies, his work. But not for much longer now." The cruel small smile she has on grows. "You, my dear, are a toy. Just a toy to fill his time and needs. A pretty one this time..." Her fixated eyes on me taper. I don't think she even blinks. "So please don't get your hopes high." That's it, I have had enough, more than enough. Although he never actually said it out loud, I know just how much Reeves cares for me.

"Listen," I start with an intimidating voice of my own.

"No, you listen," she cuts me off. "Did he once even imply that he has feelings for you? That you might be anything but friends?"

I open my mouth to oppose but snap it shut in bitter recognition. No, he didn't.

"Let me ask you this: how many times has he left you to run to me?" Cold sweat trickles down my spine in tandem to a surge of bile that rapidly swims up my throat.

"What's up with dessert?" Reeves voice reaches us from the door. Katie, on cue, adjusts her sweet mask. She sends her hand to hug me and plants a friendly kiss on my cheek.

"Oh Reeves, I like her so much," she sings.

I'm not sure where to look or what to do anymore, I'm too exasperated and stunned.

And hurt.

Reeves helps us carry the ice cream bowls to where Beth and Stanley wait in the living room. I make a great effort not to meet Reeves' eyes, or Katie's. When the Evans fall into conversation about a property they might purchase, Reeves inches closer to me.

"Hey, you feeling well? You're kind of pale." He gives me a second check.

I grab the opportunity with two hands. "I'm not feeling so good. Maybe I'll just leave now. I can call for a cab."

"No," he says firmly. "I'll take you home." I don't know what to feel anymore, tears clog my throat when I try to find my words. I'm following Reeves on autopilot as he excuses us, telling Beth I'm not feeling well. I return Stanley's shake and Beth's hug with manufactured gestures. When Katie hugs me next, showing a magnificently performed concern for my wellbeing, I feel like sprinting out the door and never looking back. Regretting that I came here in the first place.

Luckily, Reeves lets me be and keeps silent all through the drive back. I try to convince him that it's better if I sleep by myself, but he doesn't even want to hear about it. He tells me that there's not even a slight chance that he'll let me be alone with the way I look. Adding so much more to the turmoil already wildly twirling inside of me.

It's on the tip of my tongue to confront him, tell him what Katie just told me, tell him that I'm falling for him, and that I can't go on this way. But I don't. I want to think it over before talking to him. I need to understand what I want to tell him first, before I actually do.

The realization of what I need to do, or better yet, stop doing, surges through me after a not so extended, painful diagnosis of our relationship so far. With the first tear rolling out of my eye while I lie in the dark next to a sleeping Reeves, it becomes clear, too clear. I should just let him go. If this is how I feel now, I can't imagine what will happen to me if he breaks my heart, which all the signs so far have shown that he eventually will. Yes, I can do it. I can be without Reeves. I could really do it. Just like I could drink decaf coffee, champagne without fizz, and dance without music.

It should be back to basics for us, the right and feasible thing to do is keep him as a friend and friend only, nothing more than that. Sadly so, including pulling the plug on the benefits part of "our deal." No complications. I should close the part of my heart that has his name written all over it and maybe start seeing other people. Seeing other people should help take my mind off him.

The comprehension compresses my lungs. I can hardly breathe but I know it's the right thing to do. Right now, I miss Patrick more than ever, and I wish I could talk to him. He always knew how to make me feel better. And it seems both people who I want the most aren't mine to have. Not Patrick and apparently not Reeves.

CHAPTER 25

Reeves

I take the stairs to the level below almost as a reflex. It's a habit I've adopted, a customary visit to Nia before heading out. It's one of our things, one of our many things, that is. I'm bathed, donning Jake's unofficial uniform, all black attire, though I'm not even working this evening. I'm meeting Jake for some stuff that he wanted me to help him with, and we'll probably hang out at the bar. There's a pretty cool local band playing later.

I think about the new rituals we've developed, Nia and me. It brings the pull to my lips, the one I've been constantly wearing lately, to lift even higher. It's been a while since I either ended the day or began a morning without saying hello to her and hanging out together. It will be a lie to say I'm not more than enjoying it, waiting for it. Somehow, her company, our being together, just makes everything... better. Much better. I shake my head at the half summersault my heart does as I take the last step in the hall to her apartment.

I stop short and my brows sink as my eyes meet the guy standing with his fist midair, debating if to knock or not, on Nia's door. He is all dressed up and... what the fuck is that? He has a goldfish in a plastic bag in his other hand.

What's going on here? It's quite obvious the dude's nervous. Putting one, two, and lame three (a fish, really?) together, I realize he must be some sort of... *date*? The insta-burn inside of me can only be described as red possessiveness.

In less than a beat, I'm pissed. *Majorly*, pissed. Hot-headedness takes over the greater part of my mind as I pass by him and lean with my shoulder on the doorframe, scrutinizing him with twisted lips. Like a juvenile dimwit, I cross my arms over my chest, giving him a clear display of my known-to-intimidate biceps. He eyes me for a moment.

I narrow my eyes at him. "Can I help you?"

"Err. I'm here for Nia," he says, still observing me suspiciously.

"Is she expecting you?"

"I'm here to take her on a date." If I was pissed off so far, it just took a greater momentum; I need to kill the urge to punch his face in.

What in the name of the ever-loving fuck? She's dating now? Not that we've ever declared being exclusive, or declared anything for that matter, but still, she is in *my fucking bed* every night! My heart quickens together with the skyrocketing of my temper. And the bitter sting of our whatever-we-have-going-on meaning shit to her is borderline painful. Not wavering my eradicating stare from Fish Guy, I knock on the door with the back of my fist, still facing him.

"Just a sec." Nia's voice comes from behind the door, light and elated, inflating the irate bubble I'm nursing. Her eyes ping-pong between the two of us, me and the person who she dates, *who is not me.*

I cringe, gazing at her. She looks like a disguised version of herself. I hate the way she looks on so many levels I can hardly count.

She looks damn hot in that tight, too short napkin of a black dress. But her hair is held up in some weird 'do and she has too much makeup on. She looks like one of those slutty Barbie wannabe dolls, and what irritates me the most; it's all for him.

"Oh, hi, Kenneth." She smiles at him. The stretch on her lips broadness as she turns to me, but quickly withdraws when she meets my livid eyes. "Hey you…" Her voice is a degree lower.

I don't let douchebag thread in a word. With one hell of a production of a smile, looking only at Nia, I say, "I was about to ask if you want to join me to Jake's, but apparently you already have plans for tonight."

The effort she puts in composing her response is more than visible on her face. She opens her mouth to speak but instead of hearing whatever she is about to say, I lean forward and brush my lips to hers.

"Enjoy, babe," I say in an Oscar winning act of indifference. Nia just holds her words in and sends me a thin smile that has an edge of something that I'm not sure I can fathom. When her date lifts his hand, showing her the marine pet, it takes all of my strength not to turn back and shove the fucking fish down his goddamn throat.

~ ~ ~

Ted, one of the bouncers at the bar, gives me one look before saying, "Whatever it is, try not to kill anyone on my watch…"

I nod with an irate twist on my lips. I guess my mood is written all over my face. I grab two beer bottles from the bar and make a beeline to Jake's office. I have zero desire to play friendly with anyone this evening.

"Who stole *your* candy?" Jake asks as soon as he gets off the phone. He observes me with slanted eyes, nodding a thanks at the beer bottle I left next to him. I mimic his position, sitting down, flinging my legs to rest on his desk.

I take a generous swig, wiping my mouth with the back of my hand and say, "Nia is on a date tonight."

Jake shakes his head and takes a breath through his nose. "You fucking moron."

"Man?"

"Man!"

"What in the hell?" I jerk up to sit straight. Glaring at Jake, I peel the label from my bottle.

"What did you expect?" he asks, mildly annoyed. "You don't keep a chick like Nia on the backburner." I grimace and he takes it as a cue to continue his lecture. "Either you have your head stuck so deep inside your ass or you're into someone else, like Katie… Otherwise, I can't, for the love of fuck, understand why you haven't grabbed Nia by now and told her you want her."

"What does Katie have to do with it?"

"Do you want Katie?"

"No." *That* I'm certain of.

"Then why do you stop yourself from going to the next level with Nia? It's more than obvious to everyone around that the girl has the greatest crush in the history of crushes on you." My lips reflexively jump up, hearing this. "She is in love with you, you fucking, blind idiot."

I roll my eyes. "And this comes from the man who screws through the yellow pages while fantasizing about his ex-wife? Excuse me if I don't run and embrace what you're preaching."

"I'm the opposite of the person who you want to pick a fight with, Reeves." We have a short stare down till Jake breaks it. "You don't have to embrace anything I say. In the meantime, your dream girl, who fucking wants you, is on a date with some tool. Yeah, you're doin' a gnarly job by yourself."

I process what he just told me in silence.

"Let's review the shit we're supposed to and then you go somewhere to chill off," Jake says and I nod, still explosively irritated.

"I guess we are done," Jake concludes about an hour later, after we've reviewed bios of new prospects and recruits and went over some ongoing projects.

I stretch back onto the chair, dropping my propped legs from the desk. "I'll hang out at the bar with Dan, you coming?"

"Later, I need to get rid of some emails." Jake pivots my way and studies me for a long moment. "You okay?"

I blink in affirmation and stand up. "Thanks, man," I say, and head to the door. Jake drops his head in an exaggerated nod, his straight strands covering his eyes.

I set the empty shot glass next to the one that I emptied less than ten minutes ago. Dan leans closer behind the wooden plank, gazing at me before he speaks.

"Another?"

I shake my head.

"Get you something else?"

"Water."

"Hey, handsome." Eileen plops into the stool next to mine, draping her hand on my back in a semi-hug. "What's up with the mood? You snippy 'cause Nia is here with someone?"

I cock my head, my forehead creasing. "Here?"

She tips her chin toward the small dance floor next to the stage. I slowly turn to where she gestures. Nia and the fish-twat are standing, swaying, next to the band, seeming to be in deep conversation. When Nia drops her head back laughing in genuine enjoyment, my hands roll into fists. Her date sets his drink on a table and takes Nia's hand, pulling her after him. She smiles and they start dancing to the song in the background. My blood sizzles in my veins.

"Hey." Eileen's hand drops to my thigh. Reluctantly, I turn my head back. "So you guys are not together? I thought you were."

"No, we never were." I signal for Dan to get me another shot.

"Oh." She keeps silent for a beat. "I need to talk to Jake, coming back in five." Not that I really care.

I turn back to someone's hand on my shoulder. It takes me a minute to recall who the voluptuous redhead grinning at me invitingly might be. When she slowly licks her lips, the recognition clicks in; it's the stalker-redhead I almost did in the toilets a few months ago. This one has a tendency to appear out of thin air whenever I feel like kicking anything alive. "Hi. How are you?" she asks, shoving her tits in my face.

"Good." I down my drink, knocking the empty glass on the bar with a thump. I shift my head to look behind her, at Nia and her date. I can feel the vein in my forehead popping when his hand pulls her deeper into him.

"You want to dance?"

My eyes move from her to the cozy show the dating couple puts on and back. For a span of moment, Nia lifts her eyes and our stares collide in flames.

"Yeah, let's dance." I tug the playboy bunny after me.

"Oh, let me just get rid of …" She leaves her drink on one of the round tables we pass, trying to keep up with my rapid steps as we make our way to the dance floor.

Just like I suspected, my dance companion doesn't fail me and starts grazing against me as soon as we reach the space next to the stage. Nia's eyes round as she sees me a few steps from her with my eager dancer. Once Red turns her back to me and rubs her ass against my groin, Nia's eyes become wild. She narrows them at me and turns to pull the same maneuver on her more than thrilled date.

I spin whatever-her-name-is by her hand, grab her ass, and pin her to me, her gigantic tits smashing against my chest. Nia grimaces and moves to press her cheek to Fishman's chest. When she turns to him and starts giving him a standing lap dance, I almost lose it. We each scrape against our partners while having an angry stare-off.

I'm infuriated by this point, every time Nia's body gets as close to his, another seam of my nerves tears. Dancing with our partners, through flickering lights, loud music, and smoke, our eyes play war. A sudden epiphany illuminates in my head, we are having a fight. Wordless, but nonetheless, a fight. A serious one it seems, hitting each other with blows below the belt using other people. I'm not sure how it started, not sure what caused Nia to fucking flip on me in the first place. I'm not even sure what about, but it couldn't burn more. Who am I kidding? It goddamn cuts me to the bone.

I loathe it.

A new song begins and our moves slowly turn into dry humping. Pulses of anger travel through my blood seeing Nia like that with someone else. Sparks are flying from the intensity of our stares. Nia is the first to break our stare, not long after the lady grazing her assets on me kisses me. Nia casts her eyes down, gloom washing over her delicate face. My next breath is a sharp intake. Nia's sudden sadness calls for a fracture to expand within me. Immediately, I let go of Red. Drops of panic infiltrate my anger.

Nia says something next to her date's ear. From where I stand, it appears that she tries to ease him off her. She speaks again and he shakes his head with a smile. When she sends her hands to his chest and pushes him, I can hear my heart hammering in my ears in tandem to a heat wave that covers me.

It's when one of his hands pull Nia tighter, and his other grabs a fist full of her ass that I see red. All the anger that I've been carrying in me explodes at once. Seeing only Nia in front of me, I push whoever is in my way till I'm inches away from her alarmed face. I clutch her date from behind and throw him to the floor. I bend to grab him by his shirt next, my eyes slicing his.

Something takes over me. Something dark and fierce that's channeled to my fist before it hits the guy's nose. I can sense the crack of bone against my knuckles. I keep holding him as he loses balance. My next blow meets his side and he groans, jerking back. Shut off from my surroundings, I pummel him repeatedly. Nia's cry at the same time as someone grabs me from behind finally stop my trance.

"Have you lost your mind? What have you done?" Nia screams at me, terror dominating her eyes.

I try to shake off the hold on me, only to learn both Jake and Ted are dragging me backward. Nia sinks to the floor on her knees next to her, now bleeding, date, petrified. Because of me...

"Get him out of here," Jake orders before joining Nia on the floor to check the damage I've caused.

"Come, let's get some fresh air," Ted mutters, his hand hooked around my shoulder. I let him guide me out.

My mind works in slow motion as I try to calm down my erratic breathing and the insanity that took over me.

"What the fuck, dude?" Ted asks as we reach the night's crisp air. I shake my head and slump back against the concrete wall, tipping my head back with shut eyes. I push in a heavy breath through my nose. What have I done?

"What were you thinking?" I snap my eyes open at Jake's bark. He gazes at me, the muscle above his jaw noticeably ticking.

"I wasn't." My voice comes out low and regretful. Jake observes me for a few beats. "What's the damage?"

"Broken nose. Probably a beautiful shiner come morning. He'll survive..." His eyes still assessing me. "You totally lost it..."

I nod, true. "He grabbed her against her will."

"Still, there are ways to deal with situations, Reeves." Jake shakes his head, dips his hand to his jeans pockets and coldly says, "You need to sort your shit out."

I nod once more.

"I hope for your sake that he doesn't press charges."

I clench my teeth so hard, my jaw starts to throb. "Where's Nia?"

"In my office with the guy."

I inhale through the stab in my chest, pushing myself off the wall, taking a step toward the bar.

"Where do you think you're going?" Jake moves to block my path.

"To see her."

"No, you don't. I'm not letting you inside tonight. Go home, Reeves. Calm the fuck down first."

"I'm not going anywhere before I talk to her."

Jake narrows his eyes at me, rubbing his prickled jaw. "I'll get her out here," he says through a sigh.

"Thanks."

He shakes his head again, in frustration this time. "You and I are going to have a serious talk tomorrow." He disappears behind the bar's heavy door.

Minutes drag by as I wait for Nia to come out. A message from Jake on my phone about ten minutes later clears things up:

She doesn't want to talk to you right now. Go home.

I don't. Knowing Jake, I'm more than positive he tried his best to get her out here. Just like I'm sure he took care of the wounded fish guy.

I'm not sure even how much time has passed when Nia comes out of the bar with Eileen. I tilt my head that's been resting on the wall, consumed by thoughts and worry. I came to two conclusions while beating myself up, waiting;

I need to go back to therapy.

I want Nia to be mine like I've never wanted anything before.

"Nia." I take a few steps forward to reach her. She scowls, seeming disoriented and shaken. "Wait up... I need to talk to you."

She crosses her lightly trembling arms over her chest. "I don't want to speak to you now."

"Nia..." I send my hand to her arm, making her flinch and jolt back.

"Don't touch me," she says firmly, a tear leaving her eye. My heart leaps to my throat, as I watch the tear roll down her cheek.

"I'm sorry, can I take you home? Can we talk? I need to talk to you," I beg.

More tears drop from her eyes and she bites her lip. Ice trickles down my back at the fear in her eyes. And once she starts to talk, words gush out of her mouth in a stream, each word like a wrecking ball swing to my gut.

"Don't take me home. I don't want to talk to you. What have you done? You scare me. I don't want to be near you." Her hand moves to hug her waist. She stares at me for a stretched moment with an air of dejection. When I open my mouth to speak, she shakes her head and starts running away *from me*. Panic enfolds me and my legs buckle up as I gaze at her getting away. Once I snap out of my shock and am about to follow her, I'm stopped by Eileen's hold on my hand.

"Let her calm down," Eileen says, still holding me firmly. I shake her grip off.

"I need to talk to her." I take off after Nia.

CHAPTER 26

Nia

I seal out Reeves' calls and his hard knocks on my door. My heart is not aching, it's bleeding. A sense of immense loss smothers me, a loss of the one person who made me feel alive again, the one person *who made me feel*. My friend, my lover. A person who I can't deny that I've fallen so deeply for. With every heavy step that I take in the direction of the bathroom, the bitter illness spreads quicker than it used to for a very long while now.

I've been, to some degree, controlling my grieving episodes; they've been somehow calculated and restrained. For a while they even disappeared, Reeves made them disappear together with my nightmares. But whatever is taking over me right now is stronger, it overpowers any ability that I may have to be sensible. Tears erupt from my eyes uncontrollably. Acid climbs up my throat and I gasp for air.

The bathroom door banging against the wall shakes the apartment as I slam it open. I turn the shower on, wait for the heavy steam to veil the glass, and step inside. I flinch at the first encounter with the fiery cascade. Soaking up the water, my clothes cling to my body in burning dampness. I fall to my knees and cover my face with both hands, rocking back and forth on my bent legs. And this time the images and voices come in a clarity that overwhelms me, it's so real, I'm back in my room, in my bed, hearing the news about Patrick.

My mother's sharp cry, my father's broken authoritative timbre as he tries to calm her down. Sounds of footsteps, a duet of light and heavy cricking on the old stairs leading to my room. Their faces as they appear in my doorway, a sight of fatality. My heart accelerates, and the familiar hopelessness and immense pain sinks in and feasts on my soul.

Their heavy, stretched, almost unreal voices as they tell me what happened. As they tell me that Patrick took his own life. They tell me, and I conjure the visions before my eyes. I see nurses in white uniform running to his room. I see an illuminated bathroom with a twisted sheet dangling from a high showerhead. I can even smell the medicine mixed with soup scent the facility he was kept in always had.

It turns my stomach. Silent cries of desperation that leave my mouth blend with the murmur of the falling water. I shake my head, crying for losing him, crying because it was me who killed him. It was me who made him die. *Crying because I need Reeves.* My skin stings with the heat of the water that covers me now from head to toe. My clothes feel heavy, drained with the scorching water. I can't take it anymore. I cannot. I need Reeves, I need him to take it all away, because this time, it's bigger than me. I can't handle it anymore. Panicked, I step out of the shower and rush to the front door.

I run up the stairs to the level above, leaving a trail of puddles that drip from my sodden attire. I knock at the door once and it opens to a display of anxiety, concern, and tenderness in Reeves' eyes as they look back at me. Without saying a single word, he wraps me in his arms, covering me with every muscle, sensitivity, warmth, and security that is him. I let out a painful cry. Sobbing, I meld into him. For a long moment, he lets me hide inside his shielding hug. He says nothing, but radiates an abundance of protective strength as he lifts me to be held in his arms. I wrap my legs around his waist, my face buried in his neck as he carries me to his bedroom.

He releases me gently till I'm standing on both feet before him. He leaves me for less than a breath and comes back to tower over me. Reeves drops to his knees and slowly takes off my shoes, one after the other. He unties my sweater and lets it slide to the floor. With nothing but a gentle stare, he starts peeling my clothes off, piece by piece. With a soft towel he dries my glowing, red skin. A twitch of pain hovers over his features as the harm I've caused myself is revealed to him.

In one swift move, he peels his own shirt over his head, the shirt I've managed to wet in a matter of a few stretched moments. He takes me in his arms again and carries me to the bed. Reeves lays me on my side and slides to embrace me from behind, so close, till our bodies unite in a human puzzle. He lifts the blanket over us and deepens his embrace around me. Painful sobs inflamed with uncontainable shudders and pants leave me as I let myself melt into his hold.

"I'm here for you," he whispers to my ear in a low, soothing, voice. His healing embrace on me tightens. He leaves a soft kiss on the crown of my head. I turn around and melt into him, burrowing my face in his neck, crying into his warm skin. I cling to him so desperately, as though he is my source of life. Which in a way he is, he is the only one who can take my pain away. It feels like I'll never be as protected if I ever let go.

"Cry it out." He kisses the top of my head, his voice rasp yet gentle. "I know it's painful. Cry. I'm not leaving you." He deepens his hold on me, reassuring my broken heart. He dismantles me, slowly and painstakingly. Layer after layer, he peels off my barriers and clothes until I'm naked—physically and emotionally, naked. I am completely bared before him, body and soul. It's a blanket he covers me with, but I know that it's his heart that wraps me to truly feel as warm and protected as I finally do.

For the first time since forever, I cry with all my heart. For the first time, no one tries to sooth me and tell me it's going to be okay. Because it will never be okay. Patrick will never live again. He'll never laugh with me again. He'll never be mine again.

Even though Reeves has no idea what I'm crying about, he seems to understand me, to know exactly how it feels, and what I need from him, and from myself. And he lets me do it, silently absorbing my grief, not even once attempting to stop me.

I'm weak and weary by the time I am left with no more tears to shed. I feel empty but in a liberating way. As the room falls silent, Reeves turns to lie on his back and slides me on top of him so we are chest to chest, heart to heart. He kisses me softly.

"I'm sorry I've scared you," he says, oceans of remorse in his eyes backing his words.

"You cannot be violent ever again."

He nods in determined affirmation. "Talk to me." His voice is so supple and caring, gently crumbling the remains of my walls.

"I killed my brother." I gasp.

Reeves' brows pull in. His body slightly edges below me, but he doesn't let go.

"He is dead because of me." We are both silent for a pause. Reeves kisses me again, this time even softer. "Patrick was five years older than me. He was also my best friend. We played together all the time as kids, we fought a lot, made each other's lives a living hell from time to time, like any siblings are meant to, but always loved each other very much. I looked up to him. He was my smart, beautiful, caring big brother. When we grew up, I was even a part of his gang—I used to go out with him and his friends. ..." A knot tightens in my stomach and I close my eyes. "Manic depression can be controlled, the symptoms are usually harmless to everyone beside the person suffering from the disease. But there are times...

"Patrick was diagnosed with bipolar disorder by his late teens. For the first couple of years we all learned how to cope, how to help him, and us. It's a hard thing to get used to, especially when the person suffering from the disease is one of the people you love the most."

I heave heavily, having Patrick's handsome face before my closed eyes. I flutter my eyes open into attentive green ones. "The worst times for me to deal with were feeling Patrick's pain when the mood swings ended, and he was mortified, ashamed, and truly repentant regarding what happened. Time after time it broke my heart."

Reeves cups my cheek, giving me his empathy, care and utter attention with one single look.

"He was usually very responsible with practicing the treatment, he took medications when needed and never missed his weekly therapy sessions.

With our support and his dedication, his illness was, to a degree, controlled. That is until it wasn't..."

The lump forming in my throat silences my voice. My eyes gloss over as I recall images from the events and finally the night that started a rollercoaster big enough to have my brother take his own life at the age of twenty-five.

Reeves' expression fills with pain as he watches me shudder and for new tears to leave my eyes. I press my cheek to his chest and shut my eyes forcefully.

"He was going through a stressful period—midterms, our grandma passing away, his girlfriend leaving him—his mood swings had increased drastically. He was mostly down." I take another needed breath. "He went out with his friends one night, which I encouraged. I thought it would do him good and that he needed a break. He ended up drinking too much. When he returned home, I was alone in the house. Later, we were told that perhaps it was the alcohol that triggered it. Whatever the cause was, the mania was strong that night, strong enough to turn him violent.

I heard things crashing to the floor, sounds of glass breaking, and went down to the kitchen to check what was going on. Patrick didn't even notice me at first. He was smashing dishes, his eyes full of rage." As I say the next words, Reeves' arms wrap around even tighter. "When I tried to talk to him, calm him down, he attacked me. I knew he wasn't controlling any of the violence he directed at me, and I was both scared for me and him." A sharp exhale leaves Reeves lips with my name in it.

"I came out of that night with shiners, split lips, and a broken rib. Patrick came out of that night mortified and ashamed. A few days after, my parents called me for a 'family talk.' We sat around the kitchen table over apple pie and milk when they told me that they came to a conclusion together with Patrick that it would be best if he was admitted to an open ward facility where he'd be treated and have time to rest.

I resented the idea. I hated it, thinking he was going away from his own home because of me, because he'd hit me. Patrick reassured me that it was his idea and that my parents said they would support him. He was there for less than two weeks before they found him hanged in the shower. He left a letter, addressed to me."

I cry so hard into Reeves' chest and he lets me, comforting me in his warm hold.

"He wrote that he loved me and that he was sorry for ever hurting me. I didn't want his apology. I didn't care for an apology. I wanted him back."

I tremble under Reeves. He kisses my head and gently pulls me deeper into him. After moments of hugging me in silence, when I start to shiver, Reeves leaves the bed only to come back with a sweatshirt which he helps pull over me. He then gets back into bed, settling with his legs straight. Leaning on the headboard, he sits me astride him. He takes my hand in his, and threads his fingers into mine.

"I feel so guilty," I say.

He pulls me closer to him and dips his head to kiss me. "I know," he says. "It's the hardest thing. That's how I feel about Ben's accident. I feel like I could have prevented it."

I blink at him.

"Go on…" he coaxes softly.

"I feel guilty and I'm so mad at my parents for going through with it. I can't let go of my anger toward them. And I can't tolerate violence—it scares me, repulses me—it's the reason my brother is dead." I look Reeves straight in the eyes. He nods, confirming he understands the gravity of my words. "You can never again act like you've acted tonight."

Reeves' hands move to frame my face. "I will not. I promise you, Nia." He brushes his lips to mine. "It's not an excuse, but seeing fear in your eyes, having that guy grab you like he did, hit me so hard." He pulls me closer to him and our breaths mix. "Now listen to me, I'm done. Nia. *We are done.*"

My brows sink together.

"We are done playing this game we've been playing for far too long. I got jealous tonight. You know why?"

I tilt my head, and he hovers closer.

"Because I want you, like I've never wanted anyone before. You make me happy. I don't want you seeing anyone else. I want you to be mine."

"What are you saying?" My words funnel between us in a soft whisper, followed by my racing heart.

"I'm saying that I want you to be mine, and so much more. I'm saying that *I need you* and *want you.*"

"Are you sure? We are like two grenades waiting to explode..." I say shakily, because I want him, I want him so badly that I can hardly breathe. But I'm afraid it's what I've just told him that makes him take pity on me and give me what I want.

"Don't two negatives make a positive?" He gives me a sweet side smile. I can't help for my lips not to curve up.

"Are you willing to deal with all my baggage? You have enough of your own to take me with mine."

He nods. "Our scars and wounds are a great part of who we are. And who you are is so amazingly beautiful. I've been fighting myself, for the life of me I don't know why, not to tell you this. I want you so fiercely it's almost unreal. Without the baggage you bring with you, you wouldn't have been the you who I'm totally crazy about."

I bite my lip, fighting happy tears this time. "Maybe sometimes we need to be completely shaken up, maybe even tore apart and suffer, so we'll be able to be at the place we're meant to be, with the one we're meant to be. I guess everything, sick and painful as it may be at times, does have a purpose. I know I've found my purpose, I can't imagine me without you. I don't ever want to imagine that." His lips hover next to mine. "Are you with me?"

Okay, here goes. Although this is something I'm not so inclined to bring up, especially at this moment, but I got to.

"I've asked you this already and I'm going to ask it again before telling you what I'm about to tell you." I push out a tense sigh. "Are you sure there's nothing going on between you and Katie?"

"Why are you bringing this up now?"

"Because that's what she told me."

"Hold up, what? When?"

"After dinner. She told me that you two apparently have this grand plan to be together, that you love each other and always did." Anger seeps to Reeves' expression.

"I love Katie. Like. A. Sister. We don't have any grand plan and we sure are never going to be together. *Nia, I'm telling you I want you.* Only you! So, I'm asking, are you with me in this?"

It's a whisper that leaves my lips next, a whisper into his mouth, but we both still hear it clearly, together with the arsenal of emotions it carries.

"I love you, Reeves."

When he kisses me next, it's a kiss so tender, so warm, so emotionally saturated. With his touch, he gives my words back to me. We kiss for hours, just kiss, long and profoundly. Our hands caress each other as if it was for the first time. We love each other through our touches till I'm too exhausted to keep my eyes open.

Reeves doesn't sleep this night and I know it because each time I turn through my sleep and open my eyes to him, he is watching me. The next time when I blink my eyes into his, the room is enfolded in soft, pre-dawn light. Reeves stretches his arm for me to nestle on his chest.

Half asleep I say, "I'm tired, I'm so tired of always being torn, every smile that I smile feels like a betrayal. Each time I laugh I feel like I shouldn't. How can I laugh and enjoy life when I took the ability to do so from someone else, from someone I loved so much?"

"I'll make you smile, Nia. No matter what it'll take of me, I'll make you happy. I'll even find you your happy date."

I lift my drowsy eyes to his and smile. "You make me happy." Not long after, I finally feel Reeves' steady breath beneath me and close my eyes, calm and content.

CHAPTER 27

Reeves

My smile is threatening to rip my face in half as I look at the note Nia left on my pillow this morning, again. I'd step into hell with the wildest of smiles, without even the slightest of hesitations to feel as I feel right now.

Had to go, early class... See you later.
Love u,
Me.

How did this happen? She really loves me? It wasn't just something she'd blurted last night under a pile of emotions.

Even though this day has been a total bitch. Having Jake scold my ass off for my brilliant performance last night. Having a mid-year call with my dad which always ends up with me feeling like someone has just pummelled my gut. Having the most awkward coffee in the history of awkward coffees with Katie. She was crabby in an "I got my period and someone ate my cookies" kind of way. When I tried to find out what was wrong, she almost bit my head off. All in all, I don't care. I'm too excited to see Nia soon, all the rest can really just go to hell.

It's true, time tends to crawl when you're waiting for something you really want— your favorite song to start, your favorite dish to arrive when you're starving. Time fucking drags when you're waiting to see your girl.

~ ~ ~

"Here's your drink. Just don't beat me up," Dan says, sliding a glass my way. They've been giving me shit, Eileen and Dan, for the last half hour about me losing it last night. They both snicker at Dan's last witticism. I shake my head with a friendly-warning gaze.

"Okay, that's the last I hear of it, one wrong word more and *I will* beat you up, Dan. And you, I'll just lock you in the storage room." I look at Eileen, saying the last part with a tug of my lips.

"I'm game, Reeves, as long you are locked up with me." Eileen winks, making sure her voice has a sultry lilt. They grin at me in unison.

"Do you still have your job?" Eileen plants her elbows on the counter, talking low enough to make our conversation private.

"Don't worry, I still got my job." It was never at risk, not that I'm about to explain to anyone about my special terms of employment with Jake.

"I'm glad, you know I kinda have a crush on you." She winks again, and I chuckle. We both know it's just a friendly tease; she loves her cat and mouse thing with Dan.

My phone buzzes in my pocket. I get it and read a message from Nia.

Can you meet me in the toilets in 5?

My lips pull up so hard and fast, in a nanosecond my face is lit up like a Vegas strip.

Dig where you're going w/that. No to the toilets though, there's a room at the back, second door from the toilets, be there.

I'd be lying if I said I'm not already semi-hard.

As I spot Nia a few minutes post-text, entering the bar with a cheerful group and a very joyful Alex, I make my way to the notorious backroom, boner still intact.

She doesn't even have a foot in before I grab her and pin her against the door I've just kicked shut. My mouth swallows her yelp of surprise.

"Hi, beautiful." I lunge my tongue inside her sweet, sweet mouth. My hand flings her thigh around my hip. Instinctively, her hands reach my neck. She absorbs my kiss with smiling lips. I lean back to look at her.

"Oh, hi there." She grins.

"Hi, yourself." I lean in and bury my tongue in her mouth again, determined.

"Reeves," she mumbles through our vacuumed lips, "hey." She brings her hand between us and lightly pushes my chest back.

My brows constrict thickly as I reluctantly ease back. I cock my head, prompting her to explain this ridiculous pause.

"I wanted to talk to you before we go outside and join everybody."

"Listening." I kiss a freckle just above her collarbone.

"Can we keep our thing private?"

I stop short with my lips next to another tiny dot, and my eyes tip up. Not feeling the love for her hesitant tone, or the words that just left her sexy lips.

"What do you mean?" I slant back, studying her expression.

"I'm just not ready to talk about... There are some really nosy people out there. And well, Paul is Kenneth's brother. I think it's better not to shove *us* in his face." The mentioning of fish guy rubs me the wrong way, to say the least. "Please?" She leaves a supple kiss on my lips.

"Fine." I twist my mouth and help her to her feet.

"I'll go out first," she says. She brushes her hand on my chest before turning on her heels. "I'll make it worth your while later."

My lips reflexively radiate joy. Yeah, I'm a guy. That just made everything okay.

I grab her arm before she reaches the door. "*Your home* this time, Nia." I say it gravely enough to convey the weight of my solemnity. A surrendered sigh and a short nod confirms her acquiescence.

As Nia joins her friends, I go hang out with Jake in his office, counting the minutes till Nia and I split out of here to be together, alone. I aim a dart at the board as I listen to Jake tell me that he spoke to Hunter yesterday. Not that I haven't seen this one coming. I know full well that I'm not going to like what I'm about to hear.

"I'm sorry man, I had to," he says after telling me that he told Hunter about my outburst. My immediate exasperation is channeled into my throw. The arrow collides with the pierced dock foam with a distinctive thud. I stay with my back to Jake, listening to his next words, moving the last arrow from hand to hand.

"You might be out of the intel circle for the time being, it's up to him to decide, I'm just giving you a heads-up. Now, as you can imagine the offer from a couple of days ago is off the table, I've assigned that job to Malcolm this morning." Jake pushes out his next exhale. "Hunter said he'll drop by to talk to you. He wants you back in therapy."

I turn back to look at him.

"Reeves, there's one thing going all caveman, beating up whoever touches your girl, it's a completely different song losing control on a job. No matter how you put it, you still lost control." There's nothing that I can say in my defense; he's absolutely right.

"Will you?" Jake shrugs off his jacket, throwing it at the back of a chair.

I watch my fisted palms and release the grip. "I'll schedule an appointment with Dr. Barnes."

Jake takes a couple of steps my way. With his hand curling around my shoulder, he says, "It's the right thing to do." I nod. "And I'm sorry that I had to take back the job offer."

"I assumed you would. I wasn't going to take it anyway. I don't want to be away for such a long time."

It's his turn to nod. "Wanna join the people?" He tips his chin toward the bar.

"Yeah," I answer, still considering what I've just agreed to. I hate therapy. I can't stand talking about everything that I'm trying so hard to keep tucked away.

Walking out of the corridor that inhabits the storage room, Jake's office, and the toilets, my eyes skim the room. When they land on a smiling Nia, my lips arch. Nia's group starts a semi-slurred, but much elated, "Happy Birthday, Alex," as Jake and I reach the bar. We turn our heads to the loud crooning that's followed by whistles and cheers.

"Yo, throw me the Partido," Jake calls to Dan, who in return flings a half empty Tequila bottle over the counter right into Jake's waiting hand. "Get some glasses," he asks of me.

"To the birthday girl," Jake holds a shot glass in the air moments later, prompting everyone at Alex's table to raise their own full glasses. When we throw back our shots, Nia and I do it with locked stares.

"So, how old is the birthday girl?" Jake eyes zero in on Alex's deep cleavage. She slants her gleaming eyes at him and he gifts her with his trademark crooked smile. She slowly drinks him, running her eyes over his faded jeans, dark, tight tee, prickled jaw, and straight, unruly auburn hair. The girl has so much sass in her eyes that it's almost impossible not to smile. "Old enough for everything naughty big girls can do." She cocks her purple spiked head sideways with a devilish grin.

Jake's head drops back with a chuckle which makes me wonder what the current status quo between Carmie and Jake is. It usually varies from "seeing" other people while together. To "seeing" other people *together*. Or the last one which is a great rarity: not "seeing" other people at all. I'd go with either option one or two, higher stakes on two, given Carmie is currently still living with Jake.

Validating my assumption, Jake doesn't dawdle much before turning a seat next to Alex and sits himself with his chest pressed to the chair's back. He leans in and whispers something to her attentive ear that ends with both regarding each other with a knowing smirk. I'm far from being a prophet, but I see a threesome in the near future.

Checking how I could thread a chair next to Nia's, my eyes catch a glimpse of a blond, wavy halo entering the bar's space.

It's time I had a serious conversation with her. Due to her dinosaur with cramps mood this morning I didn't get to that earlier when we met. I leave the group and head toward Katie.

After our usual kiss-hug greeting ritual, Katie asks me to dance with her which I dismiss by telling her we need to talk. She tells her friends that she'll be right back and follows me to Jake's office. I close the door behind us and face Katie, donning a firm expression.

"What did you tell Nia?" I forego the kid glove treatment I usually give Katie.

"Um, what do you mean?" A light flush spreads on the apples of her cheeks. Her hands, much more incriminating, knot together.

"Katie…" I look at her pointedly. Her head dips and her eyes move to her fidgety fingers. I take a step forward and take her clutched hands in mine.

"Katie, you're the closest thing to a family I got. I care about you immensely." She lifts her light blue eyes to mine. Her white cotton dress clad body stiffens as she waits for me to go on. With my free hand I caress her cheek. "Please don't abuse that. You know I could never stay mad at you. You know I'd do anything to make you happy, right?"

She utters a soft, "Yes."

"Can I ask you to do the same for me?" I hold her timid stare. "Katie, *she is* my happy. Nia is *my happy.*"

She gives me a reluctant affirmation which is followed by a compromising nod. "Are you guys together now?"

I clearly hear the undercurrent of dejection in her voice, however, I guess I need to hand it to her as it is. There isn't really much I can say to embellish or soften the fact that Nia and I *are* officially together now.

"We are. Please treat her nicely next time. Can you do that for me?"

I find it somewhat immature that her answer is a shrug.

"It doesn't change anything between us. I'm still here for you, just like it's always been. Anything you need, Katie. You know that, right?"

"Yes," she answers, still not exactly the happiest camper.

"Let's get back so I can buy you a drink."

"You better…" She finally smiles at me.

Nia's eyes burn at us as we step back into the bar. Her stare retreats when she notices Katie giving me a hug after I buy her a drink.

When I reach them, Paul, fish dude's brother, glares at me. Alex's hand is already on Jake's thigh, and Nia is focused on whatever the blondie next to her is saying. Since Nia is bunkered on both sides, I take a seat opposite her. My irritation spikes when I think about her ridiculous request, which I'm not sure why I've agreed to, to play it as though there's nothing between us. I reach for my phone and text her.

I talked to Katie.

Nia grabs her device and checks the message. She shifts her head to look my way and shrugs.

I told her about us.

This time her eyes jolt to mine, I nod with a hint of a smile.

Told her you're my happy.

The stunning smile that lights her face is incredible. I notice how she is making a visible effort to look attentive to whatever the blonde beside her is chatting about in her ear. Each time Nia steals a gleaming peek my way, my smile grows bigger. I just watch her, my chair slightly leaned back by the press of my foot on the table's leg, peeling the label from my bottle. I plead guilty to obsessed; I just can't take my eyes off her.

Everyone—those who are intoxicated and those just lightly buzzed—shoot the shit for too long. Just when I'm about to go all caveman on Nia, throw her over my shoulder and take her home, to hell with whatever I've agreed to earlier, she beats me to it.

I literally spit the next swig of my drink as Nia asks out of the blue, "Who's up for a game of Scrabble?" I'm in love…

"Good game. Big fan," I say with a humored bite.

"Are you any good?"

"I can hold my own."

"You do, huh?" she teases. The pull of her lips is mighty adorable. I nod, my eyes jumping with mischief. It seems like everyone at the table is either too shitfaced or has lost interest in our little exchange.

"You up for a match?" She pretends to crack her knuckles.

I snort a laugh. "Oh, believe me, I couldn't be more ready."

"I'm so going to own your ass…"

She grins at me while I rock back on my chair, my eyes already stripping off her clothes. I stand and gesture with my hand, over the packed table, for Nia to go ahead. "After you, darlin'."

We meet at the table's end where Alex is about to give Jake a lap dance. I bring my hand to the small of Nia's back, looking to guide her out of the bar, when Jake's voice stops us.

"Already leaving?" His straight strands fall to the side and his grin could not be more wicked.

"Yeah, we're going to play Scrabble," Nia replies enthusiastically. I stifle a laugh when I meet Jake's knowing, cocky smile.

He raises a glass. "Happy fucking!"

Nia turns into the brightest shade of red. I take her hand in mine and pull her after me.

"Smooth, babe," I dip my head to whisper next to her ear. She rewards me with an embarrassed glance and bites her lips. "For what it's worth, I thought you looked incredibly sweet covered in red."

She looks at me from under her lashes, smiling. She then throws back a glance at the group we've just left, and shrugs in a "whatever" kind of way before inching on her toes to kiss my jaw. I shrug in the same way and turn to hold her face in both hands and give her the kiss that I've been dying to give her the entire evening.

"Take me home," she breathes heavily into our kiss. I'm hopelessly in love with this woman.

CHAPTER 28

Nia

I lie in my bed, covered by a light blanket, and watch Reeves study my body religiously, with his mouth, not leaving any area of skin un-kissed, untouched. Having him explore it reverently, I think about how he cleanses my soul, stripping me to my core each time I reveal another piece of me to him.

"I'm scared," I say cautiously.

Reeves leaves a kiss on my knee and pivots his head. "What of?" he asks softly. He turns to sit cross-legged at my feet. Taking them in his hands, he starts kneading. "Tell me," he says with dramatic flare.

"I've become dependent on us, on you."

His face softens.

"I'm scared of what will happen if we just don't..."

"Nia, that won't happen. This co-dependence goes both ways. I can't begin my day or go to sleep at night without you, or the thought of you."

"I've let you in so deep inside, to my weakest hidden places," I whisper.

"I couldn't be more grateful for your trust in me." He brings my foot next to his lips and softly kisses the spot below my ankle. He brings my other foot for the same intimate, simple gesture. "Nia, like I've said before, you're inside my heart, and it's not a temporary thing." His eyes liquefy into mine. "It feels permanent." I lose him, once again, to this thing that complicates his mind. Apprehension suffuses me as I watch his thoughts cloud his face. He seems to be having an inner battle before he finally squares his eyes with mine.

"I wish I could tell you more. I wish I could share with you *my* darkest turbulence."

My chest tightens. "Why can't you?"

"One of those 'if I tell you I'd have to kill you' things." He smiles a smile that has nothing to do with amusement. He seems tormented.

Words run stale on my tongue as I try to speak. Instead, I inch to my knees and move to straddle him. I wrap my arms around him and he buries his face above my bare chest. He sighs.

"There are visions etched in my memory that I could never erase. One damn thing after another. Getting shot at, blown up, losing friends..." The last fragment holds so much pain, a thin layer screens my eyes at the light shudder wavering his voice. "There are some triggers that I don't think I'll ever get past..."

I kiss the softness of his shortly cropped head.

When he lifts his eyes to mine they are also covered with a thin shiny layer, his face full of torment. "You take it away," he says, low.

I nod, my heart pounding forcefully in my throat. I know what he means. It's the exact sentiment he infuses in me.

Eyes locked with mine, he inches closer and kisses my lips. The air around us thickens with emotion and ache, and mostly with the deepest connection one can share. We are bound in this thing of ours that no one who hasn't shared loss, and found someone to hold on to, someone to love, can understand.

In utter silence, where only our eyes converse, he lifts me with one hand and gets rid of his boxers with the other. My panties follow. Guiding himself under me, he eases me down to slide over him. We let out a breath of redemption as we unite. We are eyes to eyes, heart to heart, intimately linked. We never leave each other's stares as I slowly glide up and down around him. He holds my thighs, it's only our middles that move to meet in unhurried yet intense thrusts.

"Slow down, beautiful... I don't want it to end," Reeves whispers as I build up and accelerate my pace.

He brushes my hair to the sides of my face and brings his mouth to connect with mine. We move against each other in soundless, blissful absorption. I sink deeper on him, my eyes drinking his green irises in, and I'm countered by a sweet, caring smile. When I can't hold it anymore, I let go and drop my head to the nook of his neck, reeling from my ecstasy and the love I feel for him. I pepper soft kisses along his neck as he joins me with a few slow and hard final pounds. Blissfully intoxicated on each other, we embrace, letting the warmth of our connection flood inside of us.

~ ~ ~

"Nuh uh." Reeves snatches the remote control from my hand. When I try to get it back, he pushes me with one hand to the sofa till I'm flat on my back. "We're not watching any of that crap."

"Give me back the remote." I squirm under his sprawled palm on my navel. As I manage to almost sit up, he moves to straddle me. He grabs my hands and pins them over my head, with his other hand pointing the remote at the TV.

"It's not funny," I squeal.

He shifts to look down at me and wickedly grins. He bends to smack a juicy kiss on my mouth. "It's not funny, it's highly amusing."

Finally finding something to his liking, he turns my way again, this time with dancing eyes and a devilish smirk. "I found your porn, babe." I press my cheek to the sofa, turning to look at the TV, to find out what the hell he's talking about. I burst up laughing as I see the opening credits of G.I. Joe on the wide screen.

"Oh yeah, baby." I mimic Austin Powers. It's Reeves' turn to laugh.

Instead of salivating over the man in uniform on the screen, I gape at my own man as he brings another handful of microwave popcorn to his mouth. Truth be told, he does a much better job of speeding my heartbeat than his double on the screen. He looks so relaxed and content sitting with his legs resting on the coffee table, grey boxer briefs, sexy dog tags on a sexier defined, bared chest.

An almost forgotten emotion surfaces, one I haven't felt in more than 1095 days. An emotion that tickles at my heart. *I'm happy.* No inhibitions, no undercurrent of gloom. *Happy.* Genuinely happy. And it's all because of him, because Reeves is *my happy.*

"What?" He sends a popcorn kernel to land on my nose.

I pop the puffed seed to my mouth and smile back. His own grin broadens.

"Wanna combat my brains out?" I wriggle my brows, dropping my off-shoulder shirt further down to reveal the swell of my breast. At once, the popcorn bowl is set on the table, and I'm yanked back by my legs to lie on my back. A very distinctive bulge meets my middle when a mighty eager Reeves lands between my legs.

"Ma'am, yes, ma'am. I'd be honored," he says next to my mouth, and we both chuckle in unison.

Until we don't laugh anymore.

I keep silent, okay maybe not, it's more akin to producing breathy sounds while letting Reeves adeptly fulfills his duties.

~~~

"Oh God, I want to die." I bury my face in Reeves' chest that slightly trembles with his chuckles. I shake my head, inhaling his scent, a splendid combination of freshly showered, light softener powdery scent, and masculine musk. His arms clad in a long sleeves, white undershirt enfold me tightly.

"It wasn't that bad," he says, humor dominating his voice.

Okay, maybe Mrs. Perry catching us in a hot and heavy session at the studio, after hours, is not the end of the world, but it's still beyond embarrassing. God, I'll be mortified if she ever mentions it again.

I came to the studio to dance by myself. Something I haven't done for a while. Something I've missed fiercely. We planned for Reeves to pick me up and go to dinner. He surprised me by arriving earlier, after a run and shower, to watch me dance.

Apparently, Reeves' reaction to watching me dance is the equivalent to my reaction to him in uniform... Hence the embarrassing moment in which I was pinned against the floor to ceiling mirrors, panting, grazing against an equally heavily breathing Reeves, when I froze to the sound of high-heels. As I froze, so did the tapping. And when I looked over Reeves' shoulder, it was directly into the blue eyes of my highbrow boss.

"Carry on dear, there's nothing here I haven't seen or done."

I swallowed hard.

"Good evening," she sang. The tapping continued and I watched Mrs. Perry sashay away, adorned by a tiny, yet mischievous, smile. Which brings me to this moment where I still feel my face radiating heat.

"Seriously, not that bad," Reeves repeats through a chuckle.

"I'll have to find a new job," I say, and his smirk widens.

"Just make sure you don't hump anyone during the interview."

I feign a scowl that I'm not able to hold for too long when my traitorous lips pull up.

I lock up after us and slide my hand into Reeves' waiting one. We pass by a few shops and a couple of restaurants when he says, "I want an encore later tonight."

My eyes travel to his.

"You were saying?"

"I was saying," Reeves opens the door to a small Brazilian place and gestures for me to step in first, "that I want an encore later." His hand hovers at the small of my back, guiding us to a table for two by the window. "Only this time you'll be dancing naked, *on me.*"

The guy at the table next to us chokes on his drink. Reeves flashes me a naughty smile and I shake my head in return. We place our orders with the friendly waitress and toast my upcoming performance.

While we dig into our dishes, Reeves asks me more about Patrick. My reaction and the comfort I feel telling him about my big brother are the same as what I felt when I first let him inside my bedroom, where all my home and family mementos reside—I do it with ease. I want to tell him, and though the perpetual twinge is very much intact, so is a new air of a desire to share, a desire to tell Reeves everything.

It's been more than two weeks since we made our "official" transition from just friends to – so much more. These two weeks were one of the best times that I had in a long while. There isn't something monumental that I can put my finger on and say: that's it, that's what made it as wonderful as it was. It's everything. It's just simply being with him. He makes me happy, and he doesn't make me forget, he makes me accept.

"I love the way you look at me," Reeves says, pulling me back from my short reverie.

"How is it?" I ask, utterly indulging in the food that I've missed so much. Feijoada with Farofa, I'm in food heaven.

"The way your eyes shine, your beauty… It's even brighter than before." He takes my hand that's resting on the table and kisses it softly in the center of my palm.

"I'm happy," I say.

Reeves' hollering phone snatches his attention. "Stanley." Silence falls between us as he listens attentively for a few long moments. He takes a sharp intake before his hand drops mine and moves to hold the back of his neck. "Is she okay?"

I tense and stare at him, curious, waiting for his next words.

He pushes an audible sigh before asking in a strained voice, "Where are you?" Another pause. "I'll be there soon."

"Fuck," Reeves utters. "Fuck." His hands move to hold his buzzed head. His eyes drop to me, "It's Katie, she's in the E.R. We need to go."

"What happened?" My hand reflexively flies to my mouth.

"She took pills." His words are sharp and woven with dread. A stark reminder of how you can never really know what's going on in someone else's mind.

"God, is she okay?"

"They pumped her stomach."

As Reeves' hails a taxi, I ask in a small voice, "Are you sure you want me there?"

His response is a piercing look followed by a fierce, "Yes." Even though I truly believe it's not my place, I'll be there for him in case he needs my support. The ride to the hospital is a nail-biting fifteen minutes in which Reeves is locked up behind worried eyes and a flexed jaw.

Tears clog my throat and I am thrown back at the sight of Katie's parents. The lack of color in their faces and the pools of dread in their eyes hit too close to home. It slams my heart from side to side inside my ribcage; it's my own parents that I see before my eyes.

Reeves covers Beth in a hug while talking to Stanley over her shoulder. I manage to catch only pieces of sentences given our distance, my shaken condition, and their low voices. What I can clearly see is the relief in Reeves air as he closes his eyes and drops his face to the crown of Beth's head.

With an aim to give them some privacy, I walk out to the courtyard and do something I haven't done for too long now. I take my phone out of my denim jacket and call my parents. This time, I wait anxiously for them to pick up, and it's a very different kind of apprehension than the last times that I answered their calls. This time, I want to talk to them, this time I miss them and want to tell them just how much I do.

"Nia." My mother's voice over the line is breathy. "Are you okay?"

My stomach coils. It's me who put this worry in her. "I'm okay, Ma. I miss you." My voice breaks.

"Oh baby, I miss you so much. Every day."

"I'm sorry, Ma. I'm sorry for everything."

I'm sorry for blaming them for my self-hatred. After more than four months since I've left home, I *really* talk to my parents. My dad joins the call and I begin an unstoppable word marathon when I tell them all about the last few months. About everything that matters. Before ending the call, they make me promise to call more often and offer to buy me a ticket to visit home for Christmas.

For a moment, caught up in my own emotional bubble, I forget where I am. I tuck the phone back inside my pocket and go look for Reeves. I'm more than relieved to notice vitality has returned to Beth and Stanley's cheeks when I stop to talk to them. They wait on a peeling, grey bench at the reception, holding hands and quietly talking. They both look up at me, though an air of relief colors their expressions, they still seem to carry mounds of concern. Stanley nods and Beth gives me a weary smile.

"How is she doing?"

"Better. Reeves is with her now," Beth says.

"Room forty," Katie's father adds.

Wrapped up in my thoughts, I make my way through the long hall, planning to wait for Reeves near Katie's room. There are so many things running through my mind. I feel sorry for Katie's parents, I'm happy to have spoken to mine, I miss home. The thought of how Katie's actions might affect Reeves leaves me troubled. I'm mad at Katie, for whatever reason she chose to do what she did, just as I'm mad at my own brother for the same reason. When one decides to give up, he takes the burden off himself, but when he does, he leaves his loved ones with the heaviest rock that they'll ever have to carry. One which will never, ever, leave them.

As I finally shake my pensive state off, I realize I've passed the room that I was looking for. I retrace my steps toward the right place and stop short, hearing Katie tell Reeves, "But I love you." My breath is sucked out of me at once. I don't stay to hear Reeves' response, I just start walking away.

I hurry my steps to get out of there as fast as I can. I don't want to hear Reeves' response, and I don't want to hear the rest of their conversation either. I know how Reeves feels about me, though he's never literally uttered the words. Without the slightest of doubts, I know. By what he shared with me so far, by the way he looks at me and the way he touches me. I just know. But I also know that I can't let myself get hurt again. I can't let myself be involved in so much drama. It isn't healthy for me, nor for my healing heart.

A thought I try to push out keeps gnawing at the back of my mind, amplifying with every step that I take to get away, what if after all he does have feelings for her? Stronger than the ones he has for me? Maybe it's better not to find out at all and hold on to what he offers me right now, him, on his own terms. With the latter I could live, the other option is too shattering to even consider. I should cease tearing myself apart. I should get out of here, everything about the place or what led us here is clouding my mind, bringing back fears and insecurities that I shouldn't be nursing.

I stop by the Evans, hug them goodbye, and walk out of the hospital.

CHAPTER 29

Reeves

"Augh," I roar through gritted teeth, holding myself from punching a hole through the wall outside Katie's room. I couldn't be more infuriated. How could she do this to her parents? What a selfish, stupid, immature act to pull on bereaved parents who still mourn their first-born's loss. How could she fucking do it to them, to me?

There's a burn of anger whirling in my gut as I prop my arms on the wall and drop my head between them. I need to calm down before facing Beth and Stanley; I promised Katie I wouldn't tell them the truth. I guess the writing was on the wall all along, or maybe reflected from her eyes, the message I was too damn blind to read.

Katie told me that she didn't really try to take those goddamn pills and it all kind of got out of control. Apparently her plan was to call me and tell me that she took them. She thought it would finally push me to admit that I have feeling for her. She even set an entire scene for me in her room, leaving several pill bottles spilled on her nightstand. What she didn't expect was for her mother to find her crying, surrounded by a vision that could only insinuate one thing. From that point, everything just went out of control. Katie was too ashamed and freaked out to come clean. One thing led to another and she found herself having her stomach pumped in a hospital. This time, I was more than clear when I told her it would never happen between us, that I'm with Nia, and it's not a temporary thing. She made me promise not to tell her parents what really happened and I agreed on one condition, that when they finally get home, she will.

I take a deep breath and go look for Nia. I need to get out of here before I lose my mind.

"Thank you for coming, darling." Beth kisses my cheek. I hug her while scanning the room for Nia.

"Let me know if you need anything," Beth nods.

"She'll be okay," I tell them both as Stanley pats my back. I warmly smile at Stanley, glad to notice a bud of a smile on his stress-lined face.

"Have you seen Nia?" I ask as we part.

"She left about five minutes ago…"

"Left? Where?" Unintentionally, I snap.

"Oh, I thought she told you she was leaving. I think she went home." Beth trades a curious stare with her husband. I leave the Evans and hurry toward the sliding doors. Why would Nia leave without telling me? I jog a few good minutes till I spot her a couple of yards ahead.

"Nia." I grab her shoulder and turn her back to face me. My stomach twists fiercely to her tear stricken face. I stare at her in alarm.

"What happened?"

She shakes her head. "Is Katie okay?"

"She is," I grunt. "Are *you* okay?"

She nods with a faint smile that doesn't reach her worried eyes. I take her hand and pull her to a less crowded spot, next to a closed store. I brush the moistness under her eyes with my thumbs, framing her face with my hands.

I lean down to kiss her lips. "Why were you crying?"

"Reeves, I can't do this." Her voice comes out so weak that I need to ask her to repeat what she said, hoping I've misheard her the first time.

"It's taking so much out of me, I can't do this."

Fuck. With some fear that she might run away, I prop both my hands at each side of her shoulders on the glass window. "What do you mean, what happened?"

"What happened with Katie brought everything back. I heard her tell you that she loves you. I know you care for me, but the thought that maybe it's not enough… It's the power of this thing between us, it just keeps growing stronger and stronger. I feel like I'm losing control. I can't lose *you*, I just can't."

"You will not lose me, I won't let you," I say, starting to panic. "There's nothing I want more than you."

"It's too much. I feel like I'm losing control over myself when it comes to you."

I take a deep breath and close my eyes. My heart is about to pound out of my chest.

I don't intend for my words to come as loud and harsh but they do, "You want to talk about control and loss? When you told me you loved me, it was the first time since Ben died that I didn't regret taking the loaded gun out of my mouth."

Her eyes fill with tears again and her lips begin to tremble. "I want to lose control when it comes to you, with you. How many times do I need to tell you, I'm crazy about you. I'm not letting you go." I grab her face in my hands and kiss her so forcefully my breath hitches. I lean back and kiss the trail her tears left. I hold her in my arms till my own heartbeat calms down. "I'm tired, it's been a long day. Let's just go home."

"I'm sorry," she whispers.

"Don't be. Just stop doubting me," I say, fatigue lining my words.

~ ~ ~

It's the sweetest sound. I relish in Nia's soft, contented sigh when she leans her head back on my chest as we soak in a warm bathtub. I slide one hand to rest on her stomach, drawing small circles on her skin.

I bring my other sodden hand from under the water, letting drops drip from my fingers to her nipple. I watch the little drop trail down the pink peak, fascinated. She lets out another sigh, this time a tad breathier when my finger moves to hover over the pointed crest, lightly circling it. I dip my chin to press my lips to her smooth shoulder. She tilts her head up to reward me with an easy smile.

"I can't believe she did that." Nia pivots her head back to stare out the window. I wait for her to go on, caressing her arm from shoulder to palm, raising bumps along the way. I end the trail by linking our fingers together underwater. "What a selfish thing to do. If she loves you as she claims she does, why would she do anything to hurt you?"

"I don't know, really. Katie doesn't have a mean bone in her body," I say, squeezing our intertwined fingers. "And I still don't believe that she feels that way about me. I think she is confused and going through a hard period. It was an obvious cry for attention. I hope *you* didn't think for one moment that I might feel the same way about her." I push out an irate exhale thinking about what Katie put Stanley and Beth through.

When I'm about to tell Nia that she has nothing to ever feel insecure about when it comes to us, she makes me snap my parted lips shut by saying, "I need the reassurance from you. I guess it's a part of the shattered-heart syndrome."

I'm not sure why, but I find it so hard to tell her the words she wants me to say. Maybe it's the side effect of my own traumatic past.

"I'm with you, in every possible way. More than you can imagine. We're together," I say.

She stirs the water around us while turning to face me. I'm hyperaware of everything about her as she inclines her face to touch her lips to mine. Her body, soft, warm, soaked, and naked on mine. Her faint scent of honey and now soap. Her heart beating against mine.

She rests her cheek on my chest. I envelope her in my arms, although she'd just simmered my blood for a completely different contact. We lie in leisured silence until Nia breaks the prolonged, quiet moment, "Aren't Carmie and Jake together these days?"

"Really? Why would you bring *them* up *now*?"

"I don't know, I was just thinking about Jake and Alex, it looked like he was about to give her a *very* personal birthday present."

"I'm pretty sure the 'birthday present' was eventually given by both Carmie and Jake."

Nia's head shoots up and I can't help but snort a laugh at her wide eyes. She lightly flushes as she murmurs, "That's kind of hot."

"Don't even think it. I'm not sharing."

"Oh, God, I didn't mean… Not us, God, no. Just the thought of them…"

"Turns you on?" I say, raising an eyebrow.

She bites her smile. "I can help with that…" I grin, pressing her by her perfect, perky ass against me.

"Hold up," she states, and starts inching up.

"What are you doing?" I ask, not the greatest fan of her sudden withdrawal. And… she's out of the tub.

"Where the hell are you going?"

"Hold that thought while you wait for me in bed, I'll come back soon." She winks.

I shake my head with a smile.

~ ~ ~

Holy. Sweet. Fucking. Hell. I think I just died and went to heaven. Because the vision in front of me is definitely out of this world. I can't unglue my eyes from Nia. My pulse is throbbing over every inch of my skin, especially the very strained part.

"Touch yourself," she says with a bite of command and my breath hitches. I slowly stroke the bulge in my boxers.

"Take them off for me." There's fire in her eyes.

I push my pelvis slightly up to do as she orders. My spellbound eyes bore into Nia as she threads her thumbs through the sides of her soft pink boy-shorts, slightly pulling the fabric down. I swallow hard, watching my perfection of a girlfriend dance. She's swaying sensually to the music in my bedroom in goddamn high heels and lacy underwear. For the last most precious minutes, she's been dancing, stripping for me slowly, and with heated ardor, peeling her ruffled plaid skirt and white button-down blouse off.

When I was lying on my bed waiting for Nia, I never expected that I was in for the most erotic striptease I've ever experienced. I had to fight myself from pinning her to the wall and devouring her the minute that she entered my bedroom with a skimpy school girl uniform and those killer heels.

"Christ, you're hot," I breathe, stroking up and down my shaft as I gaze at her turning her back to me.

She unclasps her bra and throws it my way, looking at me over her shoulder. She turns to face me again. She runs her palms over her shimmering, mocha skin, passing over her long, delicate neck, taking her time as she caresses her plump breasts. I tighten my grip around myself as she unhurriedly shimmies down her panties.

"You're killing me here," I croak, prompting Nia to send me a seductive smile. "Dance your ass over here, *now*."

Slowly, she swings her curves to the bed. She stands on all fours at the edge of the mattress and starts to slowly advance my way. Hand after hand, her curves undulating, her bare chest teasing in easy moves. I watch her, enthralled, my lips slightly parted.

"Oh God," I pant and drop my head back as her mouth closes around me.

CHAPTER 30

Nia

For the first time in too long, everything around me seems to be donning a rosy hue. Stark reminders of pain still appear every now and then, and yes, I do, from time to time, feel low, but it's a different kind of low. A low in which I feel safe enough to let myself experience those feelings, to deal with them.

Something Reeves said the other day has somehow changed my perspective about myself. *"When you told me you loved me it was the first time since Ben died that I didn't regret taking the loaded gun out of my mouth."*

In a way, this bond that has been steadily deepening between us has made Reeves hopeful for a chance of a brighter future, one that isn't leaden with atonement. His admission was unconsciously a reflection of my own healing that has been gradually progressing since the day I met him. I've been going through a personal rehabilitation process of letting culpability morph into acceptance. My own purge, from guilt. And he brought me there, with his friendship, with his ease at making me genuinely content. He helped me discover my old self, the one that I disconnected from the day that I became consumed with repentance. As it seems, love is even potent enough to restore your belief in yourself.

He made me look at the world with brighter colors. I feel whole again, as much as one can truly feel whole when a piece of your heart was taken away for good. I've come to accept losing Patrick, I've come to accept that it wasn't my parents' fault that he moved to the open ward. I've come to accept it wasn't *my* fault that he did what he did. There isn't a day that passes in which I don't think of him and miss him immensely, but as I do, the weight of the loving is greater than the pain.

"Hey, where did you go?" Reeves' voice cracks through my thoughts.

I turn back to him with a thin smile. I shake my head, communicating all is okay. He keeps his stare on me till he's reassured that I'm fine and turns back to listen to Jake and Dan talk about an order they should make for the bar.

Dan, a small towel thrown on his shoulder, notes down whatever Jake is saying. My gaze wanders around the space, it looks so different in daytime. The front doors are open and the bright sun illuminates the space. The daylight colors the room in a foggy shade that still looks somewhat smoky even with the light breeze funneling through the wide-open front doors. The place looks muted, even the small stage and the huge Hendrix photo doesn't look as cool in broad daylight.

Reeves, who's sitting on a stool next to me, is utterly engaged in a conversation with Jake, that seems to hold much more than Dan and I can decode. The name Hunter has been mentioned many times by both in less than a few minutes. I study Reeves' profile, my eyes trailing over his strong jaw, and the hint of his deep green irises. Even with his casual jeans and long sleeve grey undershirt, he makes my heart twitter. We've been practically inseparable for the last couple of weeks, post-Katie mess, which shortly after, she apologized for to Reeves. She said she was sorry and agreed with him that it was a selfish, thoughtless thing to do. I force the memory away; I don't want to think of drama when it comes to us, we truly have had enough of that.

I slide a hand over Reeves back. "I'm going out for some fresh air."

He holds up a finger at Jake and pivots my way. "You want me to come with you?"

I shake my head and leave a chaste kiss on the side of his mouth. "I'll be back soon."

I run in my head the question my aunt asked me when I visited her earlier today, finally, after the long months I've been basically living a few blocks from her. She asked when I am planning to visit home. I've been pushing the thought aside for the longest time, but I believe that I'm ready to go home and face some things I finally should.

I lightly cough at the smell of smoke reaching my throat before I notice Carmie leaning on the wall, tapping the ashes of a half burned cigarette off. Carmie, as ever, is a vision of badass beauty. Her endless, skinny legs are bare under a denim miniskirt. Her milky skin peeks between the skirt belt and a worn AC/DC tour tee. Completing the look is her leather jacket, a feminine version of Jake's "uniform."

"Hey." She blows a white puff from the side of her lips.

"Hi."

"Looking great, Nia." She takes another drag.

"Thanks. Coming in?"

"Yeah, to say goodbye." She whistles smoke out of her pouty lips, grazing the small bud on the wall before tossing it to a trashcan.

"You're leaving?"

"Yeah. I always do." She pops a mint in her mouth.

"Why?"

She raises an eyebrow.

I shrug. "It seems like you two have it good together."

"We do." A ghost of a smile hovers her lips, but they quickly bounce back to her perpetual hard look. "Sometimes the big ol' L word is not enough to tie you down. Sometimes the urge to taste life and fulfill your dreams is greater than being with the one you love." She twists her mouth. "In my book of rules, I always choose me. *I* would probably never hurt me."

I frown, weighing her words.

"Go ahead, ask whatever's on your mind."

"Has Jake ever hurt you?" She circles her hand around my waist, gesturing for me to come back inside with her.

"Oh yes, he did. *Twice*. The first time he made me fall so desperately in love with him. The second, he chose himself over me." As we approach the men, she whispers in my ear, "Yeah, I still am more than crazy about him."

I plant myself between Reeves' thighs, still contemplating my short chat with Carmie. Reeves' hand reflexively falls to my lower back. He bends to kiss me, inches from my ear.

"Kiss me, handsome. I'm going to miss your lips." Carmie puts her game face on, smiling teasingly at Jake. As opposed to her, he doesn't make an effort to conceal his discontentment.

"So don't," he grunts. She just pulls him by his hand.

"Excuse us kids, this is an adults' conversation." Jake follows Carmie toward his office with a jaw that's ticking like a time bomb.

I turn to snuggle under Reeves' massive arm as he finishes the last of his orange juice. He presses a kiss on my head. "Wanna leave?"

"I love you," I whisper. Reeves' expression oscillates between adoration and edginess. His lips part, ready to say something, but unfortunately close right back shut. I just lean in and kiss him again.

~ ~ ~

The subtleness of Reeves lips on my skin seeps through the warm spots he leaves to my very core. I close my eyes, savoring his touch. We are both sprawled on my bed, my head nestled on my plump pillow, and his on my bare stomach. I gaze at my fingers that lightly dance over his shoulder and neck.

"I think that I'm ready to go home for a visit," I say idly, indulging in the intimacy we share after our easy lovemaking. Reeves' head rises to glance between me and some family photos that I have on my dresser.

"That's good, I'm glad for you." He turns to lie on his side, cheek pressed to my navel, gazing at me. "Did you tell your parents yet?"

"I mentioned that I might be visiting for Christmas." Reeves' finger moves to draw tiny circles on my collarbone. "I want you to come with me. Would you?"

His brows crease as he considers my request. "Yeah, sure." The easiness in which his answer comes staggers me for a good moment, in the best of ways.

"Yes?" My eyes widen in glee.

"Yeah."

"You would?" I can't even try to contain my excited surprise.

"Why do you look so surprised? You should know by now that there's nothing that I wouldn't do for you."

My chest expends to no end. *He has his own ways to tell me just how much he cares.* I hurry to straddle him, raining kisses all over his face.

"Thank you, thank you, thank you." I continue my attack, not leaving an inch of un-smooched skin. He kisses me back over a smile as I finally land on his mouth.

"If I knew this would be your reaction, I'd agree to more things."

"You already do." I wink. "Pfft, you're totally wrapped around my finger."

I squeal as he rolls us over, ending with him on top of me, his thigh between my legs. His teeth scrape at my neck, descending to my collarbone.

"Wrapped around your finger," he murmurs to my skin. "So right…"

I grin, enthusiastically absorbing his touch.

CHAPTER 31

Reeves

Watching Nia dance has become my favorite leisure time activity. There are more than a dozen good looking women showcasing their goods for an enthusiastic crowd at the small dance floor in the bar, but they don't even hold a candle to her. My eyes feast on her and her only, because there's nothing else in this universe that I'd rather watch. Her hips sway to the music, revealing a sliver of taut olive skin. Her tight jeans end low beneath her navel, her white halter-top kissing the skin just above it. Her dark, luminous strands fall heavily, framing her delicate face while hovering over her perky breasts. Her eyes are closed, her pouty lips slightly parted, reminding me of her ecstasy face, right before she falls to pieces under me. My heart tightens as I watch her, thinking of how much I love her. How much I need her. How much she's changed my life for the better.

I turn on my stool to get my drink, to a display of a salivating Dan and a gaping Jake. I throw a handful of salted peanuts at Jake and rise to slap Dan on the back of his head over the counter.

"I swear, if you two don't stop stripping down my girlfriend," I warn. Jake snorts and Dan drops his gaze to the floor, bringing his damn protruding tongue back inside his mouth.

"Well," Jake says, shrugging, "can you blame us?" His prickled cheek lifts to reveal a teasing smile. I flip him off before taking a swig from my whiskey.

"Hi there." Contently, I absorb Nia as she settles herself between my parted thighs.

"Hi." She leans in for a gentle kiss. She takes my drink, gives it one fleeting look that's followed by a nose wrinkle. Craning her neck to look behind my back, she asks, "Moscow Mule?"

"Sure," Dan's voice follows.

"No scotch?" I ask her as she returns to look at me with a light smile.

She shakes her head and kisses my lips. "No," she answers, kissing me deeper. "I need something lighter."

I thread my fingers through her hair, murmuring, "I just watched you dance. You keep doing this, I won't be able to hold myself..." She tilts back to look at me, and her hands drop to rest on my thighs. She blinks playfully.

"Hold yourself from doing what?" she asks with a honey dripping voice. I grab her ass, pulling her deeper into me, for our middles to meet, where I can show rather than tell. My much tangible demonstration buys me a damn adorable vision of a lightly flushed Nia.

"Thanks," she says to Dan who sets her drink next to us. I can't hold my laugh at how croaky her voice comes out. Nia downs half of her drink in one generous gulp. She wipes her mouth with the back of her hand and smirks at me. I grin, gazing at her with my head cocked.

"I see lettered tiles in your future, handsome," she says in the oddest drawl, I swear she sounds suffering.

"I more than dig the fortune telling, but what's up with the weird voice?"

"What? Didn't you like my gypsy impersonation?" I tilt my head back, laughing.

"Babe, you sounded constipated."

"Whatever." She rolls her eyes, feigning a pout. "Let's go play..."

~~~

I turn my head from the TV to look at the ceiling, sinking deeper onto the couch's plump pillow. I brush my fingers through Nia's hair that's scattered over my bare side. She purrs in serenity, leaning into my slow caress. She plants a kiss on my skin and continues to watch whatever is on now. I lost track of what we were watching long ago, letting the ease that surrounds us take over me. I've been lying here with this amazing woman tangled between my legs, this woman who makes my breath hitch each time she laughs.

I've been trying to find the words to tell her just how in love I am with her, but something has been stopping me. I can't put my finger on it. What is it that doesn't let me take my final guard down? I couldn't be more certain about what I feel for her, how intense it is, and how clearly I see her in my future. But it's as if something inside of me denies me from taking the final leap to tell her "I'm completely yours."

"Reeves, I think your phone is ringing." Nia's drowsy voice bursts my heavy bubble of thoughts. I stretch my hand to the back of the sofa to fetch my phone and still to the name on the display.

"I need to take this one." I leave my words in the air, waiting for Nia to let me stand up. She smiles at me, slouching back on the sofa as I make my way to my bedroom.

"Hunter," I say and swallow hard. I'm anticipating the lecture of the century for hitting that prick the other day or a scolding about why I haven't seen a therapist yet. I freeze as he tells me that he needs my help with something. When he mentions the name that turns my blood to ice, I close my eyes, lean my forehead to the wall, and listen. At the same time an illumination of what's been holding me back with Nia seeps to the soil of my recognition, I need a closure first. A retribution.

"... Since you know this group better than anyone, as I've mentioned before," Hunter says, referring to the "Erie Group" sleeper cell investigation that I was leading, the same one that saved thousands of lives from a planned attack on a football stadium. The same one in which we lost Ben. "I need your help with a couple of things." It's not a request for assistance, it's a clearly stated order.

"What kind of help?" I ask, my heart beating out of my chest.

"We'll talk about it tomorrow. Can you make it to my office tomorrow morning at eight?" *His office*, it's serious this time. Adrenaline washes over me at the hopeful thought he might be cooperating with Jake after all, and that there's a slight chance I might get to be a part of the current case.

"Sure, I'll be there at eight, sir."

"Thank you." The line goes silent.

~ ~ ~

"Why aren't you sleeping?" Nia asks with shut eyes, nestling deeper under my arm. I kiss her hair.

"Soon," I whisper and continue piercing a hole through the ceiling in the darkened bedroom. It should be around two a.m. by now, but sleep is the last thing on my mind. Adrenaline and anxiety are pumping through my veins as I consider all the possibilities Hunter might need my help with. I know sleep is not an option for me, not until I find out what tomorrow will bring.

~ ~ ~

I press the heels of my palms to my eyes, repressing an urge to shout. I blink forcefully and raise my head for my eyes to run over the nine faces looking back at me from the mug shots lined up on the wall. Five of them are new to me, three I know personally, and the last one's face has been etched to my memory, for life. Every twitch of his muscles as he nodded the execution of my best friend. My eyes move from the colorful pins dotting the map next to the photos and back. I can't believe they are operating from the same station they did three years ago. As Hunter said, simple and clever, the last place we might sniff around.

Since I led the investigation the last time, working undercover as a part of their operation, Hunter thought I would be the best person to give exact details of the operation and the actual facility. I can close my eyes and see any scrape of paint on the wall, the dusty floors, the underground room where they kept the spider diagrams and some of the ammo. I pace the narrow room, carefully studying the wall, memorizing every new detail.

I stand here by myself waiting for Hunter, Green, and Agent Koby to come back from another meeting. Hunter's preface, prior to my meeting with his team, as we set in his office, still lingers in warning.

"Reeves, you are going to be exposed to every little detail of the investigation, you *will not*, in any way, take it with you when you leave. Not even here." He pointed to my head with his cigar. "We need your help, but that's where it ends."

And yet, here I am, having my thoughts cause a colossal storm in my head. I know where A.Z. is, I can reach him with no sweat. I can blow his fucking head off and finally have my closure. But I'm fully aware that at the same time I'd be blowing to hell the current investigation, and probably the rest of my life. And there's a fat chance that I'd be spending it behind bars if I take that path.

Hunter sees me to my car when I finally leave. Street lights illuminate our steps through the pitch-black night.

"I really appreciate your help. I'm well aware of just how hard it must have been for you to go back there."

I nod, flinging my car keys from hand to hand.

"Reeves, the moment you step into your car, you forget everything you saw today."

I don't look him straight in the eyes because I know I can't promise that. Because I know he'll see right through my thoughts of how I'm burning to do the one thing I shouldn't.

He claps my shoulder, forcing me to grace him with a look. Our eyes spark in the dark, his with warning, mine with determination.

"I'm sorry to be doing this, but it's for your own good." He pauses. "I'm having you followed till I'm convinced you won't do anything reckless." The last part comes through an exhalation. I'm about to protest and halt, realizing that not only is he absolutely right to do so, but that it's indeed for my own benefit.

"Sure," I say low, an assent loaded with frustration.

"Thank you." He finally lets me go, patting my back.

~ ~ ~

It was a quiet night. I was wrapped up in my thoughts while she was buried in dance steps and music for a show that she is putting on with the girls. We made love and I held her in my arms throughout the night, afraid to let her go, soaking in every bit of all that's exquisite, calming and sweet, that is my Nia.

"Hey, you're squeezing me like it might be our last goodbye," she said through a laugh just before leaving in the morning, pressing a brief kiss on my cheek. Little did she know just how apt her words were.

~ ~ ~

I lean with one hand on the brick wall where I'm hiding, a few yards from where I'm going to soon determine how the rest of my life will play out. I shake off the thoughts of how earlier today I ditched Hunter's guys who were following me to Nia and how we left off this morning. Thoughts of my father, Ben, Katie, Beth, and Stanley, and even the mother I never knew, all twirl together in my head. Faces, eyes, fragments of conversations, snippets from better times, bits from worse times, all run before my eyes. I shut them tightly, focusing on the one person who makes me want to retrace my steps back to the car and recall what I'm seconds away from doing.

Nia.

I clutch my stealth phone in my fist. Two beats pass before I start a text message, taking a deep breath that doesn't reach all the way through… and press send.

Nia, I love you. Reeves.

I switch the phone off right after. Whatever happens today, at least she'll know how I truly feel. I close my eyes again, going into focus mode, where there's only one aim on my mind. I bring the unmarked gun from my belt, load it, and walk against the wall toward the back door. Wind whistling next to my ear and the thudding of my heart are the sounds leading me toward my closure.

CHAPTER 32

Nia

A tender warmth of fulfillment suffuses me as I watch the girls perform the dance we've been working so hard on. I move with them, imitating their airy, small steps and twirls. The last tunes come and they all bow, holding their little hands in a pink chain of adorability.

"Wow," I shriek, my voice is too elated to sound any less excited. "This was perfect, way to go!" Smiles and gleaming eyes respond to my compliments as they sit in a semi-circle around me. "You should be so proud of yourselves. You did such an amazing job." I repeat some information about the last practices we'll have before the final show and let them run off to their waiting parents.

"I'm so excited for them," I tell Alex as we make our way to Jake's.

"Me, too. One of my girls said her grandparents are flying over just to see her perform. Poor girl, the pressure..." We both laugh but my smile withers as soon as I check my phone again. No answer from Reeves yet. I texted him right after I left his apartment this morning, it felt like our goodbye was somewhat odd in a too intense kind of way. I just wanted to make sure he was fine, and that whatever had him preoccupied is over. But he hasn't answered since, not to my text and not to the few calls that I made to him. Strangely enough, his phone has been off for the greater part of the day.

I try not to worry, however the fact that he was somewhat distant last night doesn't make it any easy. He told me that he had a lot on his mind with work. Also the way he hugged me when I left today had me thinking he didn't really want me to leave, but he said nothing so I assumed I might be reading something that wasn't there.

"What can I getcha?" Eileen asks. She has this bright smile, one that pours out of her eyes. A tad on the naughty side, but I guess that's what helps her get huge tips. That and the swells under her tight shirt, of course.

"Just water, thanks." I rub my temples. "Any chance you have some pain killers? My head is killing me."

The bar is still relatively quiet, just a few patrons having a drink after work. Even the music is considerably mellower, softly playing in the background. Things usually pick up in a couple of hours. I couldn't be more thankful for the quiet-ish noise, though.

"Jake has a first aid kit in his office, try there," Eileen says, handing Alex our drinks. Alex tips her chin, pointing at our regular table and I nod back in confirmation.

"I'm coming, just give me a second."

Alex's expression takes a mischievous tone. "Ask him if he has something for me too…" She winks and I inwardly cringe. I still find Jake and Alex's flirting as well as Jake and Carmie's relationship hard to digest. The whole free spirits, let's all get naked together, it's a bit too much for me.

Although the door to Jake's office is wide open, I still knock on the doorpost. Jake's messy auburn mane and piercing eyes peek from behind his screen.

"Nia," he calls in his graveled lilt.

"Hi." I send him a small, side smile. "Eileen mentioned you might have some pain killers in here?"

"Sure, come in." He pulls his chair toward a metal cupboard. "Have a seat."

He puts a little white container next to me and bends to a mini fridge. He lets a water bottle roll toward me on the table before sinking back to his wide, worn-out chair. Jake's legs rest on the massive desk.

"You okay?" He gets rid of the cap of his water bottle.

I pop a pill, down it with water, then bob my head. "I'm fine, just a minor headache. Have you heard from Reeves today?"

Little creases form in Jake's forehead. "Nope. Trouble in paradise?" The side of his mouth twitches.

"No, paradise is fine. I just didn't, umm, well, nothing really."

"So, you two are serious, huh? He's a good guy..." Jake's features morph a shade graver. "He's a *great* guy."

"Yes," I answer on a breath, "he is."

"He'd probably deprive me of my next breath if he ever heard I said this, but take it easy on him, he's been through a lot."

I nod, a whole new seed of sympathy blooms in me toward Jake.

"The last thing I'd do is hurt him, anyway. I care about him very much," I say, countering Jake's intent look. Our intense moment breaks as Jake lifts his feet from the table and accidently knocks over his bottle.

"Shit," he swears under his breath. The water spills all over, forming a little pond on his desk, drowning some scattered papers. He makes his way to the door and calls over his shoulder, "Wait up, there's something I want to tell you."

I try to save some of the floating documents when I get a text message. My heart rockets to my throat, saturated with emotions, when I read the content of the message.

Nia, I love you. Reeves.

I blink at the phone, then blink again. I don't think there was anything that I wanted more than for Reeves to tell me these three little words. "Tell" being the keyword. Goosebumps raise my skin and my heart spirals around my ribcage as I press send, trying to call him. Confusion takes over when I learn that his phone is off again. When the muddle wears off, I check the message again to find out it was sent from an unregistered number. What's going on?

"Nia... Nia?" Jake's voice invades my musing. I blink at him with everything Reeves dominating my mind. He gazes at me while pressing a stack of paper towels to the wet mess on the table. "You all right?" he asks.

"Yeah, yeah, do you mind if I make a short call?" Jake slants his head toward the back of the room to a small pantry.

Still fogged by the message, I murmur a quiet, "Thanks," and step away. Jake turns to sink into his chair, discarding the soaked papers into a bin under his desk. I shift to stand with my back to the room when I try Reeves' number again and again.

"You two don't answer my calls now?" My heart jumps and I jolt back to face the room at the sound of the raspy, loud voice. The combination of the gravity and fury that's barked at Jake makes me flinch. From where I stand, I can see Jake staring with mild confusion while stretching his hand for his mobile.

The man, wearing a perfectly fitted dark suit and an intimidating glare gazes back at Jake, rigid. Jake studies his phone for a short beat and before he is able to comment, the man adds in an artic tone, "Where is Mitchell? *Where. The fuck. Is Mitchell?*"

"What do you mean?" Jake's voice counters with his own bite of chill. My breath is held at the air of concern lacing his words.

"I don't want another one of my boys' brains blown aw…" says the man who stops short once he notices me. Jake's head slowly turns to follow the guy's eyes and stills on me.

"That's Nia, Reeves' girl," Jake says, not bothering to tell me who I was just introduced to.

"Have you spoken to him in the last few hours?" asks the picture of authority and intimidation.

I shake my head, words fail me as panic starts spreading through me, *another one of my boys' brains blown…*

"Did you have any contact with him today?"

"Nia, it's important," Jake says, the look on his face telling me he knows something I don't.

"Hmm, I left his apartment this morning." My fingers wrap tightly around the phone in my hand till the plastic bites into my flesh. "And haven't spoken to him since…"

"I see." Narrowed blue eyes burn into me as though trying to get inside my deepest thoughts. I hug my waist, in a way, trying to protect myself from the menacing stare.

I lower my gaze to the floor, having an inner debate whether I should mention the text I just got. Jake seems to trust this guy, perhaps I should say something.

"What is it?" Jake's voice reaches me, low and urging. I send him a wary glance.

"Miss, if you care about your man, you better speak up."

"Hunter?" Jake sends him a bothered look.

Hunter? *Hunter.* Reeves and Jake mentioned the name a few times before.

My voice shakes as I tell Jake, "He sent me a message about five minutes ago." The palpable sigh of relief heaved from both of the gentlemen mouths' dazes me, while the weight of their worry seeps into my recognition.

"Can I see this message?" Hunter extends his hand forward, leaving it hanging, demanding. I take a few steps, followed by the men's severe stares on me. Cautiously, I hand my phone to him and bite my lips.

He gives the phone one short peek, another my way, and says, "From a burner." Jake's silent curse tugs at my nerves.

"Wha... t's... wrong?" I stammer, begging with my eyes for Jake to let me know what kind of trouble Reeves might be in.

"Nia," Hunter says, both Jake and I turn to look his way. "I need to talk to Jake alone. Can you please make sure to call Jake if there's any signal from Reeves?"

"Can you please tell me what's going on?" My hand moves to my chest, unconsciously trying to calm the painful thuds.

"We have a reason to believe he might be... somewhere he should not be."

I twist my lips in unconcealed scorn, offended by Hunter's vague brush-off. I open my mouth to protest when Jake interferes, making me close it right back. "I know how to reach you if needed." Very clearly dismissing me.

"Jake, can you at least promise to let me know if he contacts you?" Jake's jaw tightens, but he still nods affirmation.

My posture and mood fall free in complete harmony as I make my way out of the room. One of them closes the door behind me. Making my way to the bar, my head throbs with pain and anxiety. I rub my temples, processing the last few minutes.

Although they tried not to include me in whatever they were discussing, they were clear about Reeves being in some kind of danger. Inwardly, I shudder at the thought of something happening to him. At the same breath, I convince myself not to take my imagination into any dark places, as I'm not sure I'd be able to come out whole.

"Hey, Nia." Alex waves my way, momentary pulling me out of the ring of worry tightening around me. I nod at her and shortly join her and a couple of friends of hers who I haven't had the chance to meet yet. They talk around me as I gape ahead, warming a cold drink in my tight hold. I hear their voices pass through me but don't really listen to what's being said. My attention is fixated at the hall leading to Jake's office. My mind is set on waiting for Hunter to leave so I'll be able to try and talk Jake into telling me what's going on.

My head jerks up as I see both men walk through the bar tables' maze. I try to catch Jake's eyes but he seems absorbed inside his own mind. Jake leans to tell Eileen something and not long after Hunter pushes the exit door open, leaving with Jake in tow. The looks on their faces blow another hit right in the middle of my stomach.

A familiar plaguing feeling starts spreading its vines of venom through my bloodstream, and without much attention to Alex or anyone at the table, I stand up with a start, needing to get away. I run out of the bar, hugging myself, rapidly passing cafés and stores, rushing to get behind my closed door. Behind my bathroom closed door. Everything in my peripheral view becomes a blur as tears gloss my eyes. With the last bit of hope, I knock at Reeves' door. I wait for some stressful, long minutes, but he doesn't answer. At this point, I need his breath inside me. I need it desperately, so *I* could breathe.

Next to the door leading to my apartment is when I become hollow, preparing myself for what's next to come. I rummage through my bag for my key. Voices in my head whisper of fear, of loss, of Patrick, of Reeves.

I narrow my eyes to lead the way through my dim living room and stagger back. I'm paralyzed by the vision in front of me. I'm glued to the floor and I'm afraid to blink, to blink him away. He sits on the sofa, in a halo of weak evening light. He raises his face that's buried in his hands to look my way. Through the murky space, I notice that his eyes are gleaming with pain and my heart collapses down into my stomach, pulling at every emotion in me. I suppress the tears in my throat as I gape at him.

He stands up and as though I'm about to disappear into thin air, he quickly strides toward me with fast, determined steps. My heart is drumming so wildly that it sends my blood viciously rushing through my veins. As soon as Reeves reaches me, his eyes melt into mine. In hurried, anxious motions, he threads his fingers through my hair and gazes at me as if I am the only thing that can save him. His lips crash to mine, and I'm torn deep inside as I feel the moisture on his bristled cheek. His kiss leaves me breathless. It contains so much gloom, desperation, and… hope.

"I love you," he says to my mouth, pulling me deeper into his hold.

"I love you," I quietly say back, saturated with emotions I can hardly contain.

"Are you okay, are you hurt?" I run my eyes over him, searching, not even sure what I'm looking for. "Jake and Hunter, they said you might…"

Reeves breaks my words. "I didn't, I couldn't." He kisses me once more. "I couldn't lose you."

EPILOGUE

Nia

Six months later

"God, ouch!" I cry and bite my lips, breathing through the sharp pain.

"Ssshhh…" Reeves attempts to sooth me. "You're kind of loud, babe." He cranes his neck to look at me. "I warned you it's going to be uncomfortable, try to relax."

"Uncomfortable? It. Freaking. Hurts!"

"Loosen up, babe."

"Stop babe-ing me! I told you, it hurts! And stop smirking!" I chide. "It's not fair you're the only one enjoying it." I take a deep breath, trying to calm down. "Ouch, ouch!"

"We can't stop now," he says, a hint of plea in his eyes. "Why did you ask for it in the first place, really? It was your idea." A bud of a smile roots on his lips. "So, try to relax your muscles and enjoy the ride!"

"For us… For our happy," I say and send him a thin smile, the only one I can produce under the continuous piercing pain.

"You rock!" He winks at me, his full-blown smile almost blinding me.

I gaze at this heart quickening smile and go back to a similar smile that initiated this "lovely" discomfort.

It's one of our lazy weekends. I don't think we've got out of bed for two days. Only in cases of emergency, of course. Opening the door for the fast-food delivery guy or attending nature callings. Oh, and there was a shower or two somewhere in the middle. But that was kind of it, the rest of the time it was Reeves' comfy bed, and us…

I'm leisurely lying with my head resting on Reeves' abs, reading a book, enjoying tranquillity in its calmest form. I squeal when without any prior warning I find myself flipped over to be straddled atop heavenly filled boxer briefs.

"A date!"

"What?" I frown at Reeves who looks as excited as I'd be if they ever invented calorie free ice cream.

"How about today?"

The creases on my forehead multiply.

"I found the date."

"Huh?"

"You said you wanted a date that would make you smile each time you thought of it. So, how about today?" Reeves grins at me, a full-blown Reeves smile. Heavy duty material. My lips pull up at the side, said grin comes highly contagious, what's a girl to do?

"It's great... Today is great. Can you start making sense, though? I can't deal with crazy... I've only had one cup of coffee."

He props his arms on the bed and leans forward to kiss me again, utterly elated. "The date in which I told you that I'll be asking you to spend the rest of your life with me in the far future. Our happy date."

A layer of traitorous happy tears cover my eyes.

"I love this date," I say in bliss, peppering his face with endless, tiny kisses.

"We're done." The pierced guy who's been hunched above me for the last half hour says. I thank him and carefully observe the dark roman numbers now decorating the inside of my wrist.

"I love it!" I beam and turn my head to the person sitting on the chair beside me, the person who just got the same date inked to his skin, my boyfriend, my, according to the date imprinted on me, future fiancé. He smiles back, and there's an air to his eyes that wordlessly tell me just how much he loves me.

As we leave the tattoo studio, Reeves tugs me to a nearby wall. Facing me, the points of our shoes touching, he narrows his eyes at me. With a

which justice was served. A closure where A.Z. was read his rights and will decay in prison. A closure where I am a free man, literally and figuratively, able to start a life with a cleaner conscience and my girl.

Nia's voice pulls me back to the present. "There's nothing I'd want more, and anyway we've been practically living together already."

My eyes trail from her mouth to her joyfully shining eyes. My lips slowly pull up at the notion of how easily she'd agreed to move in with me when we get back home.

"You know I don't do sleeping without you anyway."

I lean in to press my mouth to hers. When she parts her lips for me and her tongue enthusiastically takes over control, my hands urge to touch her, all over. Soft, delicate neck skin, swell of the most amazing set of tits, ass, her round, perky ass. Her hands move to my neck and I shift my weight to lay her back onto the mattress. I settle between her legs, sliding my hand under her loose shirt.

"Reeves," she utters breathily, "we can't." She pulls back. I groan, leaning deeper into her. "Reeves," Nia scolds through a moan. She jolts back, flushed and bothered and supremely beautiful. She shakes her head. "They are still up."

Reluctantly, I flip to the side and slump my head onto the pillow next to her. Nia watches me with a hint of a smile. My face radiates playful annoyance as I point with my hand toward the tent at the crotch of my sweats. Nia's eyes follow the gesture, and she lets out a light giggle.

"Shower to your left, for cold water turn the handle on the right," she says and my lips break into a smile as I grab her by the waist and settle her atop where she wants me to pour cold water.

"Reeves," she says my name through a laugh. "C'mon, my parents are right below us."

"Okay, okay, one last kiss, c'mere you," I rasp.

"Now." Nia pats my chest. "I'm going down to join my parents. As much as I hate to see great things go to waste, you get the situation in your boxers down and join us." She winks and closes the door behind her. I beam at the shut door and sink my head back onto the pillow. I crane my neck to survey the room, again. Soft buttery tones, many dancing keepsakes and touches of a younger Nia.

We've been visiting Nia's parents for a week now. Nia finally reconciled with them. A long talk, tears and hugs concluded months of pain, anger, and detachment. A week in which I got to peek into Nia's past, and had the pleasure of getting to know her parents.

We'll celebrate Christmas together in a couple of days and then I'll be leaving for a week by myself. I'm leaving for the trip, a short version though, I was planning to have over three years ago, after we were supposed to take a break. Me to travel or disappear somewhere in nature and Ben to be with his future fiancée. Finally, I'm taking that break. I'll be trekking in the Panatal region here in Brazil, the world's largest tropical, most amazing, wetland area. It's not the best time of year to do so, if you are not so much into massive rainfalls and mosquitoes. I think I'll survive some water and a few winged insects, I did, after all, survive worse. Nia will meet me right after in Rio for our last week before we head back home.

There's so much to deal with upon return. Decisions to make, therapy to continue, officially start a new together with my girl. Maybe I'll take Jake up on his offer when I get home to manage the bar while he tries to give Carmie what she always wanted. For the first time in their rocky and intense relationship, Jake will be the one going after Carmie, putting her, her career and goals, first.

I'd be lying if I said I haven't considered it more than once since he offered. Managing the bar could be the perfect solution for me, for the time being. I think it's time I had some stability, some normality, some happy, and a whole lot of Nia.

~ ~ ~

Seven months later, Cleveland, Ohio

"I did it," I say in a low voice, brushing away dry leaves that have congregated on the dusty stone. I bend my knees, sitting on the cold ground, yanking out a bundle of long weeds that's littering the short grass. "I trekked in Brazil and it was surreal." I swallow a breath. "And I met Nia's parents. They're good people." Another deep breath. "God, bro, I can't do this…It's so hard." I bury my face in my palms.

"I'm so sorry, Ben." I bite my quivering lips. "I'm so sorry that I didn't stop them. I'm so sorry that I betrayed every promise that we ever made to always have one another's backs." I try to stifle the lump rapidly swelling in my throat. I brush the moisture from under my eyes and hold my palms together, resting them on my lips. I gaze at Ben's name engraved in granite letters. "I know you wouldn't have it any other way. This is what we were expected to… But still… I feel like I've let everyone down by not being able to save you."

I think about how from the first day we enlisted together to being honorably discharged from the Army to being recruited later by the FBI, we were of the same mind, Ben and I. With great honor and determination, doing the very best we were trained to do. We always knew our lives would be in danger, and it's been, so many times we've lost track. But I never imagined that I'd ever have to sit still and watch him go. I never thought I'd have to lie to his family about how he left them. They were told it was a training accident, and I had to back it up, no matter how much I hated doing so. I never thought that I'd be the one telling Casey that Ben was going to ask her to marry him.

I take a deep breath and everything just streams out of me. I tell Ben about Katie, about his parents, about my work with Jake, about A.Z.'s arrest. About my life without him.

I sit still for a while, summoning my composure, rerunning my last session with Dr. Barnes in my head where he told me that I should have one final closure…with Ben. Accept the fact that he is gone, and that it was not my fault.

"I'm happy now," I say in a hoarse, yet quiet voice. "Nia makes me happy. She's everything. *She* made me accept the fact that I'm allowed to be happy again. She's my saving grace." I'm still staggered and overwhelmed about my feelings for Nia.

I never felt this way about anyone. I never had the time nor the inclination to open up to anyone. Not with my past and not with the life I led. At one point, long ago, I thought I had feelings for Katie, but quickly realized it was a different kind of sentiment. A sentiment that I wasn't familiar with, either, of belonging, of unconditionally caring, of a bond relatives share. A small bittersweet smile nestles on my lips. "You'd like her." I take in a deep breath and let it slowly whistle out.

"I'm taking the job at the bar. I'll be managing it during Jake's indefinite absence. I think that I'm done with our old lifestyle, and I'm ready to try something new. Something more stable. I'm ready to begin the next part of my life... with Nia." I slowly rise to stand. With my breath held in for a strained beat, I run my fingers over the cold stone.

"I miss you, bro," I whisper and walk toward where Nia is waiting for me with a soft smile.

NOTE FROM THE AUTHOR

Dear Reader,

Thank you for taking the time to read RETRACE. I hope you enjoyed reading it as much as I've enjoyed writing it. For me, the writing of Reeves and Nia's story was a thoroughly emotional journey, there's a piece of my heart somewhere within these pages.

If you have any extra time, it would be great, REALLY GREAT, if you would leave a review where you bought it, Goodreads, or anywhere else you wish. ;-)

Also, I more than love hearing from my readers, honestly, it's the best part of the whole writing process. So, drop me an email at: author.sehrlich@gmail.com or chat with me on Facebook.

Thank you for allowing me to share my stories with you, and I hope to be re-invited to your bookshelf with my next releases.

Again, THANK YOU!
Much love,
Sigal

ACKNOWLEDGMENTS

Wow, writing Retrace was a long, bumpy journey in which my emotions were pulled from one pole to the other. While I was writing a completely different book, Nia and Reeves practically seized my mind to the point I couldn't concentrate on anything else and just had to pour their story out of me. Their story was not an easy story to tell, and I honestly would have not been able to do so without the help of some incredible people I'm blessed to have in my life.

First public gratitude announcement goes to my Liis. Thank you so much for being my right hand for over a year and for taking care of my nutty kids as they were your own. Thank you for listening and bearing my endless preaching and psychoness. And mostly, for being the amazing person that you are. I love you hard, kid.

Gal, thank you for taking care of everything when I didn't and for making me stop to breathe from time to time. And of course, thank you for reminding me, that apparently there's a whole world of living, breathing real humans outside my screen. You're SO my better half.

My kiddos, for being as perfect as you are and still loving unconditionally even with less mommy-time.

Capy, for your constant encouragement, for being the most awesome soul mate one can ever ask for.

Beth, how do I even begin thanking you? Thanks for putting up with all my crazy. Thank you for reading, honing, and answering silly questions at ungodly hours. Thank you!

My beta readers, thank you for being as passionate, patient and fun to work with. Evelyn, Liis, Sima, Hila, and Sylvie.

My favorite author on the globe, my amazingly talented friend Olivia Luck, for your support during my way too many, Psycho-writing-bipolar-syndrome episodes. And basically for being you.

Nicole Hornbaker, for your magnificent work and your priceless ideas. I can't imagine writing a book without you somehow involved.

Jenny, for all the hard work and professionalism.

Alisha from Damonza.com, for tolerating my over-the-top control-freakish nature and designing Retrace's gorgeous cover.

R. Brosh, for the valuable help and advice on Bipolar Disorder.

Bloggers, truly incredible bloggers. I cannot begin to express how thankful I am to you and your support. It's priceless.

Special gigantic gratitude to:

Christie of *Smokin' Hot Book Blog*. Kawehi, my kindred spirit, of *Kawehi Book Blog*. Michele of *Devilishly Delicious Book Reviews*. Jen of *Lustful Literature*. Beth of *Tome Tender*. Dearest Carmie and the awesome ladies at *Forever Me Romance*. The great bunch of women at *A is for Alpha B is for Books*. Alice of *All Things in the Clouds Sweet*. Bianca, aka the blogger who rocked me to my core, of *Bianca of BJ's Book Blog*. Theo, sweet Theo of *Shattering Words*, Cindy of *The Book Enthusiast Blog*, and the lovely ladies at *Love Between the Sheets*.

And most importantly, my readers. Since Layers was released I've been constantly overwhelmed by your response. You guys are truly amazing and I could have not asked for better readers.

Thank you! Thank you, and then some. Thank you for reviewing, messaging, emailing, loving, liking, spreading the word. You rock big time!

And lastly, warm thanks to some special ladies: My fav, aka Julie, Sharon, Christa M., Lies and Carmie.

ALSO BY SIGAL EHRLICH

Layers

Inner Core

ABOUT THE AUTHOR

By teen age, Sigal already lived in three different continents where she was lucky enough to experience and visit varied places, meet unique people, which only helped fuel her overly developed imagination. Currently, Sigal calls Estonia home where she lives with her husband and three kids.

Not exactly sure where they will end up next …

Sigal would love to hear from you, please visit her on her website, Twitter, and Facebook.

http://www.sigalehrlich.com/

@Sigal_Ehrlich

https://www.facebook.com/sigalehrlich.author

http://www.pinterest.com/authorsehrlich/

auhtor.sehrlich@gmail.com